OFF THE VOORTREKKER ROAD

BARBARA BLEIMAN

Printed by CreateSpace, An Amazon.com Company

Available on Kindle and other book stores

DEDICATION

Dedicated to my father, Jack, whose life experiences and stories were the inspiration for this work of fiction.

Thanks

With love and thanks to Adam, Gemma and Joel Sharples and my mother, Rita.

Special thanks to my agent Elly James at HHB Agency, to Jenny Green for all her invaluable support, to Lucy Webster for her advice and practical assistance, to Sue Tyley for editorial help, and to Henry Brown for reading and commenting on the novel.

CHAPTER 1

May 1958

Jack sat in the hushed courtroom. High in the ceiling a single fan whirred slowly, spiralling down a fug of stale air. It was unusually warm for the time of year, an unexpected last gasp of heat before the Cape breezes picked up bringing rain and cooler air.

He watched the jurors settling down. The men loosened their ties and discarded their woollen jackets and felt hats. Some took out handkerchiefs to wipe their faces, one mopped his bald head, while a young woman in a bright floral dress opened her bag, applied a dab of powder and a greasy smear of red lipstick. Carefully, she rolled up a magazine to act as a makeshift fan, flicking it backwards and forwards in awkward, jerky movements. Had they heard the stories and read the newspaper headlines in the *Cape Argus* and *die Burger*? Had they already made up their minds?

As the courtroom began to fill, a low hum of noise rose; murmuring voices, the rustling of paper, a nervous cough, throats being cleared, but Jack knew that, when the judge swept in, there would be a sudden stillness, a collective intake of breath and then silence.

He took up his fountain pen, unscrewed the lid, and pulled towards him a pad of lined paper. He wrote: 'May 7th 1958' then jotted down a few phrases to calm himself, words that he wasn't even sure he would actually use. He'd been mulling it all over for so long now, rehearsing the different permutations, one word against another, considering the precise effect of each. His training had schooled him in the need for clarity and exactitude; a word in its everyday context could mean something quite different in a court of law. Verdicts could turn on linguistic niceties and nuances; there was little room for error. His own experience too had taught him how words could open doors, break down barriers, establish fresh, revelatory understandings but they could also damage and destroy. He still hadn't fully determined what he was going to say. Any minute now he would be forced to go one way or another, choose one set of words over another and face the consequences.

What would the woman with the rolled-up fan make of it all? He'd latched on to her, as representative of a kind of South African he thought he understood well. Her small, rather bored eyes and full red mouth, her showy dress, cerise pink with flowers, made him doubt that she would be sympathetic to him. She would almost certainly be looking for something simpler than he could offer, a nice straightforward story that she could take home to her husband or fiancé at the end of the day. 'It was lekker,' she might say, 'really great. We listened to all the facts and that was that - nice and easy, the law of the land, working perfectly, just like it should. Man, I'm proud of this country of ours, proud to be an Afrikaner.' Instead, he feared that she would come away from it all confused, perplexed, probably even angry. It would all depend; on her and whether he'd judged her right, on the outcome of the trial but most of all on him and what he finally chose to say.

There was a soft buzz of talk in the corridor and then, more distantly, out on the wide stone courtroom steps, the sound of shouting. A crowd had gathered. There was a queue for the public gallery and those who hadn't secured seats were still milling around outside; tempers were clearly frayed. Earlier, buses had disgorged eager spectators out into the square and he'd had to barge his way through the crowd to get in.

The court officials hurried to and fro, whispering among themselves, sensing a possibility of trouble. Any minute now, the Judge would come in; soon Jack himself would have to speak. What if he opened his mouth and nothing came out?

The school yard. The memory of it came out of the blue, sharp and shockingly precise.

The boys are standing all around him in a circle, laughing. J-J-J-Jackie. His head is bowed. He is looking down at the red dirt of the Parow Elementary School yard. He sees his shiny leather boots, made for him by his oupa in the little cobbler's workshop at the front of his house, a present for his first day at school. The tiny black stitches trace an ant's path round the stiffened toe-pieces. His socks have fallen down to his ankles, the worn grey elastics having failed. A trickle runs down his leg, producing a dark stain on one sock that soaks quickly into the baked red dirt of the yard. He holds his arms out straight to his sides. His fingers twist nervously but otherwise he is perfectly still, like the posts holding up the schoolyard fence, like the columns on either side of the gate, like the Stinkwood tree on the other side of the street. He wants to disappear into the background.

'Mrs Uys, Mrs Uys, Little Jackie's done a wee in his broekies! But he won't tell, 'cause he can't speak!'

His trousers are wet and there is a sharp-sweet tang of the urine and warm wool on his skin. He waits for the school bell to ring so he can go inside, to the safety of Mrs Uys and away from the laughter of the boys and girls.

*****

A gentle tap on his shoulder brought him back to the courtroom. An usher, bringing him a note from his chambers, with a message asking him to phone when the court adjourned for lunch. There'd been a last minute question in a case that was about to draw to a close and Vera, his secretary, wanted to know how to respond.

Up to now Jack had been given only minor briefs, the kind of cases his more experienced colleagues avoided: petty thefts, disputes about a piece of land over in Paarl or a lease on a shop in Maitland, broken contracts, messy middle of the road divorce proceedings. A few solicitors had given him a break, trying him out to see what he was capable of. So far things had gone reasonably well, given how inexperienced he was, fresh out of his pupilage. He'd done a decent enough job and a number of judgements had gone his way. He was a quick learner, he knew that. He did his homework and the attendants at the Law Library knew him well. 'Back for another stint, Mr Neuberger? You'll be a High Court judge before you know it!' the one older librarian joked. But he wasn't fooling himself. He was still a rookie and he knew why this particular case had come his way rather than going to one of the more established members of the chambers.

He'd heard the talk among the other advocates, before he'd agreed to take it on. The new Immorality Act had just come into force and this was the first case to be prosecuted – a test case, with a lot of attention focused on it. Fineberg, a senior counsel, couldn't do it. He was right in the middle of a big case, he said, a long one, and really wouldn't be able to squeeze it in. Berman, Cohen and Ronnie Levine were also offered the case and declined.

'I don't want to get known for this sort of thing,' he'd overheard Berman telling a colleague, over coffee and a salt beef sandwich in the

Waldorf. 'You can find yourself with a reputation for cases like this and then that's all you get. It damages you. You lose the quality cases, the commercial clients. The thing is to find an excuse, like Fineberg – much too busy, dying mother, wife expecting any day – whatever it takes to get yourself off the hook.'

Big, fat divorces of gold, or diamond-mining magnates, chunky, complicated business disputes, or maybe even a good, meaty murder case from time to time – that's what senior barristers like him wanted to spend their time on.

Finally when the solicitor called, having tried a few others and had no luck, it was mentioned to Jack. He'd agreed straightaway to take it on. Mixed marriages, sexual relations between black and white – this case spoke to him, not only because of its political content, some abstract commitment to a cause, but for another reason as well. That episode when he was just a boy, in his father's shop in Parow, with Terence, his childhood playmate, the only boy he'd ever really thought of as a friend. He'd never forgotten it; it had stayed with him.

'A word of advice, Mr Neuberger,' Bob Cohen had said, when he'd heard the news.

'Yes, Mr Cohen?'

'There'll be publicity for this one. An Afrikaner in his position, it'll be a juicy one for the press. They'll lap it up. I'd keep a low profile, if I were you. Whether you win or lose isn't really all that important. It's your reputation that you want to hold on to, if you want to make your way at the Bar. Use your head, not your heart.'

Jack hadn't replied. Bob Cohen had worked as an advocate for thirty-odd years; his opinion was not to be easily dismissed or ignored. Head or heart? He'd used his head that time before, he'd listened to his parents and followed their lead, but what if he'd listened to his own feelings, if he'd struck out on his own and gone the other way? Perhaps that too would have been an equal, if different, burden to bear.

There was a sudden flurry of movement in the courtroom, the ushers moving into position by the doors, the clerk of the court taking his place behind his desk.

'All rise,' the clerk called. 'All rise for Justice Steyn.'

The moment had come. Jack stood up. He felt a trickle of sweat running down the back of his shirt. He adjusted his bib and collar, straightened his gown against his shoulders, brushed off stray pieces of lint and took a deep breath.

Justice Steyn came in through the wood-panelled door behind the bench. He was a thin man, small, with a grizzled beard and deep-set dark eyes, a long, narrow nose and a pale complexion. Not a very imposing figure, more like a librarian or book-keeper than a judge, yet able to draw on the authority of his position instantly, to command the respect of the courtroom. Gathering the folds of his gown around him, he leaned forward and opened his notebook, then gestured to everyone to be seated. Jack followed his sharp gaze as it scanned the court, resting finally on the jury. This was it. The start. The opening remarks.

'Let me remind you of the seriousness of your duties, in this case perhaps even more than most, where a new immorality law is being tested and the outcome will have significant consequences beyond this courtroom. It will be broadcast far and wide. It will send out a message, not just about the illegitimacy of *marital* relationships across races, nor just about the sex act itself between Europeans and non-Europeans, both of which have long been enshrined in our country's law as criminal offences, but about *all* sexual contact between whites and non-whites. "Immoral or indecent acts," the new law says. That is the ground that is being tested here today and you, the jury, will have to decide whether the two defendants are guilty of contravening it or not. Immorality and indecency. Two words that can mean very different things to different people. Perhaps you have your own strong views? Maybe your wife or your brother or your neighbour takes different ones? But our job is to regard them as legal terms, not just as everyday words, such as you might use in banter with friends. You will need to put aside whatever prejudices you bring to the courtroom and decide whether the defendants are guilty of immoral or indecent acts, as defined by this new law, and as a result whether they should be subject to the full weight of its penalties.'

He paused and looked towards Jack and the prosecuting counsel, Willem du Toit, sitting just across from him.

'You will hear a lot of arguments from these two learned men. They will use all their knowledge, all their cleverness and their verbal skill, to persuade you that their view is right, for let me tell you they are both very clever men. They've been trained in all the techniques of argument and persuasion. But they will also present you with evidence and with facts. And you will hear the evidence of the witnesses they call to appear before you. It is your duty to judge the two defendants on the basis of the evidence. Facts, evidence and the law. That is all that matters.'

Du Toit, his adversary. Fifty years old, or thereabouts, paunchy, reassuringly unkempt, with a florid complexion and an easy smile. He looked relaxed. His arms were folded and he had his legs stretched out in front of him, as if settling down to watch a good film at the bioscope, rather than launching into the first day of what everyone recognised to be a major trial.

'He looks like a great big, cuddly teddy bear,' Bob Cohen had warned. 'But don't be deceived. He has an enviable record of successes and, let me tell you, that doesn't come from being nice. He's ferocious. And he's cunning. Watch your back.'

He wondered what approach du Toit was going to take. The smug look on his face suggested that he thought he had every angle covered, held all the cards in his hand, but perhaps that was just part of his game plan; maybe under that cool exterior, he too was feeling just a bit nervous about what was to follow. He'd never been up against Jack in court before and perhaps he would have preferred the known patterns and rituals that he could follow with his contemporaries, men he'd trained with at university and whose careers had closely mirrored his own. A new young advocate might be more of a wild card for him than Bob Cohen or Marius Fineberg, the more senior men, whose every trick and courtroom joke were by now absolutely familiar to him.

Jack ran his eye along the rows of the jury. Nine men and three women, all white of course. What more could he tell about them? The big Afrikaner with the shiny bald head and flat, broad nose, the tall thin man with horn-rimmed glasses, dressed in a threadbare suit, the girl with the red lipstick and paper fan, these stood out. He tried to do a quick tally, to tot up the score. Four or five Akrikaner men, two Afrikaner women and one man who he thought was probably, like him, a Jew. The rest, going by their appearances, seemed to be of English stock. Their thin noses, redder skin, their choice of clothing, assumed air of refinement, all marked them out from the Afrikaners. He was a pretty good judge of these things. All those years of looking at people in his father's store in Parow had helped; he'd become adept at the art of the quick summing up, whether picking up on the clues of physiognomy, like the shape of a nose or the texture or teint of the skin, or a single gesture, such as the way a person swatted a fly, or reached across to take their change.

More women, a few more Jews, that's what he had been hoping for. They were more likely to favour his client, or so the folklore among his fellow advocates went. He might have thought of contesting one or two, to get a more favourable balance, but then what was the point? All in all, given the circumstances, it was unlikely to make a difference. He'd let it go.

Some of the jury had their eyes trained on him and on du Toit. He caught the gaze of one or two and then quickly looked away. It was an uncomfortable moment, this first hesitant sizing up of each other. He wondered what conclusions they would draw. Like him, they would probably be quick to pigeonhole him, from the physical signs that he himself knew to be fairly obvious. Dark hair, olive skin, an energetic, mobile face. He'd been told by Louis Abrams, his pupil-master, that he should practise the art of studied indifference. 'You give too much away, you know. You risk showing your hand too early. Try to be more like a poker-player. Be more like the English, with their well-known sang-froid, and keep your emotions to yourself.' But, as Renee had said when she'd first met him, 'What I like about you, Jack, is the way you wear your heart on your sleeve.' The exact phrase the jurors might use to describe him would depend on their own persuasions and prejudices. Maybe 'one of those clever Cape Jews', or 'a Litvak, a Lithuanian immigrant – why the hell did so many of them end up as attorneys?' or, and he didn't kid himself about this more unpleasant possibility, 'another Jewish kaffir-loving communist'. He'd heard that phrase enough to be realistic about how he might be regarded.

He was distracted by these thoughts and so, rather absurdly, felt a sudden jolt of surprise when his client was brought in, a court official holding him firmly by the elbow. Johannes van Heerden, a man in his early fifties, a minister in the Dutch Reformed Church, whose wife, Laura, did flowers for the Sunday service and baked koeksisters for the annual Bring and Buy; a respectable man of the church. He entered the dock, his head bowed, then briefly looked up and caught Jack's eye.

Jack had hardly been able to believe it when he'd first heard the details of the case. Of all people to be brought to court under this new law! It had pushed the whole issue right back into the public gaze; the headlines

7

in the local papers were full of it, focusing on van Heerden himself, with a prurient interest in every detail of his private life. But there had also been furious debate in the serious press. The *Cape Argus* and the *Cape Times*, the voices of the English-speaking, more liberal community, had both struggled to tread a line between raising questions and concerns, and out-and-out condemnation. What exactly were immoral acts? What was indecency? The Afrikaans newspaper, *die Burger*, of course took a more predictable government line.

If he were found guilty, van Heerden would lose his position in the church and his reputation would be irreparably sullied. What's more, with the new stiffer penalties, he faced possible imprisonment for up to seven years. There was a huge amount at stake.

'Incarceration and disgrace,' thought Jack, and his stomach churned. He tried to give van Heerden a smile of encouragement, a signal of support, the comfort of knowing that there was at least one person there who had his interests at heart. But van Heerden was standing limp, staring blankly in front of him, looking as if the first hostile word uttered might cause him to collapse under the strain of it all and bring the whole proceedings to an abrupt, if temporary halt. 'You're here now, at last, Johannes,' Jack said to himself. 'You've got to see it through to the end.'

He heard the Judge explain to his client and to the other party, the woman involved, what the procedures of the court would be. Unlike van Heerden, she seemed calm enough, standing beside her own counsel, with her gaze focused intently on the Judge as he spoke. There were warnings from him about the seriousness of the charge and reassurances about the rights of the two accused to expect that justice would be done. Jack saw his client being presented with the worn leather Bible. He heard his voice quavering across the quiet courtroom, as he swore the oath on the book.

Now it was time. Jack knew that he would have to begin, that every word would count, each weighed and measured and placed in the balance. What he said would have its impact, not just on Johannes van Heerden, his wife and his family, his church and community but also on Jack himself and on his wife Renee as well. He'd been waiting for this day, just as van Heerden had, with trepidation, and now it had come. He stood up and prepared himself to speak.

CHAPTER 2

1939

Pa's hardware store stood in Parow, at the far end of Main Road, the long thoroughfare stretching east to west across Cape Town that eventually came to be renamed Voortrekker Road, after the rugged, tough-minded Afrikaners who had settled the Cape. Parow, in those days, was quite a distance from the city centre, out beyond Woodstock, Maitland and Goodwood. Property was cheap and rentals easy to come by, so Malays and Jews, Afrikaners and English had started to crowd in, and the suburb was growing by the day.

On one side of the store was Irene's, the women's outfitters. It sold corsets and brassieres, blouses, suits and bright cotton frocks, the most glamorous of which appeared on two smiling, painted mannequins in the window. On the other side stood Krapotkin's butcher's shop, its large plate-glass window filled with pallid sausages, mounds of worm-like minced beef and lean joints of lamb hanging from silver hooks. A sticky yellow paper in the front of the shop was always black and buzzing with flies. Krapotkin was a large, pink-faced man, with hands as red and raw as the meat he handled and a voice loud enough to wake the cockerel himself. He was in the shop, from early morning till late at night, heaving dripping carcasses and slapping bloody joints of meat onto wooden boards, slicing, chopping, grinding, sawing through flesh and bone, all the while singing, laughing and swearing so loudly that my mother said that Krapotkin and his butcher's shop would be the death of her.

The hardware store had a sign painted on the front with, "Neuberger's Handyhouse", in a clear, unfussy style. It stood a little apart from its neighbours, its whitewashed walls yellowed with age, its sloping tiled roof in some need of repair. On one side of the door stood rolls of carpet, stepladders and brooms. On the other were baskets filled with dishcloths and dusters, bars of waxy household soap and boxes of washing suds. A notice in the window said, "Everything you need, from soap and rice to chicken feed!" and "10% off for bulk bargain buys!" A faded red-and-white striped awning was pulled down every morning to provide shade from the hot midday sun and wound back up every evening when the store was closed.

My father, Sam, had bought the store six years earlier, just before his marriage to my mother and I was born a year later. He worked all hours, either out the front or in the back yard, cutting wood or linoleum, measuring string, counting nails and screws, cutting strips of biltong or weighing biscuits from the big jars that lined the counter. The hired girl, Ada, helped out while my mother moved between the kitchen, the back yard and the shop front, cleaning and cooking, talking to customers, and keeping an occasional eye on me.

Where could I be found, on a typical day in 1939, four-and-a half years of age and living in the Handyhouse with my ma and pa? Occupying myself with toys? Splashing about in a tin tub of water to keep me cool in the blistering heat of the day? Playing a game of five stones with a little friend, or sharing a tasty slice of homemade melktert? No. I would be sitting in the corner of the store, on my sack of beans. The sack was high enough up for me not to attempt to climb down but not so high that I would do myself serious damage if I did. Little Jackie, aged four, knock-kneed, wide-eyed, dressed in shabby grey shorts and a grubby cotton shirt, stick legs swinging against the rough hessian of the bulging sack, sitting watching and saying nothing.

Ma would tell me stories at bedtime. Sometimes they were fairytales, sometimes family stories but often the two were mixed together, a blend of fact and fiction, magic and mundane, then and now; the biblical, the superstitious, the humorous and the sad, all woven together into a strange and complex fabric.

'Once upon a time, long ago and far away,' my mother said, 'there lived a man named Solomon, who was a cobbler. He was born into a Jewish family in a shtetl far away in Russia, a poor peasant, but clever and practical and full of hopes and dreams, a storyteller, a joker, the centre of attention at every wedding, barmitzvah, festival day or village party. He built a small wooden house for himself, he married a decent Jewish girl, he fought for the Czar, he saw his house burned and his synogogue razed to the ground, he felt hunger and he felt fear, and, finally he took his destiny into his hands and fled with his lovely wife across the wide seas, the swelling oceans to Cape Town, where he settled and had a family, a gaggle of girls, who, one by one married and left home themselves. One of his daughters was called Sarah. That's me, Jackie, your own mother, your ma. Solomon is Oupa, your very own grandfather.' She kissed me on the head and then she carried on.

'And then it came to pass that Sarah married Samuel. And they lived in a store and they called it the Handyhouse. And soon they had a child of their own, a little boy with many names: Jacob, Jack, Jankele, Little Jackie, son of Samuel and Sarah, grandson of Solomon, the shtetl cobbler, the man with a stout heart, a steel will and a voice that told an endless river of tales.

Your curly black hair comes from your grandfather, Jackie, your skin as dark as an Eastern prince's, your black, black eyes, like the 'ten a tickie' buttons your father sells in the shop. Your looks you got from Oupa, that's for sure. Maybe you got his cleverness too, with your serious eyes that always seem lost in your thoughts. But what happened to your voice, Jankele? Where oh where has it gone? Who knows? Perhaps it's been locked up by an ogre, in a great big iron box in his castle? Maybe, like a little bird, it's flown away over the seas to find its way home to its nest in Russia? It's waiting there, collecting up all its stories, getting itself ready to fly back again to Parow, and tell them, when the right moment comes?

Four-and-a-half years old; too young to start school, too old to be carried around on Ma's hip or wrap my legs round her waist and hang my arms from her neck, too big to sit in the highchair in the back room, sucking on rusks and pieces of salty biltong, while Ma, Pa and Ada bustled around me. So all day long, I sat on my sack of beans in the store, the Handyhouse, or in the sawdust on the floor, where someone could keep an eye on me. I watched the customers coming in and out, the bell tinkling as they stepped on the mat, carrying their parcels of dried peas or biscuits, candles or string.

Here was Mr van der Merwe, with his flat nose and sunburnt face, his strong, hairy legs spread wide. He had patches of damp sweat under his armpits and down the back of his khaki shirt. He scratched himself inside his trousers, like Ma told me not to. 'It's rude in public,' she said.

'Ooh yirrah! That sun's a bugger today.' His Afrikaner voice was hard like gravelly stones and each word seems to trip up his tongue on its sounds.

'I've brought you something,' he said to Pa, dropping his voice down low, till it was almost a whisper. He handed over a small brown paper envelope. 'It's not the whole lot. But it's the best we can do.'

Pa stared at him, stony-faced. 'We've been waiting for well over two weeks now. Your wife promised to pay up days ago.'

'Times are hard,' said Mr van der Merwe, shaking his head. 'It's not easy.'

'For us too,' said Pa. 'I'll expect the rest next week.'

He turned abruptly to Millicent, the Shapiro family's maid, to serve her. Mr van der Merwe cleared his throat, raised his hand awkwardly in a half-hearted farewell and left the shop.

With her yellow-brown skin, her hair plaited and knotted in tight rows on her head, Millicent was usually the last to be served, even when Mrs Shapiro had asked her to fetch back the family's groceries in a hurry. I was dark-skinned, like Millicent, taking after my mother's peasant father, as she had so often told me; not pale like Pa, or peachy-pink like some of the little English girls who came into the store, or red in the face like Mr Krapotkin, the butcher, not black-black like the boys who swept the road outside the store, or the labourers who climbed out of the truck every morning to work on the new shop across the road.

And here was Millicent, saying 'Yessir' to Pa and waiting to be served, as usual.

'Tell your madam that I don't have the crystallised fruit. I'm expecting an order.'

'Yessir.'

'And tell her the snoek is fresh from the smokery. Best quality fish. That's why it's a bit more pricy than usual.'

'Yessir.'

'And make sure you don't throw away the bill by mistake when you unpack. It's tucked inside the big paper bag.'

'Yessir.'

'At least you can rely on the Shapiro family to pay up,' Pa said when Millicent had left and the shop had gone quiet. 'A good Yiddishe family.'

'Times are hard,' Ma said. 'With all this talk of Smuts taking us into the war, people are nervous – they don't want to spend money.'

'Times are hard, times are hard. That's all I hear.' Pa sighed. 'Of course they're nervous. Aren't we all? But I've got a living to make,' and he went out the back to the yard, slamming the door behind him.

Ada was cleaning the counter, slopping soapy water onto a cloth and wiping it vigorously, her thin arms stretching as far as she could reach, in great sweeping movements. She paused to wipe her forehead.

'How's your mother, Ada?' Ma asked. 'Any better?'

I felt sorry for Ada. My mother always said, 'Poor whites are almost worse off than Cape coloureds. They have nothing.' I liked Ada. She patted my head and kissed me on the cheek. She made me bread and butter when Ma was upstairs lying on her bed with her door shut. She told me silly jokes and sometimes, if the coast was clear and there was no risk of Pa appearing, she came up close and dropped a little chewy caramel into my hand. It was a shame if Ada had nothing.

'My ma? She's so-so,' Ada said.

'Would you like a little bit of time off to go and see her?'

'Ag yes, missus. That'd be nice, lekker. But if you need me here, with it coming so soon and everything, then I'll stay. My friend Maisie's visiting Ma for me sometimes. I'm paying her a few tickies to go by the hospital and check on her. But it's not the same as me going myself. It's not long now, the doctors say. Her time's coming.'

'You're a good girl, Ada, and you don't usually ask for these things. And you're a hard worker as well. Even Sam thinks so. I'll talk to him and maybe you can go early this evening and come back on Thursday. Give you time to see your Ma.'

'Thank you missus. You're good to me.'

Ma went over and patted her on the shoulder. 'And now I think I'll go find Sam and speak to him.'

Ada came and picked me up from the floor. She brushed the sawdust from my shorts and kissed me heartily on the cheek.

'You don't know what's coming little man!' she said. 'You don't know what's gonna hit you, when your ma's time comes.' She laughed heartily, but I didn't know what was so funny. Ada's mother's time was coming;

13

Ma's time was coming. Ma's time kept coming and coming but it never seemed to arrive. And when it did, I couldn't think what it was going to bring.

Chapter 3

It was an especially hot day. I had had my early afternoon nap. The air hung heavy; the shop was quiet. There was a lull too in the hum of the flies buzzing round the biltong. Perhaps they were also feeling sleepy, just waking from their lunchtime doze?

Ma was tidying the drawers in the store; Pa was out in the yard, taking stock.

'I need to get some more chickenfeed and lucerne from Pietersen's, out beyond Paarl,' Pa muttered to Ma, coming through from kitchen, with his light summer jacket slung over his arm. 'Make sure you look after things in the store. You can do that, can't you?'

'Don't I always?' Ma replied, without looking up from the glass bowl she was polishing with a yellow cotton duster.

'Don't let old Rabinovitz buy another thing without paying his last bill. You're too soft on him. You need to set limits.'

Ma sighed. Pa didn't seem to like leaving the shop in her care.

'He's a schnorrer, that man, always after something for nothing.'

'He's sad and he's lonely. He comes in for a bit of company, that's all.'

'And no handfuls of biscuits for every child who stands there looking at you with big eyes. No paying on account either. Cash only. And,' Pa looked towards me, 'no treats for the boy.'

I didn't expect any. My father kept the lids tightly screwed on the sweet jars, with their tickie twists, liquorice sticks and sherbet fountains, and I knew only too well that the fig rolls and digestives were not for me.

'Go if you're going,' said Ma. 'For goodness' sake go.' She came behind the counter, moving heavily, and lumbered over to the stool that Pa had placed there for her.

'Don't overdo things. Use the stool,' he said a little more kindly and put a hand on her shoulder.

'Go. Please. I'll be fine.'

Pa took the keys for the old Ford, grabbed a paper packet filled with wads of notes from a drawer under the till, and went out back, to the rooms where we lived. I heard the door into the yard slam shut and the sound of the engine turning over, as Pa cranked it in vain. There was a shout of 'Blooming useless!', the creak of the bonnet being opened, more furious cranking and then finally it took, the engine humming into life and growling its way slowly out of the back yard.

Ma eased herself onto the stool and slipped off her shoes, stretching out her feet in front of her.

'Oy vay,' she said, blowing air out slowly through her mouth. 'I'm tired, Jackie, so very tired. I could really do with a nice little sleep, if only I didn't have to look after you and the store. I'm getting too big for all this work.'

Her light cotton dress was stretched tightly over her stomach and her legs, in her thick stockings, looked puffy and swollen, like the fat pink boerewors sausages from Krapotkin's next door. I wondered why she'd grown so large.

I sat on my sack waiting for something to happen, for Ma's head to nod forward and her mouth to go slack, for the store door to open and for one of the customers to walk in. With one hand I felt inside the top of the sack, and pushed my fingers in, allowing the slippery beans to flow through my fingers and roll between them. The beans rippled and swelled under my bottom as they shifted, sank and settled. Ma's head dropped down and she dozed.

At last the store bell tinkled and in came Mrs van der Merwe. Ma roused herself, stood up and squeezed on her shoes. Mrs van der Merwe was a regular customer. She came in every few days, to pick up something, always in those same old-fashioned linen dresses of hers, with her beige felt hat pinned close to her head and her old brown lace-up shoes polished so hard that they were as glossy as the paint on our wooden stairs.

'Mr Neuberger not here?'

'He's gone to Paarl to pick up supplies from the wholesaler's.'

'Leaving you alone to mind the store?' Mrs van der Merwe raised one eyebrow.

'I'm fine,' said Ma. 'Ada's here to help. And still a month to go.'

I watched Ma sorting Mrs van der Merwe's shopping. She lifted the lid from a tin and scooped out some white flour that she weighed on the scales, then poured carefully into a brown paper bag. She squeezed a roll of string into Mrs van der Merwe's basket, next to the flour, a twist of birdseed, some wooden clothes pegs and a small can of maize oil. She carefully placed on top a bag of Garibaldi biscuits that she had sealed up with a piece of sticky tape.

'There you are,' she said. 'All done.' There was a moment's silence. Mrs van der Merwe was shifting awkwardly from one foot to the other.

'Put it on the list for me, will you, Mrs Neuberger, my dear? I'm a little short this week. Mr van der Merwe's due some money from Willy Nel for a job he did for him. Willy's promised to bring it over this evening, so I'll be able to pay you tomorrow, honest to God I will.'

Ma hesitated. 'I'd like to, Mrs van der Merwe, only…'

'God's truth, I'll come in and pay tomorrow. Please Mrs Neuberger. Mr Neuberger need not know.'

Ma stood there, holding the basket and frowning.

'So help me God I'll pay tomorrow.' Her voice was insistent rather than pleading.

Ma looked at her for a moment, then handed over the paper bag.

Mrs van der Merwe thanked her brusquely. 'So how's the boy getting on?' she said. She turned to look at me and smiled so that her mouth was stretched open and her full row of teeth showed. 'Understand what's coming?'

'What *is* coming?' I thought.

'Same as always,' said Ma. She sighed. 'Still not speaking. It's a worry to me, I have to say.'

'He's only four, isn't he?' said Mrs van der Merwe. 'All children speak in the end. Have you ever heard of an adult that doesn't speak?'

'No but –'

'He'll be fine, you mark my words.' She hesitated. 'Come to think of it, though, there was that boy, the son of those people down near the railway crossing, what was their name again…Jordaan. Mr Jordaan the dentist. Their boy ended up in one of those homes for people who're not quite right in the head. Slow, he was. Retarded. I never did hear *him* speak.'

Ma frowned.

'He wasn't right in the head, that Jordaan boy. Does your boy show other signs of not being quite right?' Mrs van der Merwe asked, looking me up and down, with her piercing blue eyes.

'I don't think so, though he's not so good with his hands. He won't bang in the pegs with the little red hammer Sam made for him. A lovely little toy. Sam put a real effort into making it for him. But he just looks at it and refuses to touch it. It drives Sam crazy.'

Pa had shouted at me that very morning, when Mrs Goldstein had come in to buy a length of calico and some sewing needles, bringing her son Joey with her. Joey had seen the hammer and pegboard lying in the sawdust and made a tottering lurch for it, grabbing the brightly coloured pegs and banging them firmly into the holes. 'I made the thing for *you!*' Pa stormed, when they'd left the shop. 'Not for blooming Joey Goldstein, who's barely three years old!'

'Perhaps you should take him to see a specialist?' said Mrs van der Merwe, still looking straight at me, her icy eyes drilling into me. 'They could tell you if something's seriously wrong.'

'I've suggested it to Sam but …'

'I know, I know, they're expensive these specialists. But if you speak to Dr Meller, maybe he'll find you someone who'll do it cheap? Or why not ask your father to pay for it? Old Oupa would cough up something, wouldn't he, even if your husband isn't so keen on spending the money. Old Oupa loves the little boy, doesn't he?'

'Of course,' said Ma. 'But I don't want to go behind Sam's back. Maybe later. I have other things on my mind at the moment.' She placed one hand on her stomach.

The store bell rang and old Mr Rabinovitz came in. He was wearing his usual dirty grey cardigan and stained black trousers. He came over and ruffled my hair, then started rummaging through the brown cardboard box in the corner, with its fraying offcuts of carpet and rolls of linoleum. I pulled at my hair, to try to get it to lie flat and comfortable again.

'Look, still in his soft bedroom slippers,' whispered Mrs van der Merwe. 'He's obviously forgotten to change into his outdoor shoes.'

'Poor man. He's not the same since his wife died last year,' Ma said quietly.

Mrs van der Merwe nodded.

'And he's worrying about his family in Poland, of course,' Ma added. 'An aunt and a sister. He's not heard from them for a while.'

Mrs van der Merwe said nothing, as if all this meant very little to her; Poland was as distant and unfathomable as Venus or Mars. The talk between the Jews who came into the store was often about family back home and fears of what was happening. The words drifted around my head but they didn't make much sense to me either: troubling signs, dark clouds, Smuts and Herzog, neutrality, the war effort, obtaining visas, hiding jewellery, booking passages, trains to nowhere.

'Oh well, I'd best be going,' Mrs van der Merwe said at last. She nodded a good-day in Mr Rabinovitz's direction, then picked up her bag of goods and left.

'You'll come in and pay tomorrow morning, then?' called Ma. 'First thing. Don't forget, will you?'

'Of course not, Mrs Neuberger. Tomorrow.' Gently she closed the shop door behind her and the bell tinkled to signal her departure.

I kept my eyes fixed on Mr Rabinovitz. I hoped he would not touch my hair again, or take a soft bit of my cheek between his finger and thumb and squeeze it, as he sometimes did when I was sitting on my sack of beans and couldn't get away. He would touch or prod me with his dry, wrinkled hands, or laugh loudly and call me boychick or bubula, with that voice of his that sounded like it was being ground up into coarse mealie flour. Ma might feel sorry for him but I couldn't look at him with anything other than disgust. I watched him pick out a small roll of dark-blue carpet and look hopefully towards Ma.

'No, Mr Rabinovitz. Absolutely not. I'm sorry. My husband says no more on account. You have to pay what's already owing.' She sighed.

Mr Rabinovitz held the roll in front of him and looked at it mournfully. He placed it carefully back in the box, stood staring at it for several minutes and then turned to leave, shuffling towards the front door. Glancing back at me, he waved, with a slow, sad sweep of the hand and opened the door to go.

'Oh for goodness' sake, just take it,' I heard Ma call out to him. What was she doing? 'It's not worth much and it won't be noticed. Take it and go before I change my mind, or my husband walks in and tells me what a damned fool I am.'

Mr Rabinovitz shuffled back and seized the roll of carpet. He placed it carefully under his arm and edged his way out of the store, smiling to himself as he went and muttering, 'Thank you, bless you. It's a mitzvah, an act of goodness. God will thank you.'

When he'd gone, Ma slumped back down on the stool and kicked off her shoes again.

'God may thank me but what's your pa going to say when he finds out how soft I've been?' She looked at me, sitting on my sack of beans. 'At least I know I can trust you, Jackie,' she said. 'I know that you won't say a word.'

*****

'What's happened with the money in the till?' asked Pa when he got round to checking it the next day, after the front door had been locked and the shop was closed for lunch. He had come back late the previous evening from Paarl and had spent the morning unloading the truck and stacking the dusty sacks in the shed in the yard, while Ma and Ada minded the store. Finally, now that it was quiet, he had turned his attention to the till, adding up the notes and the coins, placing them in neat rows and piles on the countertop, licking his finger and thumb and flicking through the notes while his lips moved, silently counting.

'It doesn't tally. There's money missing.'

'Don't get angry, Sam,' Ma said. 'I can explain.'

I looked at my father. His face was turning red and the veins stood out in his neck, like thick sinewy rope. His body was rigid, his limbs stiff. Suddenly he swept his arm across the counter and sent the spools of string spinning off the edge. They turned and turned crazily in the sawdust on the floor.

Now Ma was going to cry and climb the stairs to her room. She would close the door behind her. She might not come down for hours and hours and I would be left on my own, sitting in the kitchen or the store, wondering whether she would be better by suppertime, or whether Ada would give me a thick slice of bread and butter instead of the borscht, sour cream and warm potatoes that Ma had promised.

Ada would say, as she always did, 'Ag shame, man. A kiddie like you don't need to hear grown-ups shouting like that,' or 'Seis tog, Jackie, I feel sorry for you in this crazy place!'

This time, though, Ma stood there silently. There was no crying. Her blank face, pale and waxy as greaseproof paper, was almost worse than tears and I wondered what was coming next.

Pa looked at Ma. The colour in his face had faded a little but his forehead remained furrowed, his eyes dark. He slammed the till shut, so that it rattled.

'I hope you can explain,' he said.

I sat on the rough wooden floor, tracing patterns in the sawdust with my finger, feeling the soft wood dust powdering my hand. I looked up towards Ma.

'It's Mrs van de Merwe again. She promised she'd come in this morning to pay. I felt sorry for her. She was short of cash. She promised to come but she must have forgotten.'

Pa thumped his fist down hard on the counter, making the row of biscuit jars shudder and jump along the counter.

'Don't be angry with me,' Ma said. 'I couldn't say no to her. They're still struggling after the bankruptcy last year. Her husband's not back on his feet yet.'

'You may not have noticed but we're a shop, not a welfare board. We're not in the business of helping out every blooming Afrikaner who's having a hard time. What are you doing, giving out favours left right and centre, the minute my back's turned?'

'I do my best. I try.' There was a silence. 'It doesn't come naturally to me,' she said.

He sighed.

'I didn't ask to be a shopkeeper's wife.'

'Ah, that again, how far beneath you it is to be serving in a store.'

'I didn't say that.'

'A woman with your education shouldn't have to serve customers.'

'I didn't say that.'

'A woman like you, who could have been a schoolteacher, or a nurse.'

Ma turned away, towards the kitchen. Now, though I couldn't see her face, I knew that she would be blinking away the tears.

'I've had enough of this meshugas,' she muttered wearily. 'I'm so tired of this shouting all the time.'

'So what are you going to do about it?' Pa said. There was a little note of doubt in his voice.

'I know what I'd do, if it weren't for Little Jackie, and the one on the way.'

'What, go back to your parents? Go, if you're so keen,' Pa said. 'Go crying to your parents to have you back. Go! I'm sure they'd be delighted!' and then finally, in Yiddish, 'I'll give you sandwiches to help you on your way!'

'You're just trying to upset me,' Ma sobbed.

'No,' he said, more quietly. 'I'm not. Why would I want to do that? But for God's sake, Sarah, we need to make a living. I'm trying to build this place up, make something of it. The last few years have been hard, but now maybe things are starting to look up a bit. Please, help me. No more nice gestures to Mrs van de Merwe or anyone else for that matter.'

He stepped towards her to put a hand on her arm but Ma turned away from him, picked up a pile of papers from the counter and without looking up, said, 'I think I should tell you, before you ask; I gave Mr Rabinovitz that piece of blue carpet. In case you're wondering where it went.'

'For God's sake, Sarah!' he shouted, but she was already in the kitchen. I heard her slow footsteps climbing the staircase and listened for the silence at the top, where she usually waited to catch her breath. I heard the bedroom door open and shut quietly behind her. I knew that she would be gone for the rest of the afternoon and that once again there would just be bread and butter for my supper.

Chapter 4

'Where are you going?' Ma wailed. 'Don't go.' But Pa had already grabbed the keys to the truck and was heading out the back door. I heard the truck door slam and the engine hiccoughing into life. Ma sat down heavily on the stool behind the counter. Her shoulders were shuddering.

They'd had another argument, soon after Ada left, this time about the money that Pa was giving her to spend. Ma had asked how he expected her to put food on the table, unless he gave her the money to buy it. Why couldn't she budget properly, like other women, Pa had demanded to know. 'You're clever enough, aren't you?'

That had been the final straw. She'd shouted at him that other women had husbands who gave them enough money to run a decent home.

And then he'd taken the keys and gone.

'Go for your afternoon nap, Jackie,' Ma said, sniffing into her sleeve. 'I'll bring you a biscuit and a glass of milk later, if you're a good boy.'

I went up to my bed and tried to sleep but tossed and turned in the hot sheets. My hair was damp with sweat. I thought about the biscuit and the glass of milk and of Ma downstairs, sitting on her stool. The patterns on the walls drifted before my eyes, the flowery wallpaper, the stain above the bed and the dark patch where the photograph of Auntie Essie had once hung and been taken down. I stared at the glass lampshade, with its dusty yellow light. A pair of flies circled the bulb, like little aeroplanes that had lost their controls.

Briefly I dozed and woke to hear Ma coming slowly up the stairs. She opened the door and stood there. She was panting for breath.

'I'm not well, Jackie,' she breathed. 'I need help. Pa's driven away in the truck, goodness knows where, and Ada's gone for her bus home. You're the only one here, so you've got to look after your ma, Jackie my boy. You've got to help me.'

I tried not to cry but there was a voice out there in the room, outside of me, sobbing, a high-pitched moan. Was it mine?

'Be brave, Jackie. My time has come.' That phrase again. And now it was here.

'Listen to me,' she said fiercely, through gritted teeth but then stopped midway and held her breath, seemingly unable to finish her sentence. Then all of a sudden she started to moan and when I looked down I saw her dress was wet, a burst of water rushing down her legs and pooling on the linoleum by her feet.

Now she was whimpering. 'Come with me, Jackie,' she whispered. 'We must get help.'

She pulled me out of the bed by the arm, bruising me with the pressure of her hand on my elbow. Heaving herself out of the bedroom door, she lowered herself slowly onto the stairs and slid down, one at a time, pausing for breath and to steady herself, pushing me ahead of her with one hand.

Halfway down, she stopped. I saw her bite hard on her lip, till a small bubble of crimson blood welled up. She licked it away and then, when more appeared, let it trickle lazily down her chin. She eased herself further down the stairs, then crawled into the store, keeping close to the counter, and edged towards the locked shop door. I had never seen her like this, on her hands and knees, lumbering across the dusty floor. I clung to her arm. A few yards from the door, she stopped and sank down.

'Open the door,' she said. 'Try to reach up, Jackie, and see if you can do it. Try hard, Jackie.'

I stretched up for the catch. If I stood on tiptoe I could just about reach it but it was too stiff for my small hands to pull back and I couldn't open it.

I looked out. On Main Road, it was quiet. The shops had all closed. It was that time of day when stoves were being lit and everyone had headed home, when children played in the yard and cats and dogs came back to be fed, when mosquitoes began to seek out lamps and the gazanias closed their blooms for the night, when the rubbish lorry had already passed. I looked out and saw no one. I banged on the door. Ma yelled for help but no one came by.

I stood looking out at the empty street. No one. Finally, from the corner of my eye, I saw something coming. It was Piet du Plessis, strolling down Main Road.

I knew Piet from the times he came into the shop with his mother. I'd heard Ma say, 'He thinks he's a real man now with that swagger of his,' and Ada had giggled. 'Gone girl mad,' Ma said. 'Eyeing up everything that moves.'

Ada had laughed. 'Got a few years to go before he nabs one, I reckon. Fifteen's too young to be sniffing around the meisies, the young girls.'

Now he was strolling down Main Road. Perhaps he was off to the corner shop to buy an ice and hoping that there might be a girl or two there. He passed the Handyhouse, all dark and shut up.

He was about to walk past. 'It's Piet,' Ma panted. 'Get him to stop.'

I tapped on the window. He walked on. How could I make him stop?

*****

Later, Piet told the story to everyone who came into the store: Mrs van de Merwe, Mrs Shapiro and Mikey, Millicent, April Fortune and all the others who crowded round the counter to listen and make ooh and ahh noises at the puling, shrivelled little prune who was my new brother.

'I thought it was Spot-eye the cat, that tapping noise, scratching at the shop window, trying to be let out. Something made me turn back. I looked into the darkness and saw nothing. I looked more carefully. And there was Little Jackie, standing at the door, tapping away. And there on the floor of the store was something big and lumpy, up against the counter, that turned out to be Missus Neuberger. I didn't recognise her at first. I thought it was a pile of clothes, or old curtains or something.

'I didn't know what to do. Should I go and run for help? Should I leave her and the little boy? Or should I break down the door and help her myself? Jeez, it was the most difficult decision of my life.'

Mrs du Plessis laughed out loud at that. 'You've had no decisions in your life, Piet. You're only fifteen.'

Everyone laughed.

'Shut up, Ma,' yelled Piet, blushing furiously. She was spoiling his story.

'Anyhow, I decided there and then. There was no time for help. So I pushed the door hard but it wouldn't give. And then I kicked at the door as hard as I could. First time it only shuddered. So I tried again. Second time no good. Third time round I hurled myself at it and what d'you know, the lock gave and I went flying in, glass shattering all around me and Little Jackie sitting there with it sprinkled all over him like shiny frosting. She was in a bad way, boy oh boy, was she in a bad way!'

'Yes,' said Ma. 'I was.' She was holding Sauly, my ugly baby brother, looking down at him and smiling tenderly.

'I couldn't leave her lying like that and she was shouting, "It's coming, oy vay, it's coming," so I ran behind the counter and fetched one of those rolls of cheesecloth and I rolled it all out and got it under her bum ('scuse my language, Missus Neuberger) and I did what I'd heard Ma saying she told my cousin Alice when her baby was coming too quick. I said, "Now take it easy Missus N, and don't you push too hard. Keep breathing, keep breathing," and that kind of stuff. I didn't want to look at what was happening down below because, well, you know… But then she was doing one almighty awful push like there was no tomorrow and she says, "The head, Piet, the head. You've got to pull." So what was I to do?'

'What did you do?' said Mikey Shapiro but Mrs Shapiro tutted loudly and covered up his ears with her hands. 'Too young,' she said and kept them there for the rest of story, with Mikey squirming and struggling to break free.

'There was no choice, I had to do it. There it was, all bloody and smooth, just coming out.'

Piet paused in the telling. It seemed like he had to, as his eyes had filled with tears and he was swallowing hard and wiping them away roughly with his hand.

'I shoved my shirtsleeves up to my elbows and I just took hold of the head. It was warm and soft. I could feel a little pulse beating, de dum, de dum, under the skin. I felt for the edges and gave it a little tug, just a little one and suddenly everything was out, slipping and slithering, shoulders and arms and legs and blood and a face all red and cross like Mr Krapotkin's.'

Mrs du Plessis ruffled Piet's hair.

'It's good news for some little lady who's going to marry *you* one day,' said Mrs van de Merwe. 'No doctor's bills.'

Everyone laughed.

But his mother said, 'I reckon this'll stop him thinking about girls for a while. Let him concentrate on his studies and on his swimming and high jump for a year or two!'

And then the shop erupted and Piet blushed again and turned his face away and hid it in his sleeve.

Ma carried on the story for him. 'When Sam came back late into the night, I was upstairs in bed with the baby. And what does he say? He takes one look at the baby and gives him a kiss on the head, then he asks me who in hell has broken down the store door, 'cause whoever it is is going to damn well have to pay for it!'

Mrs van de Merwe frowned and tut-tutted and said what a shame. And Piet and Mrs du Plessis quietly left the shop and headed off home, but not before Mrs du Plessis had paused in the doorway and, in a loud voice, turned to Piet to make a solemn vow, 'never to use that man's store again'.

CHAPTER 5

Mrs van Heerden had just had her fourth child. The birth was a difficult one. It had ended in a Caesarean section and, with three other children to care for, she had found it hard to get back on her feet, to keep up with the day-to-day demands of the family, let alone the additional burdens of being a pastor's wife. Even with Alice, the coloured girl he'd brought in to assist her, it was clear to her husband that she wasn't really coping. Little Beatrice, like all the children, had been a blessing from God, but his wife had definitely struggled since her birth.

'She's a good woman,' Johannes van Heerden told Jack, when he came to his chambers for that first meeting, 'a decent woman.'

It was a strange start to the meeting. Jack had set aside an hour for this first encounter with van Heerden. He had read the documents that Smit, the solicitor, had passed to him and had been appalled; the man had barely scratched the surface of the case. He'd not even talked to van Heerden himself or any of the other key people involved. Clearly, whether through lack of interest, negligence or distaste for its content, Smit was in a hurry to pass the case on and he'd made it quite evident that he'd be very happy to turn a blind eye and allow Jack to do the interviews himself, however unorthodox that might be. The papers were a mess; the defence was shoddy; Jack knew he couldn't mount a proper case without more information. So he had decided to meet the accused himself.

Now that he was here in front of him, he had a long list of questions to ask. He wanted to get the facts clear – what had happened over the weeks leading up to the accusations and formal charge, van Heerden's relationship with the woman, with his wife, with his accusers and, most important of all, whether he had decided which way he was going to plead, guilty or not. Jack hoped he might get one or two good angles, either way: if innocent, a few initial lines of enquiry that might help him mount a defence; if guilty, a way of presenting the mitigating circumstances so as to achieve the lightest possible sentence.

The first question he had actually asked his new client was a different one, a gentle warm-up to establish a relationship. He was aware of the huge gulf between them, him a Jew from Parow, brought up in his father's hardware store, van Heerden an Afrikaner with a Dutch Reformed Church background that had made him a well-known figure in his community. He was very conscious of the gap in their ages as well. He couldn't have helped but notice the look of surprise on van Heerden's face when he walked through the door. An advocate barely out of school! How could he possibly be experienced enough to handle this kind of case? He'd have to find ways to reassure his client, however much he himself might secretly share his doubts.

'Tell me a bit about yourself, Pastor. I'd like to get a sense of who you are, before we get down to the details of the case.'

But straightaway van Heerden started talking not about himself, but about his wife.

'We've been married for fifteen years now. We met at church. She was the daughter of the previous pastor, Reverend Pietersen. Laura Mairie Pietersen, the third of four daughters. It was clear from the start that we were meant for each other. Everything seemed right – everything made sense.' He paused. 'It has been a good marriage and she has been a good wife. I want you to understand that, Mr Neuberger. I love my wife. It's important that you know that.'

'Of course,' Jack said. 'That's understood.'

'Good,' he said and then, somewhat disconcertingly, he began to sob. 'She's a good woman,' he continued, struggling to speak through the tears. 'This whole business, it's been terrible for her. It's for her that I want to clear my name.'

He leaned forward, placing his head in his hands.

'This must be upsetting for you,' Jack said. 'Take your time.'

While van Heerden composed himself, Jack took the chance to observe him more closely. He was stockily built, dressed in a grey suit, rather than the dog collar and robes Jack had been expecting. His hair was springy and thick but somewhat grey. He had a wide face and a large, full mouth, straight shoulders, big, broad hands. In other circumstances, Jack could have pictured him on a farm in the Karoo, herding cattle into the coral, or driving a harvester over a field of mealies, an authoritative figure, shouting orders out across the noise to his workers.

'Shall we continue?' Jack said.

'I'm sorry for that silliness. It's been a difficult time.'

'Not silly at all, Mr van Heerden. Perfectly understandable.'

Van Heerden now spoke more firmly, holding his gaze. 'I want to know what I should tell you, so you can help me. I'll do whatever is necessary.'

Jack hesitated. He wasn't quite sure how to take this. He wondered whether van Heerden understood that his words to his own advocate were not to be said lightly, that Jack was held to a code of conduct? Was he asking for a steer, to find out how much he could say, without jeopardising his position?

'You need to tell me the truth, Mr van Heerden. And then I act upon the facts of the case, on your behalf, representing your interests as best I can. If you tell me you're innocent, I fight to prove that. If you tell me you're guilty, I make the best possible case for you. If you tell me you're guilty, I can't go into court and pretend otherwise. I can find mitigating circumstances, of course, and I can question points of law, but your admission is what will guide my actions.'

Van Heerden continued to look straight at him but there was nothing in his gaze that gave anything away.

'I suggest that we take this slowly,' Jack said. 'At this stage, perhaps you don't even understand exactly what the law itself states and what the implications are. Maybe you've read about it in the papers, big headlines and sweeping statements, the politics behind it all, but probably you don't know anything about the fine detail. I'd say you're not yet in a position to judge how your actions may have been interpreted, rightly or wrongly, so perhaps we should just start with the story. You can tell me what happened and then we'll take it from there. We'll see what kind of case we can mount.'

Jack picked up his phone.

'Vera, I think we need a pot of coffee in here. And maybe order us a few sandwiches from Lou's. Salt beef suit you, Mr van Heerden, or a smoked salmon bagel?'

'I've never tried either,' van Heerden said.

'There's always a first time,' Jack said and saw that he'd brought a faint smile to van Heerden's lips. Good to make a relationship. Not what Willem du Toit might do, or Fineberg or Cohen for that matter, but it was his way of going about it, and he'd find out soon enough whether it would pay off or not.

'Now perhaps you want to tell me the story,' he said. 'Take off your jacket. Relax. Start whenever you want.'

Van Heerden shifted a little in his seat but kept his jacket on, despite the heat. 'I was brought up in a house of God,' he said. 'My parents were good, upright people. I went to school, I read my bible, I went to church, I married young. Laura and I, we started a family. And when her father died, ten years ago, God rest his soul, I took over as minister. We are a large community and a strong one. We have over one hundred families attending Sunday services, you know. It's grown since I took over and though I can take some credit for that, so can my wife. She's well respected. People come to her for help. The women like her.

'She runs a prayer group for women and they decided that their prayers should be turned into deeds. They started visiting the poorer areas of our community, taking with them things they'd made themselves or articles they no longer needed, clothing or jars of jam or bags of koeksisters, old toys, kitchenware, anything they thought might be appreciated by those less fortunate than themselves. They go out to share their own riches with others more in need. Acts of goodness to others, daily demonstrations of their faith. This group has brought all kinds of people to our door. They come to my wife and her group for help.

'I have supported her with this. But when she had Beatrice and was so unwell, she stopped being able to keep up this good work. It was too much for her. The women turned to me for help and I stepped in. It was only intended to be for a short time, until she got back on her feet, back to her usual self. They needed someone to guide them and it seemed only right that I should do this for her.'

Jack found himself wondering where all this was leading, but he was reluctant to interrupt his client. His style of speech was rather ponderous and slow, but it might prove helpful in court; it suggested a man who thought hard, who measured his words and his actions carefully, not someone who would lightly throw caution, and his reputation, to the winds. And yet again, it drew attention to his love and admiration for his wife.

'I came across the woman while carrying out these duties for my wife.'

Now were getting closer to the nub of it, the reason why they were both here in the small office on the third floor of Temple Chambers. The woman. Agnes Small. The co-accused.

'She was a woman on her own, with two small children. Her husband had died and she had no family to speak of. Her employer went bankrupt and she lost her job. She'd come to our house to ask for help and my wife had taken her situation to heart. She was a proud-looking woman, who clearly found it hard to seek assistance and yet she was close to despair. Laura told me of her plight. And when she became ill, she asked that I should continue to help her.

'So there we have it,' he said. 'I visited her from time to time, taking with me a sack of groceries or a small bag of clothes that my wife had gathered from our little flock. I took her these things and then returned to my duties at the church, or to my wife and family.'

He looked Jack in the eye. 'It's as simple as that,' he said. 'Laura knows all about it. She asked me to go. And as for the accusations, they are malicious rumours, nothing more. People – her neighbours, others on the fringes of our community – find it hard to understand why a white Afrikaner, whether a man of God or not, should go to see a coloured woman in her home. They imagine the worst. They do not understand that all people are equal in God's eyes and that this woman is as deserving of our love and our charity as anyone else.'

Good, good, thought Jack. He would make an excellent advocate for himself on the stand, though some of his views might not be to everyone's taste. There were plenty of Dutch Reformed Church clergymen who, in the current political climate, would be happy to make distinctions between themselves and their black neighbours, who would find no trouble in squaring this with their Christian faith, as if Jesus himself had sanctioned a hierarchy of human value based on the colour of your skin. It was a relief that van Heerden's rhetoric was different. Jack would have found it hard to sympathise with him and act for him, were this not the case. But his client needed to take care in court. He mustn't come across as a liberal thinker, or, worse still, a communist. If van Heerden could be persuaded to tone down his views, he had a perfectly plausible story to tell, of charitable doing with the blessing of both God and, perhaps more importantly, his wife.

And yet… Jack couldn't help but wonder. It was all so simple, all so obvious. From his limited experience, perhaps too simple.

'Tell me about the accusations. Where do you think they stemmed from? When did they start?'

'A whispering at first, a few strange looks in church, a word of concern from my church warden, then one day a letter through my letterbox and a stone through the window. Finally, the inevitable, a knock on the door from the police. That's when Laura had to be told. I'd kept it from her, fearing for her health. "Just boys playing tricks," I'd said and got the window repaired. It was a terrible shock to her when the police came to our house. "We've been led to believe…" they said. "People tell us…" "We understand that…" – all very vague and unclear. But then a week later they were back with papers to sign, saying, "We now have sufficient evidence to warrant a charge." Perhaps you know better than me who my accusers are? The prosecution must be preparing to bring their witnesses before the court. Have they provided you with a list?'

'One or two names have been mentioned but I don't yet know for sure who they'll call. Is there anything you could have done that would have created resentment towards you? Anything that might have aroused suspicion? You did nothing beyond visiting the woman with your wife's charitable offerings?'

'No, nothing at all,' he said. 'There is nothing for which I can feel any sense of shame or remorse.'

There were other questions to be asked about the visits to the woman, how often he had gone and how long he stayed and Van Heerden took them in his stride. He was clear and direct in his answers – just six or seven visits over a period of six months, staying for ten minutes or so and once or twice a little longer, to share a drink of tea and offer up a short prayer.

So far so good, but Jack wanted to find out more about van Heerden's wife, the state of her health and whether she was well enough to be interviewed, to confirm her husband's version of the events, to him first of all and then in court if need be. He would like to meet van Heerden's wife. She was clearly a woman who commanded respect in her community. And the love Johannes expressed for her was admirable and appeared to be genuine enough. It seemed, from his account, that theirs was a marriage truly made in heaven. He pictured them together in church, or in the midst of their large family, at a charity sale or harvest festival, or kneeling in prayer together at the end of their bed. And inevitably he thought of their intimate life, alone together, and wondered whether for Laura and Johannes van Heerden that too was a model of marital happiness. That would be important to know. But it would be a difficult thing to broach with him. Van Heerden's feelings for his wife were strong; he would want to protect her at all costs. Jack knew, however, that in the end it would inevitably be brought into play, if not by him, then certainly by the prosecution. Van Heerden's marriage was going to be put under the microscope.

'Let's leave it for today, shall we?' he said. 'We'll take it further when we meet next time.'

Van Heerden nodded. 'I should get back to my wife. She'll be worried and wanting to know what has happened.'

'Tell her I'm fighting your corner,' Jack said. 'She can rely on me to do my very best for you. I'll do everything I can.'

He came out from behind the desk and shook van Heerden's hand. He liked the man, despite all the myriad differences between them, and he meant what he said. He would do his damnedest to get him off, and though he could barely acknowledge it to himself, let alone voice the thought to anyone else, he knew that he wanted to have him acquitted, innocent or not. The law was an outrage and a farce and any jury of decent men and women should recognise that. They should reject it, as a mockery of justice and basic humanity. And if he could get them to do that, wouldn't that be an achievement? An act of defiance, a small but significant stand.

He believed his client's protestations of innocence, at least at this stage, but even if he *had* slept with the woman, so what? In a civilised society, a white man sleeping with a black woman shouldn't even be frowned upon, let alone considered worthy of a criminal charge. But over the last few years things had been changing; the Nationalist government had been hardening its position even further and the few remaining remnants of the English-speaking community's values were in rapid retreat. From separate seats on buses and 'Whites only' benches and toilets, it was a surprisingly small step to these further pieces of legislation, pushing relentlessly onwards towards total segregation. The pass laws had long existed, restricting the movement of black people into the cities and keeping them confined to their 'homelands', but here was a law that seemed to him to be equally damaging, one that reached deep into people's private worlds and most intimate personal relationships – the right to express their physical and emotional feelings for another human being. To love someone of another race was no longer a matter of preference or choice; it was a criminal act. And to defend someone accused of breaking the law in such a high profile case was also a risky business. It might damage his chances of getting ordinary commercial work; there would be many who would be only too quick to characterise him as one of those new politically motivated advocates, a Jewish rabble-rousing communist. But would it also, perhaps, make him the object of unwanted attention by the authorities? He'd heard of advocates who believed themselves to be under scrutiny, nothing too obvious, just a sense of being on the Special Branch radar. The mood in the country was darkening. Who knew where it was all leading?

These things had to be considered; it would be foolish not to. Cohen had told him to use his head not his heart and that's what he'd been telling himself that he would do. He'd remain coolly analytical, forensic, do a good job and walk away with his reputation intact. He wouldn't let it damage him – he owed that to Renee. And to himself. It'd taken him long enough, God knows, to get this far; years of studying, against all the odds. His father hadn't lived to see it but his mother was able to witness it and he knew how much pride she took in his successes. Her son Jack, who had started out with so little to show for himself, an educated man, an advocate in a good set of chambers, making a proper living for himself, appearing for the first time in the most important court in the land! He had told himself that he'd have to take cognisance of this. He was building up a practice for himself and beginning to do well. It was important not to put a foot wrong. Use his head.

And yet…This case spoke to his heart, however hard he tried to deny it. The politics and the racial aspect, he'd known about before. It interested him hugely, from a professional point of view. It was a testing ground for values he'd come to hold dear. It felt good to be right at the heart of an important case, one of national importance, whose outcome would change things, not just for his client but also for his country, for South Africa as a whole. But behind all of that there were other things.

There was Terence. He remembered Terence, sitting cross-legged with him in the sawdust on the Handyhouse floor, lining up his Dinky cars for a race, or playing five stones, his head bent forward in concentration. It was hard to forget him.

Now, having met his client for the first time, he could see that there was also another aspect to it all that he would struggle to put to one side, in the interests of cool logic and professionalism – a man and a woman, a husband and wife, a marriage teetering on the brink. This was *his* case, through and through.

Head or heart? He put the papers back in the file and set them to one side. Then he stood up, pushed his chair under the desk, took up his briefcase and left the room. He locked the door behind him and as he did so his eye lingered on his name etched onto the gold plate on the door, 'MR J. NEUBERGER, ADVOCATE. He touched it, feeling the ridges of the letters under his fingers.

He'd go home and talk to Renee. He'd tell her about his day. But he wouldn't share with her these thoughts, not yet. He'd give it a bit of time. No point in worrying her; he'd just wait and see what happened.

CHAPTER 6

1940

One morning when I woke up and called for Ma, Ada appeared beside my bed instead, looking flustered and pale. Her eyes were red and puffy, as if she had been crying.

'Ag, man,' she said. 'It's a blerry good thing you slept through last night, Jackie. All hell let loose. Your ma was goin' to come and wake you and take you with her, but she decided to leave you to sleep, with all the upset and the shouting and that. She's told me to bring you to her this morning.'

What did she mean? Where was Ma? Where had she gone? What about Sauly? Had she taken him with her, instead of me, abandoned me while Sauly was by her side? And what about Pa, what had happened to him? Had he gone too?

'I'm going to get you dressed and I'll give you some nice hot Nutrene porridge and milk for your breakfast, then we're going over to your ouma and oupa's house. Your pa's busy taking stock in the store. You can say goodbye to him before we go.'

An hour later I found myself walking down Main Road with Ada, holding her hand. She was sniffling as she went. From time to time she exploded in a burst of 'Such a lot of blerry nonsense,' which then subsided into sobs again. Along the way we met Mrs Levy, who shook her head and tutted. She had obviously heard that something was amiss. Further down, Mrs du Plessis crossed the street to say, 'I always knew there'd be trouble, right from when they took over that store,' and old Mr Roach muttered, 'Well, well, well,' as he passed.

Ouma and Oupa lived three blocks down, on a side street, in a small house, bounded at the front by a high factory wall and at the back by a piece of scrubby, unused land. Oupa's workshop was in the front room. It was filled with shoes and boots, slippers and sandals, bags and satchels. In the corner, a grinding wheel usually turned. To one side was a large treadle sewing machine. At the front was Oupa's table, covered in tacks, heels, chalk, cardboard labels, paper bags, shoes in a state of half-repair. I knew it well.

The front door was open and we walked straight in. Today the wheel was silent, the sewing machine still. Ada took me with her into the back room, where I saw Ma, with Sauly sitting on her lap. Here also were Ouma and Oupa, sitting beside her. The tiny room was crowded with suitcases, wicker baskets, jute bags. Jarpe, my toy monkey, was perched perilously on the top of the pile. The small window, with its mosquito netting, had been flung open wide, but with all these people and bags in it, the room still felt oppressively hot, steamy with human sweat and reeking with the acrid tang of leather, shoe polish, rubber and glue.

'We've left,' said Ma, pulling me towards her. 'We're not going back.' She burst into tears. Sauly sensed the mood and joined in, along with Ada and Ouma, who was howling curses in Yiddish. 'May he be dead and not just dead. May he be buried in the earth,' she howled, 'not just in it but through it, to the very core. May he grow like an onion, with his head stuck in the ground.'

'Hush, Bertha,' said Oupa firmly. 'Enough.'

'This is your home now,' said Ma to me. I looked around and wondered how on earth there was going to be room in this tiny little house for Ouma and Oupa, Olive, the coloured maid, Ma, Sauly, Ada and me.

'Ada, you must go back to the store now,' said Ma. 'You'll be needed.'

'Never,' said Ada fiercely. 'I'm staying with you.'

'We have no money to pay you. Your wages are for your work at the store. You must go back now. Be sensible and think of your sick mother. Think of the hospital bills. She depends on you.'

Ada hugged Ma, kissed me and Sauly on the cheeks, burst into a new flurry of tears, then hurried off to make it back in time for the store opening.

Ma placed me on a chair in the workshop. She put Sauly in an empty chest drawer, wrapped a blanket round him, placed one foot underneath one end and rocked it vigorously with the other. I listened to the voices of my mother and my grandparents, their noisy Yiddish, and Oupa's voice the loudest of all.

He said that he understood his family was cursed, that their woes would never cease, that having five daughters and only one son was a tragedy, that a shoemaker's money only went so far in supporting five useless girls and he'd been overjoyed to get her married, that Sam had been a very good match, better than she deserved, a man with prospects. He said that under God's eyes a marriage is a marriage for life, that men are men and women are women, that there are two ways to scratch an itch, like so and like so (scratching his cheek with one hand and then bringing the other hand awkwardly over his head to scratch it again and prove his point), that Sam sometimes behaved badly, yes, badly, badly, that he was too preoccupied with money and forgot all the other important things in life, that he didn't always show enough kindness to Ma, even if he felt it.

'But,' said Oupa, 'for all that, he's a good husband to you. He's not a schlemiel. And he's not a schnorrer. He may not be the biggest brain in the world, not the great intellectual that you seem to think you are, but never mind – he works hard to put food on the table. And he doesn't go off chasing other women, from what one can tell. There are much worse men, much worse husbands, and if you had an ounce of sense in that oh-so-clever head of yours you'd count your blessings and be a good wife to him, instead of making a big meal of every little irritation and argument.'

Ma listened quietly, snuffling into her handkerchief. Ouma came and put her arm around her.

'May he get running sores and ulcers on his skin,' she muttered, 'for upsetting you so.'

'Enough, Bertha,' Oupa shouted. 'You're not helping. Leave her to think about all that I have said. She'll see reason soon enough.'

I woke from my afternoon nap later that day, to find all the bags and suitcases packed again and piled up by the door. Ma was puffy-eyed and not speaking to Oupa. He cursed the day he had ever had daughters. Ouma in turn cursed men and the ugly thing they had dangling between their legs that caused so much trouble and made men think they were so wonderfully important, and the sorrow they brought to their poor, long-suffering wives.

I listened to Ouma and Oupa and drank in all this information about my mother and my father and the adult world of men and women. If marriage was like this, perhaps I would stay single all my life, like my father's cousin Morrie, or Mr Singer the bookkeeper who came to pore over my father's accounts each year. I would save myself the trouble of having a wife. I didn't want to make my wife cry, like Pa seemed to do to Ma. Was it possible to grow up to be a different kind of man, with a different kind of life?

Ma hugged Ouma and then, helped by Olive and her son, Willie, we walked back down the street to the store, carrying all our belongings with us.

When we got there, Pa was behind the counter, in his shirtsleeves, measuring lengths of cloth. He didn't look up as Ma dragged the bags through the sawdust, out the back and up the rickety stairs. He didn't offer to help. But he came and took Sauly up in his arms and kissed him on the cheek, and ruffled my hair roughly with his hand, and I was glad to see him, which made me feel all the more confused. Ouma, Oupa, Ma, Pa – how could I decide who was right and who was wrong?

*****

That summer we seemed to be going backwards and forwards to Ouma and Oupa's every second week. The bags would scarcely be unpacked when Ma would decide that enough was enough and we would head off, back down the road again, with Sauly under one of Ma's arm and me trailing behind her. All along Main Road heads shook and tongues clicked. 'Ag, shame, man!', 'Poor little kiddies!', 'Whatever possessed her to marry him?', 'Whatever possessed her to leave him?', 'Whatever possessed him to take her back?'

One evening, as Ma lay close beside me in the camp bed in the back room at Ouma and Oupa's, trying to get me to sleep, she started to tell me about when she was young, before she met Pa.

'I know you don't speak yet, Jackie, but I'm sure you understand. You're getting to be a big boy and you must wonder about all these things that are going on. So I'll tell you the story of me and your pa. It's not his fault really,' she said. 'And it's not mine either. It's just the way things are. Not all marriages are made in heaven, you know.'

Ma paused and smoothed my hair. 'Are you listening, Jackie'

I nodded.

'I'll tell you about me and your pa and how we came to be married. But I need to go back a bit first, to Ouma and Oupa and the years before.

'When Oupa arrived in Cape Town, he got off the boat and stood with Ouma on the waterfront and the first thing he did was to ask for the synagogue, not because he wanted to pray – he wasn't frum, like the Levys or the Goldsteins – but he knew that where there was a synagogue, there'd be Jews, and where there were Jews he would find help. At Constitution Street synagogue, someone asked someone who asked someone else to give them a bed for the night and the next day they were sent on to Vredehoek, a little district not too far away. When Ouma and Oupa got there, they found themselves in another little Jewish world – hotter, dustier, than the one they'd come from, odd and unfamiliar but safe, thank the Lord, safer than the shtetl back home, where they always feared the threat of a pogrom, the burning of their house or the theft of their land.

'There in Vredehoek, they settled in among Jews but lived close to other people of the kind they'd never seen in their lives before – coloured people and Chinese, black and Indian, Afrikaner and English.

'Oupa rented a small house from an old Afrikaner doctor. Ouma lit candles on a Friday, cooked chicken soup and barley, boiled salt beef and made borscht, just like back home. She only spoke Yiddish when she arrived but by the time they moved to this house, here in Parow, Oupa was making enough for them to have a maid, so they hired Olive and Ouma picked up some scraps of Afrikaans from her, enough to buy what she needed in the shops. She bought mealies from the market and boerewors sausages from the local butcher, kosher or not. She found out how to make hot Malay chutneys and brought home new fruits from the market – mangoes, paw paws, loquats, sharp granadillas and creamy avocado pears.'

'One by one new children arrived and each time Oupa sighed as the midwife proclaimed the dreadful news – another girl! Oy a kappore - what a catastrophe! Enough was enough.

Ma was thoughtful for a moment. 'Are you still listening, Jackie?'

I nodded and pulled my knees up to my chin. Ma wrapped a blanket round my shoulders to keep me warm.

'Times were changing, the old matchmakers in the shtetl were halfway across the world, and the Jewish boys in Cape Town were all of a sudden going crazy, meshuggah, breaking with tradition and making their own foolish choices. Ouma had to do all the arranging herself, seeking out good matches for my sisters, talking to friends and neighbours, letting it be known that she was on the lookout for a good catch. Sometimes it seemed like an impossible job but in the end she found husbands, of one sort or another, for all of them, Ethel, Esther, Sadie and even Fella, with her ugly moles. All the girls were finally married and off Oupa's hands, except, that is, for me.

'By this time I was doing my matric, in the last year of school. My sisters had not been great scholars. "Dumb cows," Oupa used to say. "Useless beasts." They had all left school as soon as they could, with Oupa's blessing.

'But I was different; I was clever. I'm not boasting, Jackie bubala, really I'm not. Everyone said so. I looked set to pass my matric with flying colours. I locked myself away in the shed in the yard to get a bit of peace, away from Oupa's workshop, and I studied hard. When the results came through, I had gained the top marks in the class and my teacher came to talk to Oupa one evening, to tell him that I should think of becoming a teacher myself. I would be the first girl in the family to continue my studies and have a profession.

'Oupa said no. Absolutely not. "We'll find a husband for her, like all the others," he pronounced. "Times are tough and I can't afford to keep her for ever." There was no point in arguing, so my teacher went home.'

Ma paused. She was looking away, staring into the distance, as if caught up in her thoughts, her eyes suddenly swimming with tears. I prodded her arm; I wanted her to carry on. She wiped her face with her hand, sighed for a moment, and then continued.

'I begged and I whined, I cried and I cajoled and finally Oupa agreed that I could start my teacher-training course, but said that I would have to give up as soon as a suitable husband was found for me. I could not believe my luck. If I just got started on the course, I would have a little time to come up with a plan.

'So when February arrived, I found myself studying to be a teacher. It was wonderful, leaving the house each morning with my satchel on my shoulder filled with exercise books, pens and pencils, walking out of the Jewish quarter, and into the streets beyond, passing the Malay shops, the poor white district and from there entering the neighbourhood where the college was situated. Not far to walk but as far as leaving one country and arriving in another. In the classes I sat next to Avis Pretorius, an

Afrikaner girl, who became my best friend. I got to know Deidre Jones, whose father worked as an administrative assistant for de Beers and then there was Vicky de Wet whose great-uncle managed a vineyard in Groot Constantia. When I came home, I said nothing of my new friends.

'A year passed, with no news of a husband. Now it happened in those days that young men would arrive, out of the blue, looking for a place to stay and a helping hand to start their new lives. Like Ouma and Oupa, they would find their way to the synagogue and from there to the streets of the Jewish quarter. A cluster of new people would appear on Main Road, shuffling along with all their possessions in tattered cases and pillowcases and bags wrapped with string, looking lost and afraid.

'From time to time Oupa would receive a knock on the door from a friend wanting to know if he needed an apprentice, or, if not, just a few weeks' labour in return for a bed and food. Sometimes Oupa said yes, sometimes no; it depended on how many shoes he had waiting to be repaired and how much money there was in the box at the back of the cupboard. So we were used to the idea of a young man coming to live with us for a few weeks, sleeping in the workshop, sharing our dinner table and then going off to find a job and a home somewhere else.

'One day, while I was away studying at college, Moishe the mohel came by and asked Oupa if he would take a young man for a few weeks, to help in the store in return for a bed and food. By the time I got back from college, the young man had moved in, with his small package of belongings wrapped in brown paper and string. I thought nothing of it. Here was another in a long line of big-eyed, skinny boys, who would stay for a while and then leave. He would sleep on a mattress under the counter and eat with us in the evenings, but other than that I would hardly see him. I didn't know anything about him and I didn't especially want to; his name was Samuel, he had just arrived from a shtetl called Kupishok and that was that.

'I went to college each day and returned again, so wrapped up in my studies that I hardly noticed what was happening to turn my home and my life upside down...'

Ma was about to continue but the door opened and Ouma came in. She sighed loudly. 'Oupa wants to talk to you,' she said. 'He thinks it's time you returned to your husband again. I told him another day won't do any harm but you know your father – when his mind's set it's hard to budge him. Put the boy to bed and come to the kitchen.'

Ma looked at me and shrugged. 'I'll finish off the story another time,' she said, 'I'll tell you more of my fairy tale.'

I lay awake thinking about it, wondering what came next in the story, listening to the raised voices in the kitchen, as Oupa reminded Ma of her duties as a wife and a mother and confirmed that we would be returning home in the morning. I was afraid for Ma and Pa. What would become of them? And what about me and Sauly? We needed a fairy tale ending. I hoped that Ma might be able to provide one.

Chapter 7

1941

A little pattern had formed: Ma and Pa would row; it would be something more than the normal little snipes and querulous irritations, usually about money and the shop, rarely about Sauly or me; Ma would go to her room and I would hear drawers opening and a few small bags being filled. And then we would troop down the road to Ouma and Oupa's for a few days. There was no more talk of us staying there forever, no great scenes, no threats. I had become used to it all; this is what we did; this was what family life was like. I even looked forward to the steamy warmth of Ouma's kitchen and the closeness of sleeping on the camp bed pressed up next to Ma. After a day or two, when Oupa started grumbling and Ma began to talk again about the store and wonder what was happening there, and whether Mrs van de Merwe had paid her bills and how Pa was managing without her, we would return. Nothing was said, but Pa would kiss Sauly and me and hold us tight in his arms for a few moments, before turning back to finish what he was doing. Then, for a few days at least, there would be calm between my parents, a careful tiptoeing around the things that caused them to fight, a quiet, almost tender, peace.

In these quieter times, I enjoyed watching Pa going about his business in the store. I especially liked watching him cutting planks, the chips of wood and powdery dust flying out from the saw and catching in the sunlight like a spray of gold. Or the slicing of biltong, his strong arms vigorously sharpening the knife on a stone, then carving a pile of the finest slivers of dark, fat-marbled meat onto greaseproof paper. I appreciated his skill, so different from my own clumsiness, his control over the physical world, which seemed to allow him to do with it whatever he wished, like a great god of wood and metal and paper and stone.

Each night when he locked the door and turned the 'Open' sign to 'Closed', when the counter was cleaned and the sawdust swept away, he would come to the till to count the takings. I watched his fingers flicking through the notes more quickly than I thought possible, his lips moving silently as he totted up the figures. He scooped the tickies and the shillings out of the drawers, spreading them on the counter and with a single finger expertly flicked them one at a time into small paper bags.

At this point, if I was in the store, he would take me out the back and hand me over to Ada or Ma, saying, 'The boy needs his supper,' or 'Time for his bed now,' or simply, 'I don't want him with me any more.'

One evening, when Sauly was sick with the flu and Ma was upstairs tending to him, and Ada was away seeing her mother, Pa said, 'Come, Jackie,' took me through to the back room, put a wrapped toffee (rare treat!) into my hand and told me to be good and wait for Ma to come down to look after me.

Sitting on a chair in the kitchen, I tried to unwrap the toffee, but the wrapping had got stuck and I couldn't pull it open. It was sweet and soft and sticky and just waiting to be opened and put in my mouth.

I climbed down from the chair and opened the door to the shop. I would see if Pa could unwrap the sweet for me. I was a little nervous; I knew Pa well enough to be cautious of his temper; it could flare unexpectedly and fast. But the toffee was warm in my hand and I wanted to eat it. I pushed the door open carefully.

There was my father, on his knees. What was he doing? All I could see was his backside under the till and the scuffed leather soles of his shoes. And then I heard the sound of him prising open a floorboard under the counter. I shrank back a little, watching nervously from behind the door. Pa pulled himself up and, with his back to me, straightened his body, placing his arms on his hips and stretching. He collected a small pile of notes sitting on the counter, counted them out carefully, then squatted down and began stuffing the notes into a hole under the floorboard. Very gently he then put back the floorboard and lightly tapped the nail back in, trying it with his foot to make sure that it was firmly in place.

I tiptoed quietly back to my chair in the kitchen and waited.

'Nice sweet?' Pa asked, coming through from the store a heart-stoppingly brief moment later.

I reached out my hand to show him the warm, squashed toffee sitting unopened in my hand.

'Silly billy boychie,' he said. 'You need to open the wrapper.' He sighed. 'You need to start catching up, Jackie, my boy. You're five years old and time's passing. You must start to talk like other children do, and begin doing something useful with those nice little hands of yours, or you're going to be a great big burden to your ma and your pa when you grow up. I don't know how you're ever going to become a man like me, and make a living for yourself and your family, if you don't start doing the things that normal children do!'

Pa lifted me and put me up on the table. He kissed the top of my head. 'I want you to run the store with me one day,' he said softly, almost whispering, as if it were our secret, not something for Ma or Sauly to hear. 'You and me together,' he said. 'Think how nice that would be.' He ruffled my hair.

'You know, Jackie, I was always good with my hands. That's something to be really proud of, you know. All those clever chochems, with their fancy books and pens and paper, they swan around showing off their big brains and their learning but can they get by when times are hard? They move country and then their smart qualifications are just a bit of paper to tear up and throw in the bin. I can fix up a shed anywhere, you know, in Kupishok, in London, in New York or Cape Town. Just give me the tools and I know what to do.

'My father was a peasant – he had nothing to his name, not a bean. But I've built something here in this store. I've created it all myself. The fruits of my labour. Not much yet, I know, but it will be. My own boss I am, not some penniless serf, working for someone else. That's not to be sneered at, Jackie, being your own boss and running your own business. It's something.'

He paused and I saw his eyes go soft and vague, as he looked into the distance, beyond me, seeming to leave me behind.

'When I came to Cape Town, I pitched up at your oupa's house, with no money, no job, nowhere to stay, carrying just a small package and with only one suit of clothes. He took me in, offered me shelter for a few days, in return for a few jobs around the place. You should have seen that workshop when I first arrived. A madhouse! Your oupa was always searching for the shoes, shouting, cursing like a meshuganah. Thought he was still in the shtetl, the only shoemaker, imagined people would forgive his mess and his muddle and his crazy outbursts. He was losing money hand over fist to Silberstein, the other Jewish cobbler in Parow, who didn't lose the shoes or make the customers wait for days on end for a new heel or sole.

'I suggested some changes. I built him wooden shelves that stretched across one whole wall, with spaces of different sizes, to fit all the shoes – anything from a small pair of children's slippers to a great big pair of men's boots. I fixed and oiled the broken wheel that had been stacked in the shed and put it back in the workshop. It hummed and purred like a pussycat when I'd finished with it. I sharpened and cleaned the saws and knives and built a board with pegs to hold each of Oupa's tools – the hammers, chisels, knives, punches and strong sewing needles. I set up a book to keep on the counter, to list jobs, mark down prices and payments, and money owing. Boy, was your oupa delighted! I had an extra slice of rye bread and an extra helping of chicken for my supper each night. As far as he was concerned I could do no wrong.

'Then, what do you know? Your ouma caught on that I wasn't such a bad thing. She started thinking up little jobs that I could do for her too. So I set to work on the back room making more space, varnishing the wooden floor, cleaning out the flue for the stove. Ouma was pleased as punch – extra ladles of soup came my way, more helpings of her delicious kneidlach, fluffy and light, floating in the chicken fat at the top of the bowl.

'Ah now, Jackie, here's where it's all leading, this story I'm telling you. They asked me to sort out the shed in the back yard, full of old junk it was– a broken treadle sewing machine, old metal pots and dusty jars, springs from a discarded bed, scraps of wood. A mess and a half! Your ouma and oupa wanted it cleared. But there was someone else who thought otherwise! Your mother thought it was *her* shed, the little place where she could take her clever books and get away from everyone. One day when she came home, she found that I'd stripped the shed bare, laid sawdust on the floor and straw in one corner and brought in a clutch of nice, fat, squawking hens. She gave me furious looks, as though I was her worst enemy, but she didn't say a word. She knew that Oupa would clop her, whack, right across the head if she did.

'Well, time ticked by and I carried on staying there, sleeping under the counter. There was no talk of me leaving and finding my own home. I served in the shop, went about with my sleeves rolled up, nails in my mouth and a hammer in my pocket. Your oupa began paying me a small wage, but in the evenings I went to work for other families. I came home long after the meal was cleared away and went straight to sleep on my mattress. I saved every damned penny that I earned. Each one was building my future. I worked together with Oupa and over the din of the grinding wheel we talked about the price of leather and rubber, spirit levels, chainsaws and wood.

'And then one day he changed the subject from shoes and tools to talk of your ma. She was ready to be taken off his hands. I was young and fit and keen to start out on my own. If we were to marry, he said, he'd help us on our way, with some cash to set myself up in business. It was a good proposition. I liked your ma well enough. We didn't speak much but we'd have plenty of time for that when we were married.

'I put down a deposit on a building, bought in the stock and gave the store my name, "Neuberger's Handyhouse". Then, when the rooms at the back and up above the store were ready, your mother and I were married and moved in. I became a shopkeeper – I could work for myself now, build myself up and think about a family.'

That's me, I thought. That's where I come into it all. That's how I began.

Pa folded his arms; his story was coming to a close.

'So you see, Jackie, how important it is to work hard, to work with your hands, to be a practical man. It brought me your mother and it brought me all of this.' He opened his arms wide, to encompass the world that he had created for himself. 'That's what I want for you. One day I want you to help me run the store. Yes, we've been struggling a bit, but so has everyone, and that government of ours keeps promising that things are going to get better. When these bad times are over, it'll be a good, sound business, I know. I want you to grow up and take over from me when I'm old. I want you to do something that will make me proud of you.'

He looked at me long and hard. As usual I said nothing. Then, with a sigh, he lifted me down from the table and went to the sink to wash his hands for supper.

When Ma came down with Sauly in her arms she asked the usual question. 'Good takings? Are we going to be all right this week?'

'So-so,' he muttered, looking away. 'Just about enough to get by if we're careful... if you go easy on the champagne and caviar.'

'How much longer can we go on like this?' Ma asked anxiously. It seemed as though she hadn't even noticed his little joke.

'Don't ask me,' Pa snapped back. 'Ask the politicians and the bank managers. See if they'd like to pay my mortgage and my debts and my bill at the wholesalers, and when they've done that, perhaps they might like to consider helping Mr van de Merwe and Arnie Fortune and all the rest of our customers who seem to find it so hard to dig into those pockets of theirs to pay their bills.'

He suddenly grew serious, more sad than angry. 'If it weren't for all the troubles in Europe, I might even think about whether we'd be better off closing up shop, packing our things up and going back home to my little village in Lithuania.'

Ma came over to stand beside him. She laid her hand against his arm. 'Don't say that, Sam. You know what's going on over there. I'm not sure there is such a thing as home any more.' She sighed. 'I'll do my best. I'll make the money stretch. We'll eat a bit less chicken. And so what if I can't buy fancy shmancy clothes. Who cares? We'll get by for now, till times get better, and we'll count our blessings and thank God for being safe, and pray for all those people of ours who aren't.'

Pa patted her hand. He cleared his throat. 'I must stack those sacks of animal seed, out in the yard.'

'He's a good man underneath it all,' Ma said out loud, when he'd gone. 'He's doing his best for us and if we have to scrimp and save a bit, well, so be it. We'll manage.'

I was glad that Ma and Pa weren't arguing so much any more, but as the days and weeks went by, I began to realise what scrimping and saving meant. Ma still managed to put a plate of food on the table for Sauly and me, and for Pa, but sometimes she wouldn't sit down to eat with us, telling us that she wasn't hungry. I looked forward to the Sabbath night meals we had at Ouma and Oupa's where we would all eat our fill. Our clothes, always shabby, now had visible patches and only our shoes, made and repaired in Oupa's workshop, gave Ma some pride in how we looked. 'Proper little shoes,' she said. 'Fit for princes!'

Each evening, when the shop closed and Ma was upstairs putting Sauly to sleep, Pa emptied the till and counted out the money, and sometimes, when he thought I wasn't looking and when no one else was around, he would prise open the floorboard under the counter and quickly put a few notes into the space he had uncovered.

I said nothing. Little Jackie, the boy with no voice. I listened and watched but didn't say a word.

CHAPTER 8

January 1958

'I've been talking to the counsel for Mrs Small,' Jack said.

They were sitting in his office, on this, the third occasion that they had met. Johannes van Heerden looked concerned.

'No need to worry. I just want to make sure that the stories add up, yours and hers, and that her plea's going to be the same. I'll need to meet her, chat things through.'

Van Heerden nodded. 'Of course,' he said. 'She'll tell the truth, as I have done. There was nothing between us.'

It had become quite clear during the earlier interviews that van Heerden was going to plead his innocence; he had not had any disreputable or dubious relationship with the woman, Agnes Small. He asserted this firmly. Neighbours had misinterpreted his visits to her house, unaware as they were of the perfectly valid reasons behind them; one or two members of the church, with an axe to grind, had got the wrong idea and leapt to conclusions. Perhaps he had been naïve, in the current climate, not to anticipate the possible misunderstandings, how it might be seen by others, but, as far as he knew, naivety wasn't yet a crime in this country.

A good line of defence, thought Jack, and scribbled down these last words in his notebook, for use when he came to speak in court.

'Her counsel's not the best, I'm afraid. I don't know where she dredged him up, but he's struggling to keep pace with things, from what I can see. He hasn't even interviewed her properly yet. I've asked if I can see her myself. It'll help me get the full picture.'

*****

Jack arranged to meet Mrs Small at her home in Elsie's River. He'd asked Vera to accompany him, to keep a record of the conversation, and, in view of the nature of the case, to avoid him being with the woman on his own.

'A bit unusual, this, Mr Neuberger,' Vera said a little sharply, as he was closing the office door behind them. 'It's not usually the advocate who traipses around all over the place interviewing people. That's the attorney's job, you know.'

'Smit's not done it well,' Jack said calmly. 'There are all kinds of gaps in the paperwork and hardly any interviews. He hasn't got the facts straight.'

'So you're doing it for him?' Her lips were pursed tight and he saw that she was pulling her gloves on rather over-zealously. 'The other advocates I've worked for would manage with what they've got.'

'So you think that's what I should do? Go into the courtroom without the full facts?'

'Who am I to say?' Vera said. 'I'm only the secretary.'

'We're going out to Elsie's River, Vera. It may not be what you've been used to but I'm afraid you'll have to put up with that.'

He started off down the stairs; Vera hesitated for a moment and then followed, allowing her heels to slap down on each step a bit more noisily than was perhaps necessary.

They drove out in the old bottle green Ford that Jack had borrowed from his cousin, Isidore. It took quite some time to find the little house, down a narrow, dusty street squatting among scrubby trees and run-down buildings, with a grocery store on one corner and a fruit stall selling paw paws and prickly pears on the other.

Vera wiped the dust off the backs of her nylon stockings and smoothed down her hair. He caught the look of mild disgust on her face. He knocked at the wooden door, with its mosquito screen and peeling yellow paintwork.

A woman came to the door. She was holding one child by the hand and another came running up behind, pulling at the fabric of her floral dress. For an instant, Jack was confused.

'Mrs Small?'

'Yes, I was expecting you. Come in.'

She was quite different from the woman he had imagined. A slight figure, with dark eyes and a fine-boned face, her black hair straight rather than curly, and swept up, leaving her neck exposed. She had a good skin, creamy brown and youthful. She probably had some Malay blood in her by the looks of it. She was a young woman, in her late twenties or early thirties by his reckoning, and very beautiful.

Jack groaned inwardly. This was not what he had been expecting. A vision of her standing up in court flashed through his mind. This complicated things.

Mrs Small invited them into her small front room, gesturing towards a wicker sofa, covered with a loose, pale-blue cotton spread. The room was furnished simply, bare of ornaments, but tidy and clean. On a table stood a wedding photograph, showing Agnes Small in happier days, holding a bouquet of flowers in one hand, her other arm locked around that of her husband.

She caught Jack's gaze. 'He died just over two years ago,' she said. 'Of pneumonia. Left us to fend for ourselves. There was no insurance, no payout from his work, so I had to get a job and leave the children with a friend.'

He saw her eyes filling with tears. 'That must have been hard for you,' he said.

'Yes,' she replied simply, wiping her eyes with the back of her hand. 'But it was work – it was money. I was employed in a canned-fruit company, packing tins of peaches and guavas, for a year or so. And then, someone told me about a better job, in a bottling firm in Goodwood, so I left and started there, for higher wages. Just a few months in and the company went bust. I fell out with my friend. I couldn't pay her for the children any more and she lost patience – she needed the money herself. So there I was – no job, no one to leave my children with if I wanted to go out and get another. Times were hard. I found some small jobs, taking in sewing and mending, but that wasn't enough to pay the rent and put food on the table.'

Here in the front room, with the light coming in through the open blind, Jack could see the toll that it had taken on her, this and, no doubt, the worry about the trial. Her face looked drawn and tired.

'How did it come about that you asked Mrs van Heerden for help?'

'My mother was a Christian. She took me to her church when I was small, even though it angered my father. A woman told me that there were church people giving out charity in Elsie's River and that she had been given parcels of both food and clothes. I asked her to see if they would visit me as well.'

'And Mrs van Heerden came herself?'

'Oh yes,' she said. 'She's a good woman. She came and helped me in my time of need.'

'Did you get to know her well?'

'She came many times, sometimes accompanied by one of the other ladies of her church. They brought me small parcels of food, clothes for the children, or a little bit of money for my rent. I was building up my sewing jobs but it wasn't enough yet for us to get by.'

Jack looked at the children watching him in silence. A girl and a boy. The girl must have been about eight or nine, the boy around four or five. They looked anxious, their eyes fixed on his face, or turning to their mother's for reassurance. 'Times were hard... not enough to get by.' It was a refrain he knew very well.

'What will happen in the trial, Mr Neuberger? I'm so afraid for myself and for my children. And for Mr and Mrs van Heerden, who have been so good to me. What will happen to us if we are found guilty?'

'I hope you won't be,' Jack said. 'If all you say is true, you will be acquitted by a jury of decent people. But if not...' He paused. What would happen if the verdict went the other way? It was anyone's guess. The law was new and the van Heerden case could end up being the first one to be seen through the process, if it were brought to court quickly. There was no saying what the sentence would be – a small fine, a suspended sentence or a jail term – all of these were possible. Jack feared that there might be political interference, a signal from the Ministry of Justice that it expected stern sentences to be meted out, to make a show of how seriously the government was taking this new law.

'I've no doubt you'll be found innocent,' Jack said. 'Let's just take each day at a time and put our energies into making sure of that.'

'My advocate,' she said. 'Will you work together with him on this?'

'I'll talk to him. I'll make sure we're going in the same direction, singing from the same hymn sheet, as it were. We'll share ideas.'

'Thank you,' she said, with a look of gratitude that touched him but made a little nervous knot form in his stomach. He had a sense that she trusted him and he would need to live up to this.

'Now tell me about Mr van Heerden and his visits to you.'

Her account tallied exactly with that of his client. When Mrs van Heerden had her last child, she had been too ill to visit the families she was helping and Mr van Heerden had agreed to step in and help the women with their project. He drove them to Elsie's River and shared with them the task of taking parcels to the homes. Sometimes he had come with Mrs de Villiers or Mrs Pietersen, sometimes with Miss Joubert, sometimes on his own.

'How often did he visit you on his own?' Jack asked.

'Goodness, I'd need to think,' she said. 'Five or six times perhaps.'

'And why did he come alone on these occasions?'

'There was a lot of work to do – it gave the women freedom to go to other houses and help more people. Mostly he just brought me the parcels and left, he didn't even come inside.'

'But sometimes he stayed?'

'I was grateful to him and his family. I invited him in to share a cup of tea. I told him about my mother and her church, my childhood faith that had been lost and that I was struggling to find again. He sometimes stayed and prayed with me.'

'Did anyone ever say anything to you about this? Your neighbours, or your friends?'

'A few people muttered about me taking charity. For some it was sinking low – it brought shame on you. There were occasionally harsh words, if my little girl, Lucille, came out wearing a dress that had been given to her, or Billy had a new coat. But I put it down to jealousy. It's human nature you know – people who are struggling look over their shoulder to see how others are doing.'

She stopped speaking and sent the children into the kitchen. 'Go get a drink of milk for yourselves, from the ice safe,' she said.

When they were gone, she looked down at her dress, fixing her gaze firmly on her knees.

'I never…We never…'

Vera was shifting uneasily next to Jack on the sofa.

'That's all right, Mrs Small. No need to say anything more. We know.'

CHAPTER 9

1941

'Little Jackie's speaking quite well now, isn't he?' Mrs van de Merwe remarked, looking at me with her icy blue eyes. 'A bit of a stutter, it's true, but at least that tongue of his has got going at last, so he's not going to be one of those backward children, after all, like you were so worried about, Mrs N. I always said he'd be fine.'

When she left the shop, Ma turned to Ada, her eyes dark with fury.

'That woman will drive me to murder one day! *She* was the one who got me all worried, silly woman, with her talk of the Jordaan boy in the home for retarded children!'

'Ag man, Mrs N,' Ada replied, hands on her hips and eyes rolling up towards the ceiling. 'You take no notice of her. The woman's brain's rattling around inside her head like a little dried pea in a big empty jar. You can't expect to get any sense out of her, silly Afrikaner vrou.'

Ma tried to look stern – perhaps Ada had overstepped the mark? But then she laughed out loud.

'You're right, Ada,' she said. 'She could do with some of your cleverness!'

It had been a good few months now since I'd started speaking. Ma never seemed to tire of telling the customers about the first time she heard me talk and it caused great interest and entertainment for everyone except me, the subject of her story, who would rather not have had attention drawn to it in this way.

'We'd just eaten our evening meal and I'd put the boys to bed, kissed them goodnight and half closed the bedroom door, but instead of going downstairs as usual, I'd stayed upstairs, tidying away the laundry in the cupboard on the landing. Not long after I'd left them, Sauly had begun his usual little trick of seeing if he could climb out of his cot. He'd been trying it for a while now but I was pretty sure he couldn't manage it – those wooden bars that Sam put up were nice and high. Then suddenly, just as I'd finished putting away the sheets, I heard a voice I'd never heard before, saying loudly, "N-no, Sauly! N-no! You're a very n-naughty boy!" My words! Just what I'd have said to Sauly myself, but there they were, popping right out of Little Jackie's mouth. He was trying to stop Sauly from climbing out and hurting himself, you see. Being a really good big brother! And the words poured out in a whole sentence, just like that. A bit stuttery they were, but lovely whole words from my little boychick!'

'Aah,' they all said. 'Speaking at last. What a relief! You must be very pleased.'

Why hadn't I been able to speak like other children? Why now was it still a struggle? The words were perfectly formed in my mind but didn't seem to come out and be heard. I could cry out loud like other people, when a mosquito stung me or I fell in a bed of nettles, or if I cut my finger on the edge of a piece of paper. I could laugh, if there was something to laugh about, when Oupa told me a joke, or my cousin Isidore, the youngest son of my Aunt Fella, did a magic trick for me with his pack of cards, or when the 'Coon' Carnival passed along Main Street and we all went out onto the pavement to watch and wave. But my *words*, uttered at last, were full of stops and starts, as if my tongue were fighting my teeth and my teeth were in combat with my lips and my lips were arguing with my tongue to stop them emerging whole and pure. The more I tried the worse it became and, as time went on, I began to wonder whether I would ever speak freely and easily like other children. Any day now I would be starting school and, from Ma's worried conversations with Ada, I picked up that it might not be very easy for me if talking remained such a struggle.

Ma walked me there on the first day, along Main Road and down Silk Street, holding my hand. Sauly was in the big pram, which wouldn't fit through the schoolyard gate. He was red-faced and bawling, so Ma kissed me on the head and pushed me through the gate towards the crowd of children, then turned abruptly and walked away.

I watched her go, following her back and her swaying gait as she pushed the pram along the road till she was just a tiny figure. She was going to be with Sauly all day; she was leaving me on my own, and Sauly would have her all to himself; they would not even think about me and perhaps they might forget to come and collect me at the end of the endless hours that I faced alone at school. I would need to speak – to the teachers, to the children – and Ada and Ma would not be there to help me.

I stood at the wire fence watching the children. Boys chasing each other, kicking up gravel and dirt. Girls playing five stones, jumping into a skipping rope that slapped and slapped on the ground, or chalking hopscotch squares, ready for a game. Boys in little clusters, swapping glass marbles, or prized stamps. In the corner of the yard, Miss Fortune, whistle in hand, a little group of girls adoringly hanging onto her brightly printed red cotton skirt. And there by the big wooden school door, the head teacher, Mrs Coetzee, stout, thick-calved, brown hair pulled into a bun, dressed in a tweed suit and sweating in the heat of the February sun.

'Line up!' calls Mrs Coetzee and then again, more loudly, 'LINE UP, BOYS AND GIRLS!' The children gradually drift from their games into two lines, one of boys, the other of girls. I wait till the lines have formed, then slowly join the end of the boys' queue. Heads turn, boys and girls whisper. I've been noticed. Who is he? Who knows him? What street does he live on? What do his parents do? Where's he come from? Oh, it's Little Jackie, Mr Neuberger's son, the storekeeper's boy, the one from the Handyhouse. The one with the baby brother, Sauly. The one whose pa employs Ada, whose nephew Willie drowned in the river, whose cousin is in Standard 2, who's sweet on Clarice Schwartz, who's held hands with Jacobus Malan. The one with the st-st-st-stutter, Little J-j-jackie.

'Quiet, QUIET, children!' shouts Mrs Coetzee. 'Everyone to your classes.' And the lines file into the school, with murmuring whispers and a last rush of marbles exchanging sweaty hands and being dropped into pockets. April Fortune steers me towards the first of the doors along the corridor and into a classroom. She introduces me to my new teacher, Mrs Uys.

'This is Jack Neuberger,' she says.

'Hello Jack,' says Mrs Uys. 'Come and sit at the front where I can keep an eye on you.'

I like the coolness of her hand on my hot palm, the up-and-down waves of her voice as she tells us the story of the Boers arriving in South Africa, the singsong repetitions of numbers and the echoing of children reciting their times tables, their voices like the soft pulse of a native drum. The classroom is safe and I can stay silent, sitting next to Mrs Uys, listening to it all and not saying a word.

But at the break, in the schoolyard, I am surrounded by children. They are questioning me, buzzing round me like excited little goggas round a naked flame and when I reply, they laugh.

'What's your name?' they ask.

'J-jackie,' I say.

'J-j-j-jackie,' they repeat.

'Jackie what?'

'N-neub-b-berger.'

'N-n-neub-b-b-berger,' they laugh.

I fall silent. At last the boys and girls run off to continue their games.

At dinnertime I will have to find a place to eat my lunch, sit down in the dirt, open up my little paper bag and take out my food, the piece of wurst Ma has packed, the dry salt crackers and the three small loquats from the tree. I hope Ma has remembered to pack me the fig roll that I asked for. Is it there at the bottom of my paper bag, waiting to be nibbled slowly, so that the sweet fig seeds crunch between my teeth? Yes or no?

At the end of the afternoon, I stand waiting by the gate. Other mothers have already arrived but Ma's not there. I watch the children wandering off one by one. Has Ma forgotten me? Will I be left here, standing on my own, waiting for Ma to appear, while the sky darkens and the schoolyard empties?

And then finally I see her, hurrying along the road with the pram, her face flushed and hot.

'How was school?' she asks anxiously.

'OK.'

'Making some nice friends?'

'Yes.'

'What are their names?'

I fall silent.

'Never mind, Jackie. It takes time to make friends,' she says. 'It'll happen, I promise you.'

*****

Children often came into the store with their parents, or their maids. Mikey and Clarice Shapiro with Millicent when she collected the groceries, clutching coins to buy tickey lollipops or sherbet swizzles; the five Levy children crowded round the pram where baby Ethel was sleeping while their mother bought rice or safety pins or dishcloths; Dorothy Fortune dragged in reluctantly by her big sister April, the teacher at my school, standing fidgeting by the counter, waiting to get back out into the sunshine to play with her friends; Billy Edwards and his sister Maisie coming on their own to buy things for their ma, who was sick at home.

I waited longingly for the Edwards children's visits to the store. Maisie was fair and tall with two long plaits; her knees were grubby and her teeth were crooked but her eyes were a lovely dark blue and I thought her the most beautiful girl I had ever seen. I yearned for Maisie to talk to me but I knew that she, like all the other children who came to the store, would never stay long enough to play with Little Jackie, the storekeeper's son. They did not seem to notice me. It was as if I were a plank of wood, or a box of soap suds, a sack of beans or a bag of rice. I had no hopes of making friends with any of these children, lovely Maisie least of all.

But then there was Terence, Terence Mostert.

Along Main Road, after the bakery, beyond the barber's shop and a bit further on than the Jewish Communal Hall and the Victoria and Opal bioscope, stood Mostert's Garage, where automobiles stopped to fill up with petrol at the single pump and where the coloured mechanic Walter Hendricks could often be seen lying on his back in the oily workshop, tinkering around with a broken-down Chevy or Oldsmobile. May Mostert, who ran the garage, was a plump, friendly, hard-working woman. Her husband Simey had been ill for a long time and spent most of the year in the sanatorium at Rondebosch.

'She's a good sort,' Ma said when anyone asked about May. 'She has a tough time of it, with Simey so ill. TB, you know.'

I wondered if being a good sort was the same as being a mensch. Ma often talked about whether someone was a mensch, as if this were the biggest accolade one might bestow. Menschen were 'human beings' – honourable, good, decent people who behaved well towards others. A mensch commanded Ma's respect, and that respect, as Pa and I both knew, was not easily won. I puzzled over whether May Mostert could be a mensch, or if only men were menschen, or perhaps, and this seemed to be the case from the examples Ma always quoted, only men who were also Jews could qualify. Afrikaners and coloureds, English and Malays never figured in Ma's menschen list, so obviously May Mostert, an Afrikaner, couldn't be one, which seemed to me like a very great shame, as May seemed to me to behave very well towards people, and most of all towards me.

Simey and May had a small son called Terence who was five and a half, just like me. He often came into the store with his ma and brought with him a handful of Dinky cars that the toy salesman had given him when he had his car repaired at the garage. The cars were bright and shiny Oldsmobiles and Chevvies, pick-up trucks and big-wheeled tractors. Sometimes, while Ma and May Mostert talked about the price of candles or the summer heat, Terence brought his Dinkies over and, without saying a word, sat down cross-legged beside me and set them out in front of us. Together we cleared the sawdust around us and raced the cars across the wooden floor.

Terence had closely cropped blond hair, skin that was splashed with freckles and pale-blue eyes. Like his mother, he had a broad, open face, which I thought had a nice kind of softness to it, like a ripe apricot or peach. Terence looked entirely different from me, with my dark skin and brown eyes, my thin face and small frame. He was a lot sturdier, and these physical differences, coupled with his Afrikaner background, made us an unlikely prospect for friendship. With his good looks, he had the appearance of a boy who should have had friends in abundance, and been full of self-confidence and boyish bluster. But there was something hesitant and gentle about him that made me feel comfortable in his presence. He didn't make demands of me or expect me to speak a great deal, just sat with me racing his toy cars on the floor of the store. Looking back, I realise that, despite appearances, he probably didn't feel very sure of himself at all and, like me, had probably found it difficult to make friends, but for his own rather different reasons. I think he appreciated our brief games at the store just as much as I did.

One day Mrs Mostert asked Ma if I could come and play with Terence, in their flat above the garage. Ma looked at Pa who shrugged. Then she turned to me.

'Do you want to play with Terence?' Ma asked.

I nodded shyly and soon I found myself walking down Main Road, one hand holding Terence's sweaty palm, the other clutching one of his shiny Dinky cars.

Mrs Mostert made babotie for our lunch and I was shocked by the fierce heat of the spicy minced beef, the sweetness of the raisins and cool egg custard in which it was baked, so different from the boiled chicken and milky soups favoured by Ma. In the heat of the afternoon I played upstairs with Terence's Dinky cars and discovered that he had a whole cupboard full of other toys – a painted wooden train set with 'Cape Government Railways' painted boldly on the sides of the locomotives, a box of brightly coloured books, a glass jar of swirling marbles, a store-made skipping rope with red wooden handles, a Meccano No. 10 construction set and a small painted garage, with 'Mostert's Garage' written on the sign, looking just like the real thing. 'Walter made that for me,' said Terence, proudly.

I went to Mostert's Garage often now, walking hand in hand with Terence and Mrs Mostert down Main Road, past the Jewish Community Hall and the Victoria and Opal, and a little further on. I said a shy and stumbling hello to Walter, who looked up from under a Chevy or an Oldsmobile to give me a smile. I ate babotie and boerewors, tomato bredie and frikkadels, chewed on strips of biltong and drank ginger beer while playing with the toys in Terence's toy cupboard, reading *Babar's Travels*, or one of his many Rupert Bear books. I was in heaven.

I listened to Mrs Mostert and Walter talking and laughing in the garage and sometimes heard voices I recognised from the store, Arnie Fortune or Mr du Plessis, Mr van de Merwe or Isaac Stern, buying cigarettes and petrol or checking on the carburettor, the crank or the spark plugs.

One day, Walter came upstairs, carrying a parcel, wrapped in brown paper and tied in string. He had a big smile on his face and said, 'Hey man, a little dinges, a little something, for you, Jackie boy.' He handed it to me and then went straight back down to the workshop, leaving me to open it. Terence was hopping from one foot to another and yelping, 'Man, man, man...oh man! I know what it is, I know what it is! Just wait till you see it. Ooh, yirrah!'

My heart was beating fast. I had never been given a present before, unexpected and out of the blue, all properly wrapped up like this. I was afraid to even imagine what it might be. Perhaps it was a trick or a joke and Terence would then laugh his head off at my stupidity for being so easily fooled. Carefully I tried to unwrap the parcel, using my slow, clumsy hands to untie the knotted string. I fumbled with it, unable to loosen it. Terence jumped to my aid. Deftly he untied the knot, so that all the wrapping fell away to reveal a small wooden model of Pa's store, with the name painted in tiny little letters on the front, 'Neuberger's Handyhouse'. Terence was saying, 'Well? Well? What do yer think of it? What do yer think? Say something, Jackie.' But I couldn't speak. I couldn't breathe.

At the end of the afternoon, I carried my new wooden store downstairs and out the shop, past the workshop and went over to find Walter, who was working on a car, lying on the ground, face hidden under the chassis. I talked to his legs, the only bit of him that I could see. 'Th-th-th-th-thank you,' I said shyly and Mrs Mostert ruffled my hair.

'You're a sweetie, Jackie,' she said and then she walked me home.

Back at the store, Ma kissed me and told me what a lucky boy I was. Pa looked impressed.

'Coloured or not, that Walter Hendricks certainly knows what he's doing with his hands,' he said, admiringly. He turned the model this way and that, looking at the joints and the planing and the paintwork.

'A good job, that!' he said. 'I almost wish I'd thought of doing something like that myself.'

CHAPTER 10

January 1958

Jack had put together a list of people he wanted to interview. He was looking for character witnesses to call in defence of his client, people who would swear to the propriety and moral rectitude of Johannes van Heerden and let the jury see how unthinkable it was that a man of this kind would sully his reputation by sleeping with a coloured woman.

Van Heerden had given him some names. Mrs de Villiers and Miss Liesbet Botha were on the list, as was the verger of the church, Paulus Nel. He mentioned his wife's uncle, Martin Pietersen and his mother's old friend Marius de Wet, who had known him since he was a boy. And finally he had suggested Clara Joubert, who was a childhood friend of his wife and remained her closest confidante. All of these people knew him well and Clara Joubert in particular could give whole-hearted reassurance on the sound and healthy relationship he had with his wife. If Laura and Johannes van Heerden had been unhappy, Clara Joubert would have been the first to know.

Jack mentioned the churchwarden, Francois de Klerk. He had been one of the rumourmongers that van Heerden had talked of at their first meeting. Did he think that de Klerk would agree to be brought to court by the prosecution and speak out against him? Was it worth seeing if he could be persuaded to speak for the defence instead? Van Heerden shrugged. He didn't fully trust the man but thought it worth speaking to him. Having him on his side would be helpful; he was a man who held some sway in the community and his agreement to speak for the prosecution would not be a good thing. Perhaps Jack could help him to see that his doubts as to the pastor's propriety were unfounded and persuade him, at the very least, not to appear as a witness at all?

Jack asked Vera to arrange a series of meetings over the course of the following two days. On the first day he saw four people one after the other and was unsurprised to hear their fulsome praise for his client.

'Tell me about Mr van Heerden,' he asked Paulus Nel.

'Oh he's a man of scrupulous honesty,' Nel replied, leaning forward in his chair to give extra weight to his words. 'I have never known him to be anything other than loyal to his own beliefs and correct in his behaviour. A man of exemplary moral fibre, a true servant of God.'

'And will you testify to that effect in court?'

'Of course, Mr Neuberger. You can count on me.'

Marius de Wet was equally unequivocal. 'I've known Johannes since he was a small boy and even then he showed the qualities of faith and morality that he possesses now. He was a good boy, a good son to his mother after the death of his father. He has never swerved from the true path, of that I can be absolutely sure.'

'And before Laura,' Jack asked, 'did he take an interest in other girls?'

'He was a studious boy, a serious young man. To my knowledge, Laura was his first love.'

'And since?' Jack asked tentatively, aware that he was now straying into more difficult territory.

'Johannes has always had his mind on higher things,' he said. 'And anyway, Laura has been an ideal wife for him – they are perfectly matched. Why should he stray when he has a woman of such undoubted loveliness and goodness as Laura? He would have to be crazy.'

Indeed, thought Jack, but that had not stopped many a man before him from being tempted. Even the best of men were capable of behaving like fools when the opportunity for sexual adventure came their way. But he said nothing, and thanked Mr de Wet for his time and patience.

Mrs de Villiers and Miss Botha both told a similar story. The minister was a fine man and a good husband. When Mrs van Heerden had been taken ill after the birth of their daughter Beatrice, Mr van Heerden had shown the greatest tact and delicacy in offering to help her with her mission, assisting the needy. He had rolled up his sleeves and got on with the kind of donkeywork that some ministers might consider to be beneath their dignity. He was a good man; of that there could be no doubt.

'And you'll be willing to say that in court?' Jack asked.

'Yes, to be sure,' they both replied.

Each of these people would be a good witness. Every cell in their bodies oozed honesty, every expression they used spoke of their Christian faith; they were utterly believable.

It had been a good day. Jack felt satisfied that he was accumulating a decent body of material in favour of his client. When he went home that evening he felt confident enough to tell Renee that things were going rather well despite his early reservations; he thought that this might just be the trial that would make his reputation, if he played his cards right. She kissed him and laughed.

'That's jolly good news,' she said, 'and all the better, given what I've got to tell you. I've been late by over a week now and feeling a bit strange. It's suddenly dawned on me that perhaps I may be pregnant.'

He hugged her tight to him and kissed her. It was soon, perhaps too soon, given that he'd hoped to establish himself a bit more before they started thinking about a family but how thrilling to think that he might soon be a father. You could plan and consider all you liked, but in the end these things sometimes just happened and he couldn't feel anything other than joy at the prospect ahead. In an instant he realised that if nothing came of it, if she told him tomorrow that she'd been mistaken and that she wasn't expecting after all, he would be deeply disappointed.

Before he'd met Renee, he'd sometimes wondered whether he *should* have children. On some deep, emotional level, he wanted them, that he knew, but after the ups and downs of his own childhood, he feared that perhaps he wouldn't make a very good parent himself. It was painful for him to think that a child of his might view him in the same way that he had viewed Pa. But Renee had changed everything; she would so obviously make a good mother; he knew he could rely on that and he couldn't let his own feelings of doubt get in the way of what seemed so very natural to her. It wouldn't be fair on her.

He thought about Laura van Heerden and the way in which Johannes had talked about her. If his mother and father had been in that interview room, what might they have said about each other? He doubted that there would have been anything like the same kind of warmth. But if he'd had to talk like this about his feelings for Renee, that would have been quite a different story.

He'd met her through a friend of a friend at a charity event and had instantly fallen for her. It was a cliché he knew, but from the very first glimpse of her he believed that he would marry her, if only she would agree to it. 'This is it,' he'd thought, 'the one for me.' She was not beautiful in an obvious or conventional way, not glamorous or showy, but fresh, bright-eyed, with a lovely open smile. Her brown hair fell in a wave over her forehead and hung loose around her face and she wore a simple cotton frock that showed off her figure perfectly. There was something utterly uncynical and uncalculating about her – on that first day she met his gaze with friendly warmth, little realising the dramatic, devastating impact she was having on him. For a girl with her looks, she was remarkably unaware of her power over men, and didn't seem to use it to play silly games. And most extraordinary of all, she seemed genuinely interested in him. He wasn't especially good-looking or suave, he knew that, but she appeared to be entertained by his stories, amused by his jokes and, as they stood chatting in a small group, she gave him her undivided attention. The odd little stutter of nervousness at the start of the conversation was ignored by her, and quickly forgotten by him.

Soon after they'd started dating, he'd then discovered to his surprise that, for all her apparent freshness and innocence, she was actually a girl with quite a troubling history. She told him she had something important to tell him, and revealed that he was not her first serious relationship; just a year earlier, she'd been engaged to another man. The wedding date had been fixed, the guests invited, a house bought for them to move into. At the last moment, she had broken it off, causing a huge furore in both families, and heartbreak for the man himself. Friends who'd heard the story began to warn Jack off her; in the small Jewish community she lived in, it was regarded as a major scandal and anyhow, how could he ever trust a girl who'd done something like that to another man, with such seeming heartlessness? He listened to their warnings quietly, and then chose to ignore them. She told him that she had stepped back from the brink of marrying someone she didn't love, that she'd become trapped by her family's expectations and their pleasure at his wealth; from their point of view he was a brilliant match. But in the end she just couldn't go through with it; she was looking for something more than that, something different, a different kind of life. The intensity of her feelings for Jack were clear; there was no doubting it, and he trusted the sense he'd had about her from the very start, that she was the right woman for him. If risk it was, he would jump at the chance to take it, whatever anyone else said.

Young though they were, they had got married and now here she was, in all probability, expecting their first child. It seemed quite crazy, and utterly improbable, that someone like him had met someone like her and that now they'd be adding to their happiness by becoming a proper family. With his career taking off and this trial looking so good, he found himself marvelling at how well his life was turning out.

The next day, the second day of interviews, he was due to see Francois de Klerk and Clara Joubert. Things didn't go quite so well.

Francois de Klerk arrived late. He was a tall, thin man, with slightly greying hair and a narrow, gaunt face. Jack was surprised by his diffident expression and his anxious demeanour; he had been expecting someone rather tougher looking, a more serious adversary for his client. The man looked ill at ease and kept glancing at his watch.

'I have an appointment later this morning, Mr Neuberger. We're having repairs done to the side roof of the church and the buildings surveyor is coming to give us advice. I can give you half an hour but no more.'

'Half an hour will be plenty,' Jack said. 'You needn't worry about missing your appointment.'

'There's nothing I can tell you, anyway,' he said. 'I have no knowledge that will be useful to you.'

'I'm just speaking to people who know my client well,' Jack said. 'Mr van Heerden respects and admires you and suggested that I might talk to you.'

'Oh.' De Klerk blushed. He hesitated. 'Well, I admire him very much too.'

'You do?'

'Well, yes. He's been a very good minister. He's done a good job for our Church.'

'But?'

De Klerk hesitated. 'No buts,' he said.

Jack decided to take the plunge. 'Look Mr de Klerk, let's be honest with each other. I'm acting for my client and in order to do that I must know the facts. I need to know what's likely to be dredged up against him in court. If he has any skeletons in his closet, I'd like to see them now rather than have them jumping out to scare me in the courtroom.'

De Klerk smiled at the joke but then he became serious.

'I've had my doubts,' he said. 'I'll admit that. Someone in our community – I'd rather not say who – approached me to tell me they were concerned about the minister and a woman in Elsie's River. Normally I'd have brushed it aside, I'd have told them they were speaking a load of old nonsense... But...'

'But...?'

'But this person isn't a gossip or a scandalmonger. She's a thoughtful woman who wouldn't say these things lightly, someone who has always admired the minister.'

'And how did she come to have these concerns?'

'She's one of Laura van Heerden's little group, the women who worked together to help the needy in Elsie's River.'

Jack drew in his breath. His heart pounded.

'What gave rise to these concerns?' he said.

'She told me that Johannes van Heerden had once stayed on after the women had returned home. He remained in Elsie's River after the work was done, telling the women that he still had obligations to fulfil that did not require them to stay.'

Jack paused.

'There must be a simple explanation for this, don't you think, Mr de Klerk? Perhaps there was business to be sorted out that evening, people in the community to talk to. Why jump to conclusions, without troubling to find out more?'

'I thought that myself, Mr Neuberger. But when I asked Mr van Heerden straight out, he couldn't give me a proper answer. He was awkward and confused, muttered a few things that made no sense and then refused to say more. It made me doubt. It was his own discomfort more than anything else that gave me pause for thought.'

'I've spoken to Mrs de Villiers and Miss Botha,' Jack protested. 'They are part of the group and are wholly convinced of his innocence. Why did they not tell me this if they were there?'

'Ah but they weren't there. On that particular occasion, there were only three of them: the woman I've told you about, Mr van Heerden and one other.'

'The one other?'

'Miss Clara Joubert,' Mr de Klerk said.

'Clara Joubert?' Jack struggled to keep the shock out of his voice.

'Indeed.'

'I'm seeing her later today.'

'Well, perhaps you'd better ask her yourself,' Mr de Klerk said. 'I hope there's an explanation of his behaviour, honestly I do. Look, Mr Neuberger, I've known the minister a long time and there's no one who would be happier to hear that he's innocent than me. But if he's betrayed Laura, been sleeping with some cheap coloured girl, breaking this new law …'

'Thank you Mr de Klerk,' Jack interrupted. He didn't want to hear any more of what the man had to say on this subject. 'I'm sure he'll prove his innocence. I'll talk to Clara Joubert and one or two others and then, if it's all right with you, maybe we could speak again?'

'Of course. I hope and pray that what you discover allays my fears,' he said.

'And may I ask whether you have been approached by the prosecution?'

'I have an appointment with Mr du Toit, the prosecuting counsel, in a few days' time but I haven't quite made up my mind what to do yet. I've already postponed the meeting once, to give myself a bit of time to think. To be honest Mr Neuberger, I'm a bit confused as to what to do for the best. I want to do what's right – for our little community, for Laura, for Johannes' – it was the first time he had allowed himself to call van Heerden by his first name – 'but also for my country. My forebears fought the Zulu and settled the land and I have a duty to them to do the right thing, whatever that might be.'

'Let me talk to a few more people and I'll get Vera, my secretary, to call you and arrange another meeting before you see du Toit. Even if you feel unable to speak up for Mr van Heerden in court and act as a witness for the defence, at the very least I'd like to be able to persuade you not to appear for the prosecution. I'm sure, with a bit more information, I'll be able to allay your doubts and bring you onto our side.'

They shook hands and Jack noticed his firm grasp and the evident look of relief on his face that this difficult interview had come to an end.

'Now I must turn my mind to the church roof,' he said. 'Bricks and mortar are sometimes easier to deal with than people.'

Jack closed the door and went to sit at his desk. He pushed his chair back and stretched out his legs in front of him. He threw his fountain pen down onto the blotter in a gesture of frustration. This was all proving rather less straightforward than he had hoped. He rang through to Vera on the intercom.

'Will you fetch me a sandwich from Lou's?' he said. 'I'm going to work through lunch, so I can get my head straight before Clara Joubert's appointment. Chopped liver, with a pickled cucumber on the side, and maybe a slice of their cheesecake?'

'Yes Mr Neuberger,' Vera replied curtly. Was she sulking? There were so many things that seemed to provoke her irritation. Perhaps fetching his lunch was another thing that she felt was beneath her dignity? He wished she would take more pleasure in her duties; sometimes he thought she resented every last thing he asked of her. But she was efficient enough once she got going and took a good shorthand. She had also come highly recommended by his cousin Isidore, so it would be awkward to look for someone new, just on the basis that he sometimes wished for a more cheerful presence in the office.

'I'll go for your sandwich right now. On white bread, or rye? It's usually rye I know, but I don't want to assume that and then find that you wanted white, Mr Neuberger. I know how much you enjoy your sandwiches.'

'Rye, white, brown, whatever you like Vera. You know me, I'm not fussy. No, on second thoughts, make it rye. You're right; rye's what I like.'

'Rye it is then.'

He was just about to put the phone down.

'Oh, by the way, Miss Clara Joubert called while you were interviewing Mr de Klerk. She says she can't make the appointment this afternoon after all.'

Jack frowned. 'Did you look in my diary and suggest another time?'

'Oh yes but nothing seemed to work for her. She said she was very busy at the moment and didn't think it would be easy to find an occasion anytime soon.'

'Thank you, Vera.'

'Still want the sandwich, Mr Neuberger?'

'No thanks, Vera. I'll get one later myself. I'm not feeling so hungry any more.'

Chapter 11

I wanted a collection. I wanted the thrill of examining it every day, adding to it, labelling it, displaying it, crowing over it, possessing it wholly. But I didn't know what to collect. Terence had his Dinky cars but I knew that no one was going to buy me shiny new cars to put in a cardboard box in a toy cupboard, that I could take out and line up every day. I talked to Ada, who frowned. She looked like she was taking my problem seriously, as she always did when I came to her for advice. She swept her hand through her thin brown hair, then placed her hands on her hips and sighed loudly.

'Ag, Jackie I dunno. I used to collect marbles when I was seven like you. Spent half my life, squatting down, dirtying my broekies in the dust, looking to see if I could find one that'd fallen out of a hole in someone's pocket. And then I lost 'em all in marbles matches with the boys. They was too damn good. My friend Smoky Uys – sies tog, he's dead now – he had a hang of a big collection of insects, nasty little goggas all stuck down with pins. The butterflies were nice but the goggas, ag sis man, they were disgusting. Smoky's brother Smiley had a little box full of bottle labels. He washed 'em off the bottles his Ma bought from the store. But they only drank lemon cooldrink and gingerbeer, so that's all he ever had – loads of Stoney Ginger beer labels and SAB lemonade. Not much fun, man, just two kinds of labels. Leastways that's what I thought. What's a good thing for you to collect... I'm really stumped there Jackie. Right out of good ideas, man.'

I was disappointed; Ada, though not a child like me, seemed to have more of a sense of what children were like than anyone else, whether it was knowing the right moment to surprise me with the secret offer of a sherbet lemon, or just noticing when I was down in the dumps and cheering me up with a silly joke. Maybe it was because she herself had been one of eight children and had helped her ma bring up the younger ones, but Ada seemed to know all the street games and rhymes, all the practical jokes and pranks that children got up to; I had been relying on her.

I talked to Terence instead.

'You've got to have something really, really good,' Terence said, scratching his head, as he'd seen adults do in similar circumstances. 'Something really special.' In his usual way, he was ready and eager to come to my assistance, seeing it as a joint enterprise and a shared adventure.

Together we puzzled and pondered and I wrote our ideas down carefully on a scrap of paper: bottle tops, bus tickets, buttons, birds' eggs, stamps, stones, coins. I looked at the list hopefully but the vision of myself sitting with a collection of any of these things spread out all around me felt all wrong. Nothing brought the warm glow that I knew should come with being a proper, fully-fledged, totally committed, admired and respected collector.

'Nope,' I said, 'none of them's good enough.'

'Nope,' he agreed, frowning.

Walter and May closed the garage for lunch and we all sat down at the wooden table in the kitchen to eat frikadels and rice and Terence told Walter my problem. Walter sat and thought for a moment, then snapped his fingers excitedly.

'I got a really lekker idea for you, Master Jackie,' he said. 'It's what I collected when I was a little boy like you, seven or eight or thereabouts. My Pa got me started. He brought me some back and looked out for special ones for me. Then I started swapping with other boys – one special for two ordinaries, three ordinaries for a rare, one rare for a different rare and my collection grew and grew.'

Specials, ordinaries, rares. Beautiful, exotic, magical. What could he be talking about?

'Matchboxes,' said Walter. 'That's a lekker thing to collect. And you can store 'em by who makes 'em or by size or by picture – animals, birds, people, buildings, flowers, ships, whatever.'

'Yeah, matchboxes! That'd be nice. No one I know's a matchbox collector!'

Terence's approval sealed it; the die was cast. I went home and told Ma and Pa that I was starting a matchbox collection. Pa seemed pleased.

'Good idea, Jackie. All boys have collections. You'll make lots of friends that way.'

Soon the customers started showing a bit of an interest in my matchboxes. I moved by tiptoeing steps out of the shadows at the edges of the store, and began to talk to the people I'd known since I was a baby but had never dared to address directly.

'P-p-please Mr van de M-m-merwe. Do you have any m-matchboxes f-f-for my c-collection?'

'Course, Jackie, my boy. No problem, sonny. I get through a whole heap of the darned things, lighting that blerry useless wood burner of ours, or having a smoke out the back. Mrs van de Merwe will be only too delighted not to have all my half-empty packets cluttering up the place. I'll bring you a handful next time I'm in.'

'Hey man, how many you got now?' asked Arnie Fortune.

'Over f-f-fifty.'

'My God that's getting to be a big collection. My cousin Barry used to collect them years ago. I'll see if he's got any left up in that attic of his and I'll twist his arm to hand 'em over to you.'

'I'll get my sister in England to bring you some when she comes over on the Union Castle to visit. She's coming next week and staying for two or three months, you know,' interrupted Mrs Stern. 'They've got nice colourful pictures of ships on the matchboxes in England, England's Glory I think they're called, and yellow ones with swans.'

'Show me a rare,' said Billy Edwards coming over to look at the handful I was stacking up on the wooden floor next to the sack of beans, and when Terence came into the store with his mother, we went into the back room and surrounded ourselves with my matchboxes, looking, sorting, counting, judging. Soon Terence began collecting matchboxes too and we had regular swapsie sessions, where we weighed up the value of one over another and shared our spoils.

By the end of the summer, when I went back to school, word had spread that I had a lekker collection of matchboxes and boys approached me in the schoolyard with the offer of a swap – a matchbox found on a table in a café in Seapoint, one given by an uncle in Durban, another that came all the way from New York in the pocket of a merchant seaman lodging in Parow. I overheard Mrs Coetzee telling Miss Williams, my new teacher, that she was surprised and delighted to see that at last I was beginning to make some friends.

But now my matchbox collection was growing bigger and getting in Ma's way.

'Wherever I look there are blasted matchboxes,' she muttered crossly. 'Your room's full of them and it's just not fair on Sauly. He's barely got space to walk in that room of yours, let alone play with toys.'

'But he likes them. He says so!'

'He's just being nice. It's his room too and it's not right that he has to trip over your matchboxes all the time.'

Pa suggested that he might be able to find a space for the collection in the big new shed he'd built in the yard, to house the goods from the wholesalers and farm co-ops. He said he was sure he could give me a shelf, in among the sacks of corn and beans and rice, the boxes of cereals and cigarettes, the shoe leather and bicycles, the plates of glass, the bales of string and twine, the chaff, the lucerne and other animal feeds. Over the next few weeks bit by bit he cleared a shelf and finally labelled it with a big cardboard sign, written in ultramarine blue ink, 'Jack's Matchbox Collection'.

One evening, after the store had closed, he helped me carry all the matchboxes down and put them on my new shelf. I looked at the rows of tidily stacked boxes with pride. Pa stood with me, side by side. He moved to kiss my head but at that moment I looked up at him and he seemed to change his mind. I thought I saw tears in his eyes but I couldn't be sure. Quickly he reached for a box of Garibaldi biscuits and took it out to re-fill the jars in the store.

*****

A few days later, Mr Choudhary came into the store. He hadn't been in for a while. I liked seeing him, all dressed in white, with his cap fitting snugly over his sleek black hair, so different from the other men in their khaki shorts or their linen suits, their faces burnt and red, or leathery from the sun. Mr Choudhary always looked cool, no matter how strongly the sun was beating down on the store, making the rest of us feel sweaty, sluggish and slow.

'He's not a customer,' Ma had told Ada, when she asked why he never bought anything when he came. 'He's not here for our biltong or our biscuits. He lives in District 6, the Malay quarter. They have shops of their own and their own things, like spices for curries and things like that, to suit their own tastes. No, he's not a customer. He's here to talk to my husband about the money and the insurance.'

Every few months Mr Choudhary appeared, with his leather briefcase and a new idea for Pa to consider.

'Oh my God, not another scheme,' Ma would say after he'd left and Pa was sitting at the table with the papers spread out in front of him. But he'd helped Pa find a lender that time when they'd needed the money to buy the truck, and that had worked out fine. And he'd got the insurance to pay out when the roof had leaked a few winters back. So Ma seemed happy enough with Mr Choudhary and didn't complain too much about the time he spent chatting to Pa, taking him away from the customers and the jobs that needed doing at the store. Mr Choudhary was Pa's financial adviser, so she said, if anyone asked, and she seemed to like the sound of that, as if they were a proper business, on a good, sound footing.

Now Mr Choudhary was back, with his briefcase. Pa took him to one side of the store where they talked, while Ada looked after the customers who came through the door. They talked about the price of paraffin, of candle wax, of flax and lucerne and rice and oil; they talked about cheaper wholesalers and lower taxes, about bank interest rates and lenders; they talked about Mr Hertzog and Mr Smuts and how nothing that useless government did seemed to make a blind bit of difference, how the country was going to the dogs.

'All out of ideas,' said Mr. Choudhary, folding his arms across his body. They talked on and on, about war and economics, inflation and deflation, immigration and emigration until Pa finally said,

"We'd be better off with a King, like the English!'

Mr Choudhary leant towards him, now, speaking more softly, in low tones. I wondered what he was saying and came up closer to hear.

'Stop buzzing around us like a damned bluebottle,' Pa said crossly. 'Scram!'

Ma was out with Sauly, buying mince from the Kosher butcher on Salt Street and chollah bread for our evening meal and Ada was minding the store. I wandered into the back room and sat at the table drawing with a blunt pencil, feeling bored, wondering why grown-ups always had so much to talk about and so little of it of any interest, always money, money, money.

Pa was worried about money again. A big new store had just opened up further down Main Road. People had been talking about Woolworths this, Woolworths that, ever since the first store opened on the site of the old Royal Hotel. And now here was one, right on his doorstep in Parow. Who did that Woolworths man think he was, selling everything a hardware store sells and more – clothes, shoes, confectionery, fabrics, sticky tape, glue? And the prices, said Pa, were frankly crazy.

'Meshuggah! I couldn't buy the light bulbs and cotton reels and mops from the wholesalers for what this Woolworth man is selling them for. Right on my doorstep. Right on my blooming doorstep.'

And now the customers were beginning to shop there, even ones whom we'd come to rely on as our regulars, almost as our friends.

'It's whadderyercall it?' said Mrs Fortune, searching for the right word. 'What's that word?'

Pa was sorting skeins of worsted wool for her and knotting them into bundles. He was checking the colour to be sure that the skeins from different batches matched, then wrapping them in paper and tying the parcel with string.

'Easy. All packaged up and quick,' said Mrs Fortune. 'What's the damned word for it again? It's on the tip of my tongue.'

Now Pa was counting out buttons for her – ten for a tickie – and pouring them into a little brown paper bag. He was rummaging through the wooden drawers looking for Size 9 knitting needles, a nice big darning needle and some squared pattern paper for dressmaking. He was weighing out her digestive biscuits and fig rolls.

'Convenient,' she said. 'That's the word! It's really convenient. A convenient store, that Woolworths.'

She paid for her goods and left.

Some of his customers had started coming in quite unashamedly carrying a Woolworths paper bag under their arm. 'Just the string and the candles today Mr Neuberger,' said old Mrs Pretorius. I could see peeking out of top of the Woolworths bag many of the things she'd normally buy from Pa.

Things were not good; Afrikaners, poor whites, Jews, none of them had anything to spend. Pa said he could little afford even a tickie of that money going into some other storekeeper's pocket. His takings had dropped and they were dropping by the day.

Ma was having a hard time making ends meet. She was darning the darns on her stockings and our socks and patching the patches on our trousers. She was roasting the chicken one day, picking the meat off the bones the next, boiling the bones for soup the following one and finally, by the end of the week it was milk soup and lokshen and that was all.

'Will we g-get by?' I asked her one day, too afraid to raise this doubt with my father. 'Will we, Ma?'

'Of course,' she said, though her voice sounded less sure than her words. 'Think of what our ancestors survived; they lived on little more than the air they breathed, they suffered from pogroms and beatings, they fought for the Czar and died of their wounds, they scratched the bare soil and milked their scrawny cows and killed their skinny hens. By comparison we're in clover!

And then a few days later everything suddenly changed and the mood in our household switched from worried looks and angry frowns to frantic activity, excitement and laughter. Pa had suddenly announced that we were all going to Somerset Strand for a few days' holiday. On special days, like birthdays, we had sometimes caught the train out to Muizenberg, the small seaside resort out beyond the city centre, to have a picnic lunch and swim at the beach and then run down the platform to get the last train back again at the end of the day. But we had never had a proper holiday by the sea, staying overnight away from home, in a boarding house or small seaside hotel.

Ma looked happy. She hummed in the kitchen and sang me my favourite song, the one she'd stopped singing for a while:

'Hob ikh mir a mantl fun fartsaytikn shtof Tra la la la

Hot es nit in zikh kay gantsenem shtokh Tra la la la

Darum, hob ikh zikh fartrakht Un fun dem mantl a rekl gemakht Tra la la ...'

I had a little coat that I made long ago,

It had so many patches, there was no place to sew

Then I thought and I prayed

And from that coat a little jacket I made.

She got up on a chair to reach for the old suitcase on the top of the wardrobe and dusted it off. She sorted out clothes and swimming costumes and towels. She even found the cameo brooch that Ouma had given her for her wedding and the lacy underwear she had kept from her trousseau. She packed them in the case, blushing and trying to hide them from my interested gaze.

On the train out, Ma is smiling and Pa is smiling. They are sitting close up next to each other, legs touching, hand in hand, with the luggage in the rack above them and Sauly sprawled out asleep on a seat beside them.

'How long till we get to Somerset Strand?' I ask and realise, with surprise that my stutter has stopped.

'When can I have my egg sandwich?' Yes, it really has stopped completely. 'Will there be boats at Somerset Strand? Will there be an aquarium? Will we be staying in a Boarding House? Will we be able to walk to the beach? Will we eat ice cream? Will we eat crayfish even though it's not kosher?'

'Yes, yes, yes, yes!' says Pa, who seems to have caught the excitement, like a big bright beach ball that he can throw up in the air, and Ma seems to open her arms wide to catch it. 'A holiday,' she says, breathing in deeply and laughing, with a girlish peal in her voice that I have never heard before. 'My goodness, a proper, proper holiday.'

*****

In the train coming home I think about my proper holiday. I remember: the sandcastles and the stinging salt wash of the sea in my eyes; my sunburnt back and the soothing dabs of calamine lotion; collecting wood and stones to help with Pa's dam; poking at slippery weeds and crusty shells in the rock pools; Mrs Maree's Boarding House with the low tock tock of the grandfather clock in the cool dining-room; the stoep, the porch at the front of the house, bordered by paraffin tins filled with geraniums; the sailing boats being dragged right up the beach when the wind came up and the waters frothed and foamed; the women walking to the white church with their doeks tied tight against the wind; reaching up for loquats from the over-loaded trees in the garden and shaking them down so they fell like heavy, thudding rain; eating tea and cakes at the Strand Café and still having enough room for crayfish for supper; Sauly puking up at the harbour from too much crayfish, too much ice cream and granadilla sauce; the library on Van der Byl Street, where Ma took me to borrow a book; the smell of the books and the wonderful black ink pad and the date stamp that the lady banged hard into the ink and stamped down on the first page of my book; Ma's face at breakfast at Mrs Maree's, smiling and smiling and smiling; Pa's face at breakfast at Mrs Maree's, smiling and smiling and smiling.

*****

We arrived home. I was tired out from the walk from the station and looking forward to the drink of warm milk and the biscuit that Ma had promised me, before undressing and going straight to bed. As we got closer to the store though, something didn't seem quite right. There was a scent in the air that didn't smell like home, an odour that hit us all the more powerfully as Pa opened the front door.

I saw Ma looking anxiously towards Pa but he seemed unconcerned. He was whistling and humming as he took our suitcases upstairs and started unpacking them, and continued humming happily as he opened up cupboards and drawers. Ma and I went into the kitchen and Ma went straight to the back window, to look out into the yard. And then she screamed. She yelled. She stared into the yard, crying now, sobbing, holding her head in her hands, beating furiously at her chest. She fell to her knees and howled like a dog in pain. I pushed open the back door and ran out to see what had happened.

The chickens were lying dead in the yard, their feathers singed off to reveal dry bony carcasses. There was a heap of steaming, smoking, shivering wood, charred, charcoaled, blackened. Ashy paper floated up, sending flapping slivers and wafery fragments, some curled, some crisp, swirling around the yard. The shed was a smoking and charcoaled nothing, razed to the ground, gone.

I ran towards the steaming heap of blackened embers to see what was left but it was still too hot to approach. I turned back towards the house to seek out Ma and Pa. What were they going to do? How were they going to make this right again, as I assumed that they would? Surely Pa would know what to do; he would be able to bring the shed back to life again, with a sweep of his expert arm.

But Pa was looking out from the upstairs window, his face furrowed with a frown that belied his earlier cheeriness.

'M-m-my m-m-m-m-matchboxes!' I cried.

Pa came running down. He scooped me up in his arms and held me tight. I flailed out, hitting him, pounding his chest, pummelling his face and arms, kicking at his legs. He fought his way up the stairs with me, holding me tightly and peeled me off him, laying me down on my bed, where I sobbed bitterly.

'Be brave. It's only matchboxes.' Then he left me, closing the door behind him.

The next morning Pa was occupied in the store and I stayed in the back room; I did not want to see him. I sat at the kitchen table, refusing any offers of food from Ma or from Ada, not even a treat like a fig roll or an aniseed ball. Sauly came and put his arms round me and gave me a kiss on the cheek.

'Sorry 'bout the matchboxes Jackie.'

I stared straight ahead of me. It was nice of him to say something but I knew if I looked at him or said anything in reply I might start to cry.

Ada walked past, dragging a large sack of corn from the yard, through the kitchen and towards the store. She patted me on the head, muttering 'Ag sies tog Jackie.' I remained silent and stony-faced. ' You can start up your collection again, no problem,' she said. 'Everyone will help you. Soon you'll have more than before.' I said nothing.

Ma and Pa didn't speak much to each other either that day. Ma spent her time in the kitchen preparing food, talking to Sauly and me but only saying what was strictly necessary. Pa was in the store, filling up drawers with tacks and nails and goods from the garage, items that hadn't gone up in flames.

In the late afternoon the shop bell rang and Mr Choudhary came in. I hadn't seen him since that last time. He waited till the queue of customers had subsided, standing to one side on his own, in the shadowy corner, near my sack of beans. Then Pa lifted the gate in the counter and came out to greet him properly, with an arm round his shoulder and a vigorous handshake.

He took him out to look at the smouldering wreck of the shed in the yard. Mr Choudhary waved his arms about a bit. I watched from the yard, near the kitchen door. Pa talked to him seriously, but every now and then he glanced back towards the house to note Ma standing by the kitchen window. He was also keeping an eye on me, watching as I scuffed my shoes in the dirt of the yard a few feet away. Mr Choudhary had his briefcase open and handed some papers to Pa. He read them and signed them one by one, with the smart fountain pen that Mr Choudhary unscrewed and handed to him. I caught a few stray words, drifting in the air like the smoky ash of the shed and then wafting away on the wind: 'Old stock…new stock…replacement value…inspectors….' And then finally Pa put his hand on Mr Choudhary's shoulder. Mr Choudhary smiled, shook his hand, put the papers back in his briefcase and then went through the kitchen and the back room, into the store and out into Main Road. The store bell tinkled eerily as he shut the door firmly behind him.

*****

The next day Pa went out to Paarl to talk to the wholesalers. He was making plans for building a brand new shed and re-stocking the goods he had lost. It was a big job and he would be gone for the day, perhaps even having to stay overnight, if he couldn't get through all the visits he needed to make. Since we had no telephone in our house or at the store, he promised to leave a phone message with Irene next door to tell Ma if he was going to be delayed and only able to return the next day.

It was early evening and Ada and Ma had shut the store. Ada swept up the sawdust and cleaned the counter. She pulled down the blinds and took out the rubbish. She paused to offer me a liquorice twist, on her way back through the store, which this time I deigned to accept. Ma told her that since her jobs were done, she could go home now; she wouldn't be needed. Just as she was leaving, Irene leaned out from the window of her flat and asked her to pass on the message to Ma that Pa would not be coming home till the following day – he was still in Paarl talking to suppliers and would be back around lunchtime, all being well.

Ma put Sauly to bed and then, as a rare treat, she let me stay up with her, while she sat in her wicker chair in the back yard, darning socks and stockings by the light of a small metal kerosene lamp.

I loved to be on my own with her like this, sitting in the yard, in the gathering darkness, listening to the soft buzz of insects flitting around the light and the hiss of the grasshoppers in the grass beyond the back fence, watching her fingers tidily passing the needle through the wool, her face intently focused on the task. For once she seemed relaxed, untroubled, her face softened by the fading light and the flickers from the lamp. I felt unusually relaxed too; with Pa in Paarl there was no risk of rows, no bad-tempered looks or sullen silences, no threat of Pa's anger.

'I'm sorry about your matchboxes,' Ma said at last, holding her needle still and looking up at me. 'It's a shame.'

I said nothing.

'They meant something to you, I know.' She paused. 'You worked hard at that collection and it was a lovely one. But you can build it up again.'

I shook my head. I wasn't going to start again. It would never be the same. I could never hold them in my hands, without the pang of knowledge that they could so easily vanish into thin air, turning swiftly into ash and dust. They were, after all, just cardboard and paper, rather than the precious objects I had so foolishly turned them into.

'I know how hard it is,' she said. 'But there are compensations for us all, you know. The insurance money means that we can keep going now for quite a while, with the store. It'll help us through these difficult times. There'll be chicken for your supper more often!'

I nodded. I liked the idea of a full stomach and more treats, despite the pain of the matchboxes. 'I suppose it must be a good thing that Pa knows Mr Choudhary,' I said.

'What do you mean,' Ma replied but looked at me a little oddly.

'Mr Choudhary is good with his hands, like Pa. He knows how to make a shed burn down.'

Ma's needle went still. She sat up in her chair.

'What do you mean, Jackie?'

'Pa likes Mr Choudhary because he's good at things like making sheds burn down.'

'Where do you get all this from?' Ma asked. 'What's this nonsense you're talking?' I wondered whether she was cross but she just seemed really interested in what I had to say. I was enjoying, for once, having her full attention and it gave me the confidence to continue.

'I saw Pa talking to Mr Choudhary about the shed.'

It came back to me, the memories of that afternoon; I could see it all quite clearly, myself sitting drawing at the kitchen table, with the soft blunt stub of a pencil, bored, waiting for Ma to come home. Pa had come through from the store with Mr Choudhary. They had gone out into the yard and I had got up and climbed on a stool so that I could watch them through the window. They were surveying the yard, the shed and the garage where the truck was parked. They went into the garage, letting the big wooden door swing open behind them, then they came out again, unlocked the shed and disappeared inside for quite a while, before strolling back into the yard.

I came out into the doorway, curious about what they were doing and keen to listen to their conversation but afraid to go up close and risk incurring Pa's wrath again. I watched them from just inside the door; they were pointing and frowning, they folded their arms seriously and then finally after a long, serious pause, shook hands. I heard Pa thank Mr Choudhary warmly and smile and I thought that just as Terence was my best friend, Mr Choudhary must be Pa's.

Ma sat still and looked at me. I couldn't tell what she was thinking.

'It's good that we've got money now,' I said. 'I'd like to eat chicken for my supper. But Mr Choudhary burnt down all my matchboxes. So I don't like him like Pa does.'

I waited a bit to see what Ma would say. I wondered whether I should ask her about the other thing that puzzled me, the other bit of the whole story that I didn't quite understand.

'Ma?' I said. 'I want to ask you something.'

Ma was staring at me still; I could see that her hands were trembling.

'What do you want to know Jackie?'

'Why does Pa keep money under the floor?'

Ma's voice was low and calm.

'Does he Jackie?' Her voice was steady.

'Yes,' I said, warming now to my theme. 'He puts it under the floor when he's been counting out the money from the till. He pulls up a floorboard and puts it there, then bangs the board back down.'

There was silence.

'Why did he have to burn down the shed, if he has money under the floor?' I asked Ma. Now perhaps, I would have the answer.

There was a long silence.

'Time for your bed,' Ma said.

'But...'

'No buts. It's late.'

I felt the tears coming.

'Off to bed,' she said. She seemed angry with me now, distant all of a sudden and shaking with a quiet fury.

'I'm sorry Ma,' I sobbed. 'I didn't mean to say anything bad.'

'You've said nothing wrong, Jackie,' she said. 'But now it's time to go to bed.' With a firm hand she guided me up the stairs, undressed me at speed, kissed me on the face before turning out the light. I felt wetness on my cheek and wondered whether it was her tears or mine. Both maybe. It was hard to be sure.

CHAPTER 12

We were all crowded into Oupa's workshop, Oupa at his wheel, Ouma on the big wooden chair in the corner, Ma on a stool next to her, with Sauly sitting at her feet playing. I sat on the floor next to him, making patchwork shapes out of little pieces of leather, leftovers and shavings from the making of shoes. Ma and Ouma were talking quietly. I caught fragments of the conversation, which I tried to piece together, but while some made sense, others didn't and however hard I tried to put them together it was a struggle.

Ma was complaining about Pa. She said that Pa's holiday in Somerset Strand had been a trick, a ruse to get us out the way, not a real holiday at all. And now she was thinking of a holiday herself, a long one, on her own, just with the children. Maybe never coming back this time.

I was thrilled. I thought of days and weeks and months at Somerset Strand, playing with shells, walking on the windy beach and coming back at dusk to Mrs Maree's Boarding House for tomato bredie or babotie in the cool, dark dining room.

'I'd go like a shot, if only I could,' Ma said. 'I told Sam that and he shouted, "Go gezunterheit!"' Ma said she would definitely go if things didn't get any better; there was only so much a woman could take. But Ouma told her to try to be sensible. She reminded her of what Oupa would say. Oupa had always had a soft spot for Sam. And what's more he took a tough line on wives and marriage: wives obeyed their husbands; marriage was for ever; and above all, a married woman was her husband's responsibility, not her father's.

Ma looked at me sitting playing on the floor and shook her head. There were tears in her eyes. 'The matchboxes,' she said, 'Poor Little Jackie's matchboxes.'

When we got home, she took the suitcase down from above the wardrobe, but she didn't fill it with clothes, nor did she search for her cameo brooch or her lacy underwear from her trousseau. She left the suitcase empty but instead of putting it back above the wardrobe she slid it under the bed. I was puzzled. Were we going on holiday again or weren't we?

It was just one week into the new school term, and a few weeks later, that I came home from school to find Sauly sitting on a suitcase, raw-faced and snotty with crying, and the usual motley collection of bags and cases packed and ready to go by the front door. Only this time there were more than usual.

'What's wrong, Sauly?'

He started to speak but then burst into a fresh squall of sobs that muffled his words.

I ran into the back room where Ma was putting on her coat, hat and gloves.

'Are we going to stay at Ouma and Oupa's again?' I asked.

'No,' Ma replied curtly. 'We're going away. Go and fetch Jarpe. You might want to have him with you, rather than leaving him to stay here on his own.'

When I went up to the bedroom to find my toy monkey, I was surprised to see that the room was almost bare. I was excited but also afraid. This holiday felt different. I had looked forward to the thought of the seaside, sand between the toes, poking at crabs in rock pools and tomato bredie forever at Mrs Maree's. But now there was also an icy little splinter of doubt about leaving Parow and the Handyhouse and what would happen to Pa when we were gone.

*****

Sitting in the train, surrounded by luggage and sharing a seat with Sauly, I asked Ma, 'Is Mrs Maree expecting us?'

Ma hooted with dry laughter. 'You don't think we're on our way to Mrs Maree,'s do you? We're going to Bloubergstrand, the cheapest place I could think of. I've sold off my wedding jewellery to pay for it and it's all I can afford.'

The train pulled in to the bare little station that stood close to the promenade. The straight track followed a line of ramshackle sheds and railway buildings that looked more like a small shantytown than official station buildings. We stepped down from the train. Cheap food joints jostled with narrow hotels, their paint peeling, their signs faded.

A coloured boy, alone and customerless, wheeled a dirty yellow trolley along the front offering lemon ices and cream sodas. The beach was windswept and deserted and the wood of the beach huts was rotting, stripped bare by salt and neglect. It was out of season and stalls and shops were shuttered and padlocked. A man accosted Ma almost straightaway, offering to carry her bags. His hair was greasy and his face unwashed. His trousers were held up with a piece of string and his shirt cuffs were frayed. Ma looked anxious but agreed; we were not going to get very far with all that luggage without his help.

The man hurried ahead, despite being weighed down by all of our bags, and when he reached the nearest hotel, Potgieter's, he dumped them in a big pile on the pavement. He disappeared for a while, before bringing the owner of the hotel out to greet us.

Mrs Potgieter was a large woman, whose clothes seemed to only just cover her ample body. Her face was red and veiny, and her eyes seemed surprisingly small, like small black buttons lost in the fleshiness of her broad face. She placed her hands on her hips and peered at us suspiciously, then asked Ma a few questions about who we were and where we'd come from, how long we'd be staying and whether we would have the means to pay the cost of the room up front, which was a rule she always applied. Finally, with a long sigh, she said, 'I suppose you'd better come in then,' took us into the hallway way of the hotel. The hall was painted dark red, though flakes of paint had peeled away, revealing a bilious green beneath. The desk was of sombre, dark stained wood and the carpet a threadbare mat that had seen better days. In the ceiling a dusty chandelier barely lit up the gloom, several of its bulbs having blown and not been replaced.

Mrs Potgieter asked Ma to sign a register, then handed her a key, attached to a flapping white label.

Ma paid the greasy man a few coins from her purse for his trouble, followed by several more when he kept his arm stretched out boldly in front of her face. Than she picked Sauly up and ushered me ahead of her, up the five flights of stairs to the small attic room at the top of the hotel that had been allocated to us. Leaving us sitting on the bed, she went down to drag each item of baggage, up the flights of stairs, one by one.

'I'm hungry,' Sauly whined.

'Me too,' I said.

'It's bedtime. You'll have breakfast in the morning.'

I lay in bed looking at the stained pink stripes on the wallpaper and wondering whether Ada had closed the shop door yet and what Pa would be eating for his supper without Ma to cook it for him. Would Terence be coming into the store with his mother and what would he think when he found out that I had gone away? I wondered what Miss Williams would be teaching my class, the story of the Boer Wars or the arrival of Jan Smuts, or maybe tales of the savage Zulu tribes. Would the children still be playing jacks and hopscotch, or perhaps they had already moved on to clapping games or skipping or marbles in the short period that I had been gone? And would I still have any friends on my return from my holiday, or would they have forgotten all about me and changed their allegiances, finding new friends to supplant me? I was missing it all already, home, school, the Handyhouse, and would need to be back soon, to take up my proper place in my world again.

*****

A few days later, Ma sat me down on the bed and told me that we were not going home. We would be staying away for good. She would look for a job in a school, or she would teach the children of rich people, acting as a tutor or governess. Sauly smiled happily but I burst into tears. Already I missed my school and Mrs Coetzee and Miss Williams, my visits to Terence and Mrs Mostert and my talks with Walter at Mrs Mostert's kitchen table. I missed Pa, though not the shouting or the arguments about money. And Bloubergstrand wasn't like Somerset Strand, not at all. I hated this little room at the top of the hotel that smelled of stale cooked cabbage and mothballs, with its narrow beds and bare furniture. I didn't like Mrs Potgieter's meals of cold porridge and white bread with a scrape of margarine, or watery vegetable soup, her sago pudding and jam that Ma forced me to eat because it was rude to refuse.

Ma left me and Sauly on our own while she went to look for work, locking us into the room so that we couldn't wander off and so that no bad men could come and snatch us away. There was nothing for us to do, except play with Jarpe, or with the snakes'n'ladders board that Ma had packed to take with us or the little bag of marbles I had, at the last minute, snatched up and put in my pocket.

I knew I was supposed to look after Sauly and give him a Marie biscuit from a packet in the drawer, if he got cross or cried. I wasn't to let Sauly cry too much, Ma had said, or Mrs Potgieter would get angry and throw us out. But Sauly wanted Ma, and he wanted his lunch and he cried and cried, and I didn't know what to do to stop him. I didn't want to be thrown out to wander the streets of Bloubergstrand with all our cases and bags, so I started to sob too.

There were heavy footsteps coming up the stairs, that stopped as they reached the hall outside our room. I held back my tears and drew in my breath.

'Shh,' I whispered to Sauly but he continued his bawling.

From outside the door, there was a woman's voice, Mrs Potgieter's.

'Stop making such a damn blerry noise, you young scallywags. My husband's having a bit of shut-eye and you're disturbing him. He's getting angry, he is. If you're not quiet, he'll come up here quick as a flash, unlock that door and donner the pair of you with a slipper and then you'll be quiet, that's for certain.'

Now Sauly stopped his crying and looked at me with big frightened eyes. We waited till the footsteps retreated and then huddled together on the bed, too afraid to do anything, too shocked to cry. For once, I was grateful to have my little brother next to me, to sit up close to him and pretend that I was comforting and protecting him. I had a duty to him, and I tried my hardest to fulfil it.

'Don't worry, Sauly. Ma will be back soon. And Mrs Potgieter's gone downstairs now. She won't come back if we're quiet.'

When Ma came back a while later, she found us sitting there on the bed waiting for her in silence, huddled together.

'Mrs Potgieter says you were making a racket, you naughty boys,' she said. 'Tomorrow you must be quieter.'

'Y-y-yes Ma.'

'Why are you stuttering like that again?' Ma asked.

I didn't know.

Ma came home at lunchtime each day, in time for our lunch. And then she took us down to the beach to play on the sand and paddle our feet in the salty foam. Each morning she would go off early again looking for work, leaving us locked in the hotel bedroom.

But one morning, she stayed in bed, rather than getting ready to go out.

'I'm not well, Jackie,' she said.

I was terrified. What would happen if Ma got really ill, or worse still if Ma died? What would become of Sauly and me? I wondered if Pa knew where we were and whether he would come and find us and bring us home or whether we would have to live alone in Mrs Potgieter's attic forever.

Ma hurried into the bathroom. But soon she said she was feeling better.

'I'm not looking for work today,' she said. 'I'll start again tomorrow.'

She took us out onto the beach to play. Then things didn't seem so bad after all. The sun came up and the wind died down, we dug holes in the sand with a small spade and Ma and I built big mounds for Sauly to run at, and knock down. We buried our toes in the sand and wrote our names with sticks and shells. Away from the store, and Pa, my little brother and I were suddenly becoming friends. When the ice cream trolley came round, and Sauly and I begged and begged for a cone, Ma reached into her purse for a few coins and let us run after him to ask for one scoop each of lemon ice, chocolate or vanilla. We sat on the beach licking our ice creams. Everything else was forgotten.

And the next day, when Ma came back before lunch, she told us that, miracle of miracles, she had found herself a job as a part-time teacher at a nursery school, starting in a week's time.

'I always wanted to teach,' she said. 'I did all that training before your pa and I got married and it seemed like it had all gone to waste. But now I can do it after all.' Her eyes were bright and her face glowed. That evening she took us out to the fish restaurant on the pier to celebrate and we ate big chunks of flaky white fish in oily batter and watched the steamboats chugging past on the horizon.

'We'll stay here for a few more weeks,' she said, 'And then I'll look for a little house for us, down one of the roads close to the front, a nice clapboard house, with painted shutters and a small flower garden. We'll grow proteas and geraniums and plant a loquat tree. We'll find a school for you Jackie and I'll take Sauly with me – they say he can join the other children at the nursery. We'll build something up for ourselves, a nice little life. It will be lovely, I promise you.'

But the following morning Ma was in the bathroom being sick again, and the next morning and the next. When she came out of the bathroom her eyes were red and swollen with crying. She took us out onto the promenade, where there was a public telephone, and rang Ouma's neighbour, who had a telephone, and asked him to fetch Ouma. She waited a few moments, opening and closing the telephone box anxiously, pacing up and down on the pavement. And then finally she rang again, feeding the meter from a small pile of coins. Sauly and I stood holding onto her dress. I rubbed her stocking softly, feeling the comfort of the smooth warm wool and I listened to her crying down the phone:

'It must have happened when we went to Somerset Strand,' she said. 'On our so-called holiday.'

A pause. The scrambled but faintly recognisable sound of Ouma's voice, loud but unintelligible overheard through the earpiece of the phone, and Ma's frightened, ' Oh my God Ouma, what am I going to do?'

And then, 'Please Ouma, I'm begging of you and Oupa. Just for a few weeks, till I sort something out.'

And then again, 'Please Ouma. Ask Oupa for me. Persuade him.' And then Ouma's voice, crackly and strange, before the coins ran out and Ma, weeping, putting the telephone down. I wondered what had happened at Somerset Strand that could be so awful. Ma had seemed so happy there, Ma and Pa, both of them, holding hands and smiling and smiling.

The next morning, after breakfast, Ma talked to Mrs Potgieter and told her that she would have to terminate the arrangement. She would be returning with her children to Cape Town, she said.

Mrs Potgieter folded her arms and pursed her lips. 'You've paid up front for a month and we agreed the period of your stay,' she said. 'So there's no money back, you know?'

'But we've only been here such a short while. Surely there must be some kind of refund?'

'I told you before you took the room, it's money upfront. That's how I do things. The rules is the rules. I've got a living to make here – I'm not giving out charity.'

Clearly unable to argue any longer, Ma asked her to order a taxi to take us back later in the day, however much it cost, and then she told me and Sauly that we were going home.

*****

We arrived back at the store towards the end of the afternoon, just as the sun was creeping slowly down below the roof of the Handyhouse. Ada, hearing the sound of a car pulling up in front of the store, came running out to see what was happening. She hurried to open the door of the taxi and let us tumble out into her arms.

'Ag sies tog, Jackie,' she said, 'You look half-starved, you've gone so thin. Your legs are like a couple of pick-up sticks that could snap off just like that!' She held me close to her as if she would never let me go, kissing my cheeks with fierce enthusiasm. I held on to her tightly, wrapping my legs around her, smelling her salt-sweet skin, remembering how nice it was to feel her close to me.

Pa did not appear out on the street but when the store bell rang and the door opened, he looked up briefly from his accounts. He seemed unsurprised, as if his family going away for good happened all the time and he had barely noticed it, let alone allowed it to cause him serious concern. But he came out from behind the counter and helped Ma with the bags, and ruffled Sauly's hair before sweeping him up towards his face and planting a big kiss on his cheek. I stood and looked at him and waited my turn but for me there was nothing; no arm across the shoulder, no welcoming look, no kisses.

'What brought you back so soon?' Pa said to Ma, his voice betraying no emotion.

'You'll find out soon enough,' she said, taking off her coat and hanging it on the peg behind the counter.

I lay in bed that night thinking about everything that had happened and wondering about what was coming next. How soon was soon enough? And what would that bring? I wondered too why Pa seemed to be so cross with me. For a while now he'd stopped talking to me about the faraway day when I would be a grown man, standing by his side in the store. He didn't pick me up any more and kiss me on the head or slip a little toffee into my hand, or let me follow him around watching as he cut wood or filled bags of corn. But on our arrival home, it seemed even worse; he was barely able to look at me.

Over the next few weeks, I became quiet again. Better not to say anything than to risk saying the wrong thing. Simpler not to draw attention to myself or put myself in the line of fire between Ma and Pa. When Ma's stomach began to swell again and her legs grew thick and swollen and her dresses tightened and her movements slowed, I made no connection between this gradual change and anything that might have occurred that autumn in Somerset Strand, nor with the burning of the shed nor with what happened next.

CHAPTER 13

April 1958

Jack was perplexed. Vera had tried calling Clara Joubert on his behalf several times over the previous few days but had either found her unavailable or unwilling to agree to a meeting with him. Her excuses were all plausible enough but excuses they were, of that he was absolutely sure.

Time was moving on and he felt the urgency of talking to her face to face, to find out more about that trip to Elsie's River that had caused such consternation among his client's trusted friends and community. He knew that very soon he would have to ask van Heerden for permission to interview his wife, and he wanted as much information as possible beforehand, so that he could do so with minimum pressure. He'd been warned that Laura was still fragile, both physically and mentally, and he hoped to avoid upsetting her more than was strictly necessary. He dreaded the meeting. It would be hard for her, however gentle he managed to be. Laura van Heerden was caught up in something ugly, beyond her control, and he didn't like the thought of her suffering.

He sat in his office at his chambers with his feet up on the desk, chewing on the lid of his fountain pen. Renee had occasionally popped in to meet him for lunch and found him like this. She had laughingly complained that he looked more like a newspaper hack from the *Cape Argus* than a serious man of the law.

'It helps me think,' he said. 'And in any event, in some ways I am a bit like a journalist, investigating a story.'

'Story? I thought that advocates worked with evidence and facts not stories.'

'Oh no! The story's everything. I have to be able to tell myself the narrative – what happened, when and why, cause and effect. I need to establish the characters' points of view and tell it to myself as a coherent whole. It really is a bit like being a writer, in fact, pulling together the plotline and hoping that in the end the whole thing hangs together. Preferably with a happy ever after ending… and a conquering hero!'

'Not many heroes among your clients so far!'

'That's *me* – the conquering hero, not my clients,' he'd joked, and she'd come over and kissed him affectionately.

'Of course you are,' she'd said and he realised, with a little moment of pleasant surprise, that she had meant it; she had a touching faith in his abilities and the likelihood that he would go far.

Now he spat the pen lid out so it fell onto the desk, leaving a damp inky patch on the blotter. 'What's the story this time, Jack Neuberger?' he asked himself, but so far, he really wasn't very sure.

He stood up. He had decided; all this tiptoeing around was getting him nowhere. He rang through to Vera and asked her to look up Clara Joubert's address in the Cape Town telephone book. There were several Jouberts in the directory so he recommended searching under the name of her father Pieter Jan Joubert, in the Thornton area. Finally, after the usual sighing and grumbling, Vera came up with a matching name and an address in Jan Smuts Drive, close to the church where Johannes van Heerden was minister.

Ten minutes later he was in Isidore's Ford, winding down the windows to get some air into the hot, stuffy car. 'Thank God for Isidore!' he thought, as he drove out of Cape Town's crowded city centre and into the wide plains of the Cape flats, with its scrubby waste land and sparse areas of poor housing. Without a car, this case would be difficult and Isidore had offered him the use of his old Ford, passed on to him by his father, while he himself was working as a locum at a hospital up in Port Elizabeth.

Jack headed out towards the houses and bungalows of Bellville, an area relatively close to his childhood home in Parow. It was interesting to see this area where Laura had been brought up and lived all her life, with its tidy little gardens planted with rhododendron bushes and azaleas, shaded by fig trees and sporting well-manicured lawns. They spoke of quiet affluence; not the richly opulent mansions of Constantia, nor the big old-fashioned double-storeyed homes of Claremont, but something more solidly, simply middle of the road; an Afrikaner area for families of good, hard-working stock, making their way in modest, decent jobs.

He drove down Dagbreek Road, putting the car into second and crawling along so that he could check the numbers on the doors. Number 18 was a low, brick-built bungalow, with a small front garden and a winding path created out of crazy paving. He parked the Ford several houses further on, so as to avoid drawing too much attention to himself and walked back to the house he'd identified as belonging to Mr Joubert.

It was the middle of the day and he was hoping that Pieter Jan Joubert would be out at work, leaving just the women of the family at home. If he was especially fortunate and could catch Clara alone, all the better. He rang on the doorbell and waited.

A coloured woman came to the door, dressed in a white uniform, her hair caught up in a simple floral doek. He was in luck; she looked a little dreamy and slow, smiling up at him in a friendly way, rather than giving him the suspicious watchdog scowl that so many maids had been taught to present to strangers who came to the door.

'Yessir?'

'Is your mistress at home?'

'No sir. She's gone to the ladies' prayer and coffee circle.'

'Mrs Joubert?'

'Yes Mrs Joubert and Miss Joubert.'

'Mrs Joubert and Miss Clara Joubert?'

'Oh no!' The maid tittered. 'Mrs Joubert and Miss Evelyn, the master's sister. The coffee mornings are for the older ladies not the young maisies.'

'And Miss Clara. Is she at home?'

'Oh, she's about the house somewhere, I think. I can call her for you, if you want.'

'Thank you. I would be pleased if you would do that.'

'Who shall I say wants her?'

'Oh, tell her it's to do with Laura van Heerden.'

'Yessir,' she said, shutting the door firmly in his face. He smiled. She reminded him a bit of Olive, Ouma and Oupa's girl from his childhood. The same innocence and lack of guile and a similar lack of finesse when people called. He'd liked Olive well enough, but had not been anything like as fond of her as he was of Ada, their own hired girl, whose clever wit and warmth he remembered with great affection. He wondered what had become of her; she had stopped working for his mother and father a long time ago and he'd heard no mention of her for many years now. Perhaps she was happily married and settled, with children of her own, though from what he knew of women like her, the chances were that life would have been tough. He'd heard enough stories not to kid himself on that score.

A few moments later there was the sound of murmuring voices and footsteps in the hall, bringing him back to the present. The door opened and a young woman stood in the doorway, looking at him.

'Clara Joubert?'

'Yes.'

'Jack Neuberger. My secretary's been struggling to find a time for you to pay me a visit, so I thought I'd take the bull by the horns and come out here and find you myself. Save you the trouble of making your way to my office. I hope you don't mind.'

The young woman's face flushed red and she turned instinctively to look behind her, as if seeking a means of escape. But then she seemed to change her mind and faced him squarely.

'I suppose you'd better come in.'

'I won't take up much of your time I promise you.'

She took him into the front room. It was an old-fashioned parlour, with simply upholstered green chairs and lace antimacassars, a dark sideboard with an array of pot plants perched on top; a jade, some spider plants and, in pride of place, a large aloe. The room looked as if it was rarely used, only when visitors came to take tea, or when a church elder stopped by for a word. Perhaps Johannes van Heerden himself had sat in that big armchair, talking about church matters with Pieter Jan Joubert, or with his sister, Clara's aunt?

He sat at one end of the sofa and Clara took a seat on an upright chair facing him. He felt himself sinking back into the soft cushions, so pulled himself upright, sitting forward so that he was more on a level with her.

'Can I get you a drink? Some orange squash perhaps?'

'A glass of water would be nice,' he said. It was a hot day and he would be glad of something to quench his thirst.

She called out to the maid, who came with a jug and a tumbler, which she set down on the table beside him, smiling cheerfully all the while.

'That will be all, Sadie,' Clara said. 'Now, Mr Neuberger, what can I do for you?'

'I understand that you are a good friend of Laura van Heerden, Laura Pietersen that was.'

She nodded.

'As I'm sure you know by now, I'm acting on behalf of Mr van Heerden, working on his defence and bringing together witnesses who will testify in support of him, either as character witnesses or in the substantive matter of the charge against him. I understand from my secretary that you are very busy, so I thought I'd just come out to see you myself, to make it that bit easier for you. I'd like to ask you a few questions if you don't mind. I want to find out a bit more about your relationship with Laura and her husband?'

She shrugged her shoulders. 'It's all quite simple really. I've known Laura since we were girls, living in the same neighbourhood. We were at school together at Bellville Girls High, in the same class from the start. We grew up together, sharing our walk to school, spending our evenings and our summers playing out in the streets or in each other's gardens. We've always been as close as sisters. I am an only child, so that's been especially important to me.'

'And Johannes?'

'He was a member of our church. He was a serious boy. He kept himself separate from the other boys. I wasn't surprised though, when he started seeing Laura; he had always seemed fond of her and she of him. He was shy with girls, but with Laura he found himself able to talk. She's such a gentle person, such a lovely person – she brings out the best in everyone. And her father liked him very much. He approved.'

'Did you attend her wedding?'

'I was her bridesmaid. I held her flowers for her in the church.'

'And since then?'

'They've been very good to me. I haven't married, Mr Neuberger. Like my aunt, I've remained with my parents in this house but Laura and Johannes are like a second family to me. I'm godmother to their eldest daughter Coral, and to Beatrice, their youngest.'

'Tell me a bit about what happened when Beatrice was born.'

'There isn't really very much to tell, Mr Neuberger. Laura was unwell. The baby was born early, by Caesarian section. She was taken away from her mother to be looked after by the nurses and only returned to her several days later. Laura has been frail ever since.'

'Frail? Physically unwell?'

'Yes.'

'Mentally?'

Clara Joubert looked at him firmly. 'There's nothing wrong with Laura's mind. She's just delicate. She needs taking care of.'

'And Johannes?'

'He's been a good husband to her, as far as I am aware.'

'As far as you are aware?' Jack wondered whether he was picking up a note of hesitation.

'He's taken care of her. He's provided her with extra help and assisted her work in the community – that's very important to her, Mr Neuberger. She believes that it's her purpose in life to help those less fortunate than herself.'

'And you've also helped with this?'

'I've done what little I can. I accompany my aunt and the other ladies from time to time, distributing clothes and food to those in need.'

'In Elsie's River?'

'The project is in Elsie's River, Mr Neuberger, as you must know.'

Jack had the feeling that she was telling him only what he needed to know, just so much and no more.

'You went on various occasions when Mr van Heerden was there?'

'Yes.'

'And you were with him when he visited the houses.'

'We usually split up into little groups. Mrs de Villiers and the minister, my aunt and I, or one of the other ladies joining me.'

'But you sometimes accompanied Mr van Heerden?'

'It was rare for me to do so, but occasionally yes.'

'Who did you visit with him?'

'The Swanepoels, with their five children, living close to the railway track. The husband drinks away any money he brings in and his wife is at her wit's end. And there's old Willy Nel. His leg was severed in a farming accident, so he can't work. He depends on what he gets from charity. Then there's the Johnson twins, of course. They were left on their own when their mother died last year and we stepped in to try to help. And there were one or two others.'

'The woman who is on trial with him?'

Jack watched her reaction closely. There was no flicker of emotion.

'Possibly. I forget.'

'Agnes Small is not a woman you would easily forget.'

There was a pause.

'Why is that, Mr Neuberger?'

'She is not what you would expect. She is a refined woman, a person with genteel manners and good sense, and…'

'…And she's very beautiful. I remember her now.'

He couldn't work out whether she had only just recalled Mrs Small, or simply chosen to say so now, when denial of all knowledge might seem foolish and could take her into treacherous waters.

'So you did visit her with the minister?'

'Yes, once. She invited us in and offered us a glass of ginger beer. Johannes gave her a bag of clothes for the children and we said a few prayers together. She was a woman for whom one felt particular sympathy. She had fallen on hard times for reasons beyond her control. In other circumstances, she could have led a good and decent life.'

'On that occasion you left together, Mr van Heerden and yourself?'

'Yes. We had several other families to visit.'

'And on other occasions, you were aware that Mr van Heerden went to see Mrs Small?'

'With Mrs de Villiers, or my aunt, or one of the other women, yes.'

'Never on his own?'

Was there a moment's hesitation?

'No.'

'You never had doubts about Mr Van Heerden's behaviour?'

'No.'

Jack paused and took a sip of water from his glass.

'So tell me Clara, why it is that you have been avoiding speaking to me? If everything is so straightforward and simple, surely you would be hurrying to speak up for Johannes? He's the husband of your closest, dearest friend. They have been good to you. Wouldn't you want to help them? More than anything else in the whole world?'

'I...' Clara's lip trembled and suddenly she burst into tears.

'That last time,' she sobbed, 'when I went with my aunt and Mrs de Villiers, there was something strange, not quite right. Johannes seemed troubled; he was nervous. I noticed his hand trembling on the gear stick when we parked the car on the road outside the woman's house. I was puzzled. And then...'

She looked hesitant.

'I'm on his side, Clara,' Jack said gently. 'Both of them, him and Laura. I'm acting for the defence. Whatever you tell me, I'll try to make sure it does him no harm. But I do need to know what happened. It will help me.'

'Look I don't want to speak to you here. My aunt and my mother will be back at any moment and Sadie listens in to everything that goes on in this house. She says whatever comes into her head – she can't be trusted. I'll come to your office tomorrow, I promise you. And I'll tell you everything I know, so help me God.'

Jack stood up and shook her hand. 'Tomorrow morning then? Ten a.m.?'

'Ten a.m.'

Chapter 14

The following morning, however, Jack was forced to cancel his appointment with Clara Joubert. When he arrived at his office, Vera was waiting for him, anxiously pacing the carpet in the hall downstairs, looking out for his arrival.

'Mr Neuberger,' she whispered. She was looking animated and urgent, her normal bored expression wiped away. 'There are two strange men upstairs in your office. I told them that you were busy this morning but they insisted on waiting for you. I asked them to sit in the waiting room but they barged straight in, rude as anything. I couldn't stop them.'

'Thank you for warning me, Vera. I'll go straight up and find out who they are.'

He climbed the stairs quickly, Vera following breathlessly a few paces behind. At his office door he paused, smoothed down his hair and straightened his tie; he didn't want to look flustered. Then very gently he turned the handle.

One man, a heavy, corpulent figure, was sitting at his desk, turning back and forth in his swivel chair; the other, a leaner man, sat awkwardly in an upright chair, his legs stretched out in front of him. Both wore drab grey suits and dark ties. They looked up as he came in. He knew at once who they were.

A memory came back to him, a scene imprinted in his mind. Two men, not the same ones as these two characters who had made themselves so at home in his office, but there was something about their demeanour, the assurance and self-certainty, that took him back. A wave of nausea came over him but he fought it off.

'What can I do for you, gentlemen?' he asked, smiling broadly and reaching out a hand towards them. His heart was pounding in his chest and his hands felt clammy.

'A cup of coffee, gentlemen?'

'Ja, as oo blif.'

Afrikaans. They were clearly making a point.

He called to Vera breezily. 'Could you go out to Lou's for three coffees? And call the person I was hoping to see this morning before you go. See if you can postpone her appointment till later today.'

The large man came and stood by him. 'Neuberger,' he said. 'A Jewish name?'

'That's right.'

'Don't eat pork eh? No bacon? No crayfish? Milk and meat? Had the snip?'

Jack said nothing.

'Your people don't go to church do they? Don't believe in Jesus. Worship your own God on a Saturday don't you – little caps on your heads, bowing and praying?' He made a little mumbling moan, nonsense words, a pretence at incantation. The other man laughed loudly.

'Do your business through a sheet, do you? A little hole so you don't see your missus's dingis. That's what I've heard about you and your kind. True is it? Excuse me for asking, but I've always wanted to know.'

'I'm an advocate. I don't have to listen to this. I want to know who you are and who has sent you.'

'Doing the van Heerden case?'

'Yes.'

'You like defending people like him?'

'As I say, I'm an advocate. I defend whoever walks through my door. That's my job.'

'But this one interests you, ja? Appeals to you and your communist friends?'

'I have no communist friends. I do what I can to make a living. It's my job.'

'This one's an important case for you though, isn't it? White man, black woman. It's the kind of thing you like, hey?'

'What's that supposed to mean?'

'You like that sort of thing? That's something that appeals to you, hey? A bit of black, a bit of white. You done it yourself perhaps? With a black woman? You like that sort of thing.'

Jack said nothing.

'A Dutch Reformed Church minister sleeping with a kaffir – not good is it? An Afrikaner and a cheap coloured girl. It's important the result of this here case. First one of its kind. Look here, Mr Neuberger, you must know that no one's all that interested in a poor white grocery store owner and his bit on the side but a minister of the church, a respected Afrikaner, now that's a different story.'

Jack looked the man straight in the eye. 'This is still a country where there's a legal system, with trial by judge and jury. The jury decides who's guilty or not. Or perhaps you didn't realise that? Perhaps they didn't teach you that in school? If you've come here to intimidate me I can go to the Bar Council – I'm sure they'd be interested in your visit.'

'Don't get funny with me, Mr Neuberger. We've just come for a little friendly chat with you. Just letting you know we're taking a bit of an interest in this trial, nothing more. If you ask me for my personal opinion – and I know you haven't – but if you did, I'd say to you that this new law, you know, it's no good if commie juries just let everyone off the hook. An example's got to be made. Just my view of it, you understand.'

'Who's sent you here to see me?'

'Sent? Sent? I can assure you, Mr….'

At that moment Vera came in with the coffees. She banged the tray down on the table. 'Clara Joubert's coming at three o'clock.'

'Clara Joubert?' the large man said.

Jack groaned inwardly. Vera should have been more careful than to mention her name.

'Another case,' Jack said coolly. 'A woman wanting legal advice on the sale of a piece of land in Muizenberg.'

'Not one of your witnesses to help you get your nice Dutch Reformed Church man out of trouble?'

Jack knew that he needed to tread carefully.

'When I qualified as an advocate I swore to uphold the tenets of the legal system. My duty is to do the best I can for any client I represent, regardless of who they might be. Presumably you also swore your own oath when you joined the police force? I assume that's who you are, members of the police, and if so, like me, you are bound by codes of conduct and by legal duties. You are absolutely expected to operate within the law. I'm very sorry Mr.… – you never did give me your name – but I really think this conversation is reaching a natural conclusion. So, although it has been very nice to meet you, I'm afraid I am now going to have to ask you to leave. I have a very busy day ahead of me. I'll ask Vera to see you out.'

The man got up slowly and, as he did so, he pushed Jack's chair hard, so that it rolled backwards, crashing heavily into the bookcase and toppling over a large volume of torts and a heavy textbook.

'Oh my goodness, clumsy old me. Let me pick this up for you.' He reached down and righted the chair. With one hand, he ostentatiously dusted down the seat cover. 'I hope nothing's broken, no damage done. Come, Stefan.' He spoke in Afrikaans again. 'We have other people to see. Good day Mr Neuberger.'

When they had gone, Jack stood still for a moment. His knees trembled and it took an effort of will to keep himself upright. He took out a large linen handkerchief and wiped his face, took a few deep breaths, then rearranged the fallen books and stacked them carefully on his shelf, pulled his chair back to his desk and picked up the phone.

'Vera, call Clara Joubert. Ask her to come in right away. And tell her it's urgent. I must see her today.'

Chapter 15

1944

One day, a good few months after our return from Bloubergstrand, Mrs Mostert came into the shop with Terence. He was smiling at me and tugging at his mother's arm.

'Ask,' he said. 'Please mama, ask.'

He flapped his arms up and down wildly. Mrs Mostert laughed. 'You look like you've just eaten a hot babotie Terence! Calm yourself down.'

She turned to Ma. 'Would Jackie like to come for a day out at the beach, at Hout Bay?' she said. 'It'll be a long day, but he can sleep over at the garage so we don't disturb you coming back late. It'll be a chance for you to have a bit of a rest. It'd do you good, I'm sure – you must be in need of a break, with the baby on the way.' She paused. Sauly was looking up at her with big open eyes. ' And Saul can come too if you like.'

Ma placed one hand on her growing belly. She smiled.

'Both boys off my hands for a day... and no Sauly waking me up first thing in the morning. Boy, that'd be something!'

But then she saw my crestfallen face. Sauly was a nuisance; he cried and whined and wanted to join in all my games. If I refused, he went running to Ma to complain. If I let him play, he invariably spoiled things by ignoring the rules. It always ended up in arguments and tears and Pa or Ma would step in, crossly reminding me of my duties as an older brother and the expectation of greater maturity that rested on my shoulders. In one way or another, Sauly always managed to make trouble. And what's more, he was clearly becoming Pa's favourite, usurping the position that I had once held and now lost, seemingly forever. Sauly was quick with his fingers, keen to help when Pa constructed paper aeroplanes or little balsa wood boats. He loved weighing and measuring, playing with all the little implements that Pa had made for me when I was small and in which I had failed to show any real interest. Sauly was not my favourite person.

Ma looked at me hard, then sighed. 'Let Jackie go on his own. It'll be a nice outing for him. He deserves something good for a change.'

Terence and I shared a conspiratorial smile.

Ma packed up a small little bag with a towel and my grey woollen swimming trunks, a pair of pyjamas and a toothbrush, Sauly all the while howling in the background, ' Me tooooo, me toooooooo.' I suddenly felt sorry for him and a bit ashamed at the delight I felt at leaving him behind. Should I tell Ma that I wouldn't mind if he came along? No. It was too good an opportunity to be free of him and the rest of my family as well. I didn't say anything.

Ma moved heavily over to the jars of biscuits on the counter. She unscrewed the lids and filled a big paper bag with a good mix of the best biscuits. 'For the journey,' she said. My eyes were focused on the door, watching in case Pa came back in at any moment and caught her at it and said something embarrassing in front of Terence and Mrs Mostert, or worse still, found some reason why I could not go to Hout Bay after all. But Ma managed to hurriedly scoop up some extra fig rolls and drop them quickly into the paper bag and collect everything together for my trip to the seaside before Pa had returned from his errands.

Mrs Mostert gave Ma a quick squeeze on the arm.

'I'll bring him back safe and sound, tomorrow evening,' she said, 'I promise you.'

*****

Walter is driving the Chevy. Mrs Mostert is sitting beside him. Walter is singing at the top of his voice, a jazzy tune that makes him sound like he's laughing as he sings.

Pack up all my cares and woe

Here I go, singin' low

Bye, bye, blackbird.

Where somebody waits for me

Sugar's sweet, so is she

Bye, bye, blackbird.

From time to time, Mrs Mostert and Terence join in. I sing along, but only in my head, not out loud and the words I sing are a little different.

Bye-bye, Cape Town. Bye-bye, the store. Bye-bye, Ada. Bye-bye Ma, Bye-bye Sauly. Bye-bye Pa.

On the back seat, we sit surrounded by bags, beach balls and striped towels. I look out the window as the houses of Parow and Cape Town flash by. Table Mountain looms up, a thin layer of cloud hanging low above it, like white marshmallow, and beneath it the gardens of Kirstenbosch lush and green, with the rhododendrons in full bloom. Soon the buildings and houses thin out and are replaced by countryside: fig and loquat trees; orange groves, grassland, rocky boulders; shacks with corrugated iron rooves and dusty yards with petrol cans, old tyres, goats and donkeys; clumps of thin pine trees; an open, empty road; a black man and woman, carrying cases on their heads, walking slowly from somewhere to somewhere, with the morning sun beating down on them; a single candyfloss cloud; the dust of an open-back lorry filled with African labourers, who smile and wave as they go by; a man sitting under a fig tree with a small pile of over-ripe mangoes for sale; a large bird swooping down to catch a lizard in its beak; the wild squawk of seagulls. And then at last – at last! Flashes of bleached white sand and foamy turquoise sea.

Walter parks the car and we carry everything out over the hot sand which burns my bare feet and makes me hop and skitter down towards the cooler wet sand near the sea. He sets up the big green umbrella, the towels, the picnic blanket and the hamper in a quiet spot, not too close to other bathers. There are coloured families sitting on the sand, making sandcastles and swimming in the sea, and there are white families, sitting in a different part, making sand castles, and swimming in the sea. We sit on our own, neither with the coloureds nor with the whites, in a strip of no-man's-land dividing the two. Mrs Mostert splashes sun oil on Terence's nose and shoulders but not on mine. 'You don't need it, Jackie, with your nice olive brown skin, like a little Arabian prince.'

Terence and I fight our way out of our clothes, flinging them down any old where, forcing our legs into tight woollen swimming trunks, poking them in the wrong way, getting our toes stuck in our hurry to get down to the sea. We race out for our first swim of the day, plunging into the shallow waters and splashing wildly, as the waves crash in and suck noisily back out again.

At midday Walter takes our lunch out of the hamper, which has been packed with ice to keep the food cold, and puts the dripping containers down on the large picnic blanket. He lays the sandwiches out on the plates and, with a sharp knife, slices up a large watermelon. It splashes pink juice and pips onto the white linen cloth that the sandwiches have been wrapped in. He opens cold bottles of fizzy drink, which hiss as he pulls off the lids with his teeth. My drink tips up in the sand and it bubbles and trickles away before anyone can right it. The tears are coming but Walter only laughs and reaches into the hamper for another. Terence giggles. I smile shyly and take a big gulp of soda that explodes in my mouth, like the froth of a sugary sea.

Walter sits down on the big picnic blanket and opens a bottle of beer for himself. I watch him. He helps himself to sandwiches. He is in his swimming trunks, legs stretched out, toes in the sand. He is sturdy, though not especially tall. His arms are strong and muscular, his skin hairless and brown. The hair on his head is short. It is springy and black, with just a fleck of grey here and there. His mouth seems to take up most of his face, his teeth a little crooked but white against his dark skin.

I look at Mrs Mostert. She too is watching Walter, with a little thoughtful little smile on her face. She is plump and pale, soft and large as a cream bun, rolls of fat appearing at the top of her bright-blue swimming costume. Her hair is unpinned from its usual knot, and tangled from the salt and the wind. Without her usual dusting of face powder, her nose and cheeks are spattered with freckles. She's not the same Mrs Mostert who collects me from the Handyhouse in her tidy skirts and dresses, or the business-like woman who serves customers at the garage. Everything about her has loosened, expanded, softened.

After lunch, Terence and I build sand castles and dig ditches, then run back into the sea, splashing in the shallows, while Walter and Mrs Mostert lie back on their towels and doze, close to each other, sheltered by the big green umbrella. The warm seawater rises up and washes over me. I wonder what Sauly is up to at home and am glad that he hasn't come too. No Sauly, no Handyhouse, no Pa.

Terence finds a large piece of driftwood, gnarled and knotted and bleached white by the salt of the sea. He wants to show it to Walter, to ask if Walter can carve something out of it with his knife. We run back along the beach, scanning the umbrellas for the big green one that signals our place on the sand.

As we get close to the umbrella, I see that Walter and Mrs Mostert are not alone. They are both sitting up straight and two men, fully dressed in short-sleeved shirts and cotton trousers, are standing in front of them.

'Stay in the sea,' shouts Mrs Mostert but we are already out of the water and running up the beach to see what is going on.

'Stay away boys,' calls Walter and then, more sternly, 'Don't come closer.'

Terence and I hold back. We stand where we are, watching, unable to go either backwards or forwards. Now Walter gets up from his towel and places himself in front of Mrs Mostert, standing between her and the men. There is shouting. There are bad words.

'Pasop. Watch out you blerry kaffir-lover,' one man is yelling at Mrs Mostert. 'We're gonna donner you and that coloured bastard of yours.' This man is tall and thin, with an angular face and a long jaw. His face is red with fury.

The other man, smaller and fatter, with large sweat stains on his shirt, is yelling too. He's holding a big stick that he is swinging towards Walter, only narrowly missing him each time, like he's playing a game with him. Walter looks about to see if anyone will come and help them. On towels, stretched out, or under their umbrellas, people are reading their books or sunning themselves. Children are playing ball or digging in the sand. Everyone sitting close by has turned away, facing the sea, or looking towards the ice-cream kiosk and the café in the distance. No one acknowledges that anything is wrong.

Terence is trailing the large piece of driftwood behind him. I wonder if I should grab it and run and hit the men with it. I could bash them on the legs, whack them as hard as I can, hit them and hit them till they run away. But I don't move. I just stand on the sand watching. The tears are coming and I can't hold them back.

The man with the stick prods Walter, stabs at his feet, as if poking at a crab to make it close up tight inside its shell or scuttle away in fright. Walter stands his ground but makes no move to stop him. I don't understand why. Why doesn't he just grab the watermelon knife from where it's lying on the cloth and use it to defend himself. The man grips the stick more firmly. He grunts as he takes a bigger, faster swing which arcs towards Walter, whipping his legs so that he flinches. And now the other one, the thin one who up until now has just stood and shouted,

114

joins in, punching Walter in the face so that he falls back heavily onto the picnic blanket. He falls into the plates and left over sandwiches and overturns the hamper. Mrs Mostert screams. At the sound of her voice, the two men casually turn away and stroll off down the beach, as if enjoying the nice weather and a relaxing day at the seaside. One whistles as he walks. The other laughs.

Mrs Mostert is weeping and now faces from nearby are turned towards us, watching. But no one moves from their places under their umbrellas. They just sit and stare.

'Don't worry, May. It's OK. I'm all right,' says Walter, dabbing at his mouth, testing the damage. He spits out a single, bloody shard of broken tooth and holds it out on his hand. Mrs Mostert passes him the white linen cloth that the sandwiches have been wrapped in and he presses it to his face to stop the bleeding.

He looks anxiously towards Terence and me, to see if we're OK.

'Let's pack up, boys. It's time to go home.'

Slowly we collect everything together and put down the umbrella. Walter carries most of the bags but we help with the buckets and spades and beach ball, which we hand to Walter to put in the boot of the Chevrolet. He takes out the little plastic plug and squeezes the ball, allowing the air to slowly exhale, till the ball is a flat, flabby circle, hardly recognisable any more.

In the car, Mrs Mostert is sniffing into her handkerchief. Walter pats her knee gently.

'We're OK,' he says. 'No real harm done. We'll be fine when we get back to Parow.'

Terence, who has been sitting quietly next to me, asks, 'Who were those two men?' and his mother says, 'Just nasty men, silly men. Don't worry, we won't see them ever again.'

'Your face is all puffed up,' Mrs Mostert says to Walter. 'Does it hurt a lot?'

'It's OK,' Walter replies. 'A pity all the ice melted. It would have been good as a little icepack to keep the swelling down.'

'You want to go back home Jackie, instead of coming to stay the night with us?' asks Mrs Mostert kindly, twisting in her seat to look at me. 'You upset by what's happened and want to be with your Ma?'

I shake my head. 'I want to stay the night with Terence and you,' I say.

'Good boy,' says Mrs Mostert. She turns back to face forwards again. There is a little pause. Her voice is light, breezy but I sense something important is being said. 'Perhaps don't tell your Ma and Pa about what happened, then, eh? No need to worry them with nonsense like that. Better for them not to know. We're all fine aren't we? All done with now. I'll make a nice chicken pie for supper when we get back and it'll all be forgotten.'

I nod my head. All will be forgotten. All will be forgotten. Nothing will be said.

*****

When I got back to the store the next morning, Ma asked me how the trip went.

'Was it fun?'

I nodded.

'Did you swim a lot?'

I nodded.

'Did you eat a nice picnic?'

'Yes.'

'Did Mrs Mostert drive you there?'

'No.'

'Oh,' said Ma, surprised. 'So who drove you all that way out to Hout Bay? Not Mr. Mostert, I suppose. He's still sick in the sanatorium with tuberculosis from what I've heard. Been there for months now.'

'Walter.'

'Walter?' said Ma. Her face flushed red. 'I didn't know Walter was going with you to Hout Bay.' There was a moment of hesitation and then, 'Does Walter often go on trips like this with May Mostert?'

I shrugged.

'Is he around with you a lot, when you go to visit Terence at the garage?'

I said nothing.

'Does he sit and eat with you at the table, for instance.'

I nodded. Was that the right thing to do?

'And come and go in the house as he pleases?'

I looked at her and said nothing. Why did this matter? Why was Ma asking all these questions?

'How friendly is he with her? With Terence?'

I shrugged.

'What on earth is going on between May Mostert and Walter?' Ma said under her breath.

'Ma, is Walter Mrs Mostert's other husband?' I asked. It was a question I had often wanted to ask and it didn't seem to me to be a dangerous one. I didn't think Ma would mind and since I couldn't ask May or Walter or Terence, Ma seemed like my best bet. She would know.

Ma frowned. 'What sort of question is that?'

I went on, undeterred. 'Is Walter Terence's pa?'

'Of course not, silly boy. What put that into your head? Walter's coloured. He's the paid boy at the garage. How could he be Terence's father? Terence is white and Walter's a kaffir. And anyway it's none of your business. That's something for you to think about when you're a big boy, not now.'

There was a little pause.

'Was everything nice at the beach Jackie? No problems or anything?'

I nodded vigorously in response to her first question and shook my head firmly to her second.

Mrs Mostert had told me not to say a word. I had followed her instructions. Whatever trouble she wanted me to deny, whatever revelations she was concerned to prevent, I felt sure that I had succeeded in doing as she said. I'd not given anything away. As far as I was concerned, Ma was none the wiser and I had done my job of staying silent. Ma's frowns and questions didn't worry me too much.

May Mostert had asked me to keep a secret and I was pleased that I had managed to achieve that.

Chapter 16

April 1958

'Clara Joubert has arrived,' Vera said, speaking from the outside office on the internal phone. She sounded more alert than usual, as if the events of the morning had affected her, given her a bit of a jolt out of her usual sluggishness.

When Jack had earlier reprimanded her for mentioning Clara's name, she had replied instantly with what seemed like a heartfelt apology. Jack was taken aback by her genuinely contrite tone.

'Those men,' she said. 'I shouldn't have told them a single thing, nothing at all. I'm mortified, Mr Neuberger, really I am. It was a bad mistake. If there's one thing I can't stand it's a bullying Afrikaner policeman. Those Special Branch men, they think they can walk all over you.'

'How do you know they're Special Branch?' He'd worked it out for himself easily enough but wondered how Vera, who always seemed more interested in her nails and her bouffant hair than anything else, seemed to cotton on to the situation so quickly.

'Ag, they're all the same. I can tell 'em a mile off. I used to work as a secretary in the police station in Rondebosch and the Special Branch men used to come in and throw their weight around. Thought they'd been put on this earth to tell everyone else what to do. Us secretaries tried to keep out of their way. All except Babs McGee that is – she married one of them and boy, did she live to regret it. She had two kiddies in quick succession and then what do you know, he's off chasing fresh skirt and she's…'

He had carefully steered the conversation back to phone calls to be made, jobs to be done, but he was pleased to see that Vera had a bit more to her than he had imagined, that her basic instincts were decent ones. Perhaps that's why Isidore had recommended her to him.

Now Clara Joubert was sitting waiting to be called in. He wondered what he was about to hear; it seemed that some kind of revelation was coming but he had no idea what it would be, nor the impact it might make on the case for his client. He felt nervous and hoped that Vera hadn't noticed the little stutter as he asked her to bring Clara in to his office.

Vera opened the door and led her in. Jack jumped up from behind his desk to greet her and shook her hand. It was cool in his grasp, slender and light. She was wearing a pale-green suit, with a fresh white blouse. She had clearly got dressed up smartly for the occasion and was looking much more composed than when he'd last met her at her home, though it was hard to tell how deep this went. Maybe she was just managing to disguise her nerves particularly well. He wondered how much work he was going to have to do in order to draw out the story from her; in his experience it often took quite some time to put people at their ease and establish a relationship of trust and even longer, if they had something to hide, to catch them with their guard down; you heard a lot of irrelevant or deliberately evasive detail before you really got to the nub of it. He placed his elbows on the desk and laced his hands together, taking a brief moment to decide on a good, unthreatening place to start but before he could open his mouth to ask a question, the young woman had spoken.

'I saw Johannes van Heerden embracing Mrs Small.'

Jack tried to maintain his composure. He felt wrong-footed by the suddenness of it all and unsure what to say.

'He said nothing of this to me,' he said finally.

'Why would he? It would put him in a bad light. He must be desperate. He wants to be found innocent.'

'And you're sure about this? There could be no doubt?'

'I'm sure.'

'An embrace that was – how should I put it – affectionate? Not the embrace of a pastor to a woman in distress?'

'No. Not that of a churchman to one of his flock.'

'I'd like you to tell me all about it, so that I understand exactly what happened.'

'You won't tell Johannes that it was me, will you? I'm only telling you because I think you should know. You will know how best to deal with it, how best to help him but I don't want him to find out who told you. For Laura's sake, you understand, not his; he's betrayed my dearest friend.'

'I can't make promises like that I'm afraid Miss Joubert. You must already realise that it will come out in court – you've already talked to others. Francois de Klerk suggested I speak to you on the basis of what you'd told him.'

He thought that she would remonstrate with him, that there would be tears or that she would simply clam up and refuse to say more but she seemed remarkably calm and it quickly became clear that she had decided in advance that she would tell him everything, come what may.

'OK Mr Neuberger. I trust you to do what's right. I'll put my faith in you, and in the Lord above, who watches over all that we do.'

He asked her if she would be willing for Vera to come in and take notes, to which she agreed. He called through to Vera on the intercom and, while they were waiting, took a moment to collect his thoughts. He had been thrown by the rapidity of her revelations, ones that wholly contradicted his client's own protestations of innocence. But he was also taken aback by Clara's willingness to speak out and wondered what lay behind this and her possible motivations. Clara was clearly well regarded in her community – Francois de Klerk had spoken highly of her. The van Heerdens were like family to her; she had no reason to do them harm. If anything, her instincts would be to protect them from the terrible fall-out of a guilty verdict. And yet here she was, in the name of enlisting his support, giving him the worst news of all, confirmation that his client was bound up with Mrs Small in ways that went well beyond the charitable offices of a pastor to a woman in need.

As she sat patiently, with her hands resting still in her lap and her eyes lowered, he wondered what Renee would make of her. His wife had a keen eye; she was a good judge of character and seemed able to read people well from even the briefest of encounters. 'She's a little church mouse,' he could hear Renee saying, 'but don't underestimate the quick wit and tenacity of mice, or mistake quietness for timidity. Mice often get the cheese.'

Vera bustled in with her biro and notepad, straightened her skirt with one hand and sat down.

'Let's make a start, then,' Jack said.

The story Clara Joubert told was detailed but clear, the kind of account he always wished for from his clients, but rarely got. She had gone out with Johannes and one of Laura's group of women in the church, Mrs Fourie, early one evening in March. Johannes's car was being repaired, so Mrs Fourie had agreed to drive them there herself in her husband's red Chevrolet. They had been a smaller than usual group – Mrs de Villiers was sick and Clara's aunt and some of the other women were busy preparing for the annual Bring and Buy sale at the church – so it was just the three of them. They had stopped by the church to collect the bagged-up parcels of provisions from the store room – tinned food, tea, sugar, biscuits, rice, ground mealie flour – bags that had been put together from donations from the small congregation.

Mrs Fourie had driven them out to Elsie's River and they had parked first on Main Street, then followed a snaking trail through the town. They worked as a three, stopping off at each of the houses they had on their list and delivering their parcels. With some, it was a quick and simple handing over of the bag, with a brief exchange of words and a grateful look. Others took longer; when a lonely old woman, Mrs Mann, invited them in, they felt obliged to accept and waited while she filled her kettle, placed it on the stove and prepared them a cup of milky tea. Mr Cassim, who had had his arm sliced clean off in an accident at work, insisted on taking them on a tour of his newly dug vegetable patch, giving them a lengthy account of every variety he had so painstakingly planted.

By early evening, they were running late and still had four visits to make: to Mrs Jacobus, a single woman bringing up eight children on her own; to Lucky Marais, an alcoholic they had been helping for almost two years; to the Martins family; and to Agnes Small. Darkness was falling fast and Mrs Fourie looked at her watch anxiously. She needed to be back in time to prepare her husband's dinner and didn't want to be late. Dirk Fourie didn't much like his wife's activities with the church, especially if they made him wait for his evening meal. He had, on several occasions, threatened to forbid her having anything more to do with the Elsie's River project and coming back late yet again would give him just cause to finally put his foot down and put an end to her activities. Everyone at the church knew that Dirk Fourie was a tricky customer and that his wife tiptoed carefully around him.

Mrs Fourie was becoming agitated and pressed them to leave the last few houses, suggesting that they come back with their deliveries another day but Johannes had insisted that they continue; these people are relying on us, he had said. Tensions had mounted; there had been an argument, and tears. Finally Johannes suggested that the women go straight to Mrs Jacobus's house on their own, then drive back to Bellville leaving him to take the bags of food to Agnes Small, the Martins and Lucky Marais. He would get the bus back to Bellville when his work was done. When Clara protested, he insisted – it was the only sensible option. He would find a public phone and ring Laura to tell her that he'd been delayed.

Driving towards the house of Mrs Small, Clara had noticed that Johannes looked uncomfortable and flustered. He was sweating profusely and seemed unable to keep still. He looked towards her from time to time and then turned his eyes quickly away. She wondered what was wrong but put it down to his still feeling upset by the argument with Mrs Fourie. The two women left him on the corner of Jan Smuts Drive, with his two big paper sacks of groceries to deliver, and drove off to the small house where Mrs Jacobus lived with her noisy brood.

Mrs Fourie looked anxiously at her watch, clearly fretting about her husband, but luckily Mrs Jacobus was busy giving the little ones their weekly bath in the yard and was in no mood to chat, so they dropped the bag quickly and returned to the car. They were just heading out towards Voortrekker Road and home when Clara noticed a wallet sitting on the back seat of the car. She reached for it and opening it up discovered that it belonged to Johannes. He had left it by mistake. They would need to get it to him before driving back to Bellville.

Mrs Fourie was in a state; she cried; she was all for heading homeward and returning the wallet to him in the morning but Clara reminded her that he would need money for the bus and for his phone call to Laura; they could not leave him stranded in a place like Elsie's River without any money. It could be dangerous, even for a man wearing a dog collar, who was clearly a man of God.

Reluctantly Mrs Fourie swung the car round and they retraced their steps to Mrs Small's house on Fontayne Street, hoping that he might still be there. Clara leapt quickly out of the car and ran up the steps to the front door. She knocked on the glass window. There was no reply, so she knocked again. Still no reply, yet the lights in the front room were on. She stepped off the path and went to look in. There were signs of life, tea on the table, a cigarette in an ashtray still burning, but no one there. So she walked round the back to see if they were out in the garden but there was only a single scrawny hen poking away at the dust. The kitchen light was on and looking in, from the growing darkness of the little yard, she saw a man and woman locked in a close embrace. To her horror, she realised that it was Johannes van Heerden and Mrs Small.

Flustered and confused, she hurried back round to the front of the house and retraced her steps down the path to the car. As Mrs Fourie drove off, she burst into tears.

Clara finished her story with a little shudder, whether of sadness or disgust, or renewed horror at the memory of that evening, Jack found it hard to say.

'I told Mrs Fourie what I had seen, our Reverend, Johannes, Laura's husband, hugging and kissing the coloured woman. In my shock I forgot all about the wallet and we drove home to Bellville with me still clutching it firmly in my hands.'

'What was Mrs Fourie's reaction?'

'She was angry. She said she always thought the Reverend and Laura were a bit soft on coloureds but she hadn't thought he'd take it that far. A kaffir lover; it was shameful. I tried to tell her not to say anything to anyone else, not till I'd talked to Johannes, but I could see that she had no intention of listening to me. She would park the car, run into her house and call out to Dirk to tell him all about it. That's what she's like.

'She dropped me at my house and I went straight in and had supper with my parents and my aunt. I didn't say a word though I could hardly force myself to eat a bite of the food. At around nine o'clock there was a knock on the door and Francois de Klerk asked to speak to me privately. Dirk had been to see him. Mr de Klerk asked me to tell him exactly what I'd seen and I had no alternative but to do so.

'The next morning I went to see Johannes to give him his wallet. He was out at the church, preparing for the Bring and Buy. Laura invited me in, but I refused; I made an excuse that I had errands to do for my mother. I couldn't face seeing her, knowing what I knew, so I gave the wallet to her and left.

'The rest you know. Dirk Fourie has been to see me on several occasions since that night. I don't know who it was that went to the police but it wouldn't surprise me if it were him. Others might have tried to sort things out within our community first, but not Dirk. He's no liberal, you know, like Johannes and Laura. He was out on the streets campaigning for the Nats last time round.'

'And you? Your political persuasions? Are you a Nationalist as well? Do you agree with this new law they're using against Johannes van Heerden?'

'That's my business, Mr Neuberger, not yours.'

There was silence.

They had reached a conclusion. Jack wasn't sure he could get much further but he needed to be clearer about Clara's intentions with regard to the court.

'You know that the prosecution will call you? They'll want to make full use of every last bit of what you have to say. They may ask you to act as a witness on their behalf.'

She nodded.

'And if you do that, I will have to cross-question you to tear holes in your story. I'll have to try to prove that you were mistaken.'

She nodded again.

'Will you let yourself be used for the prosecution?'

'I'm in a turmoil – I'm not thinking straight. I need to decide what to do.'

Jack thought, once again, that for a woman in crisis and confusion she seemed remarkably calm.

'Will you let me know when you do decide? Or give me a call if you think of anything else that might help your friends. They are still your friends, aren't they?'

There was silence.

'Well then, Miss Joubert, thank you for coming to see me. Thank you for your time.'

He turned to Vera. 'See Miss Joubert out.'

Jack sat back in his chair. He picked up his fountain pen and chewed the lid. Her story was flawless in its detail, entirely plausible and desperately worrying for his client. He remembered his first reactions on seeing Agnes Small, his shock at her refinement and her beauty. What would a jury say when confronted by the testimony of Dirk Fourie and his wife, the story of Clara Joubert and the glowing youth of Agnes Small? The odds were rapidly stacking up against Johannes van Heerden and the worst news had come, ironically, not from one of his enemies but instead from one of his dearest friends. He would need to fix up to see van Heerden urgently, to confront him with these latest revelations and see what he had to say.

He was just mulling over the best way of handling it when there was a knock on the door and Vera entered.

'Sorry to disturb you, Mr Neuberger,' she said, 'but I just wanted to say something about the case and that woman who was in here just now.'

Jack sat forward in his chair.

'I followed her down to the lobby and watched her go out onto the street. There was a man and woman waiting for her in a car. She got in the back and they drove her away.'

'What kind of car was it, Vera?'

'A red car, I think.'

'A Chevrolet?'

'Maybe. It all happened so fast. I couldn't really say for sure.'

CHAPTER 17

1945

Pa's Ford was giving him trouble. There seemed to be something wrong with the starter motor and he was constantly having to go out and ask people to help him to get it going with jump leads. It was driving his neighbours crazy; it was driving *him* crazy, and Ma too.

'That car's nothing but trouble. I don't know why I ever bought it in the first place. The blooming thing never starts up when I need it to.'

'Take it up to Mostert's Garage to be fixed,' Ma said. 'I'm sure that they'll do a good job on it.'

'It'll cost a pretty penny, 'specially if there's parts to be replaced. They charge the earth for these things.'

'Then use your secret little stash on it – I'm sure you've got enough to cover it.'

Pa hit the roof.

'What stash?' he roared. 'Still on about that blooming pot of gold I'm supposedly hiding from you, that your sneaky little spy of a son told you about? You should be ashamed of yourself believing a little boy over your own husband.'

'What's it for, Sam, that money of yours?'

'There is no money damnit! What a kvetch you've become, nagging away from morning till night. Is that what you learned from your mother, to kvetch and complain and drive your husband crazy with your nonsense?'

'A woman has the right to know what her husband's up to with his money.'

Pa shook his head. 'Not in this household, she doesn't,' he said, ''specially when she's no help at all when it comes to looking after it, when she gives it away, hand over fist, to every poor customer who comes in with a hangdog look and a sob story.'

They were back on that familiar treadmill of accusation and recrimination. The birth of my baby brother Mikey a couple of years previously had seemed to make things even worse, with Ma being tired and preoccupied and Pa resenting the fact that she had less time than ever to spend in the store or devote to making his life easier. I tiptoed away. Pa was quite capable of switching tack and turning all his fury onto me. When he referred to me now, unless in anger, it was almost always indirectly, as 'that son of yours', as if he had relinquished all claims to me, and all responsibilities; now I was hers, not his any more.

Meanwhile Sauly seemed to bask in his affections.

'A chip off the old block. Just look at his skill with that model he's making!'

He provided him with balsa wood and glue, with little bricks and wooden train tracks. Where Sauly was concerned, it seemed that money wasn't a problem – the means were found to buy him little bits and pieces to fuel his new interests. For me though, there was never a penny to spare for books or paper, even if it was for schoolwork, or to start me off on my Jewish studies, to prepare me for the bar mitzvah that, like all Jewish boys, I would be having when I was thirteen.

Though Pa shouted and complained and resisted the idea of taking the car for repair, the day it failed to start altogether he threw up his hands and accepted that he'd have to send it up the road to Mrs Mostert's garage. Walter arrived to collect it in the pick-up truck, coming in the back way through the yard gate to talk to Pa and make the arrangements, rather than through the store. I saw how shy he was with Pa, looking down at his feet, or off into the middle distance, rather than meeting his eye. But as he left he glanced over and gave me a big wink and a smile.

'Coming to play with Terence again soon?' he asked.

I looked at Pa.

'Whenever it suits Mrs Mostert for him to come,' Pa said.

Two days later Pa drove the car back from the garage and parked it out front, on the main road. It was newly polished and waxed and looked a treat. He came into the store beaming.

'Won a prize Mr N?' Ada asked. 'Your lucky number come up?'

'The car – it's all fixed,' he said. 'Good as new. That Walter's done a decent job on it. Sorted out the starter motor without replacing it. And

Mrs Mostert's not charged me for it either. Not a penny. Said it was just Walter's labour and, given that Jackie and Terence are such good friends, she'd not go to the bother of writing out a bill.'

'Nice woman, that Mrs Mostert. But what's going on between her and Walter Hendricks is anyone's guess,' Ma said drily.

'What do you mean?'

'Ask that son of yours,' she said. Now Ma too was disowning me. 'He can tell you better than me.'

'What are you suggesting, Sarah? That May Mostert is having an affair with Walter?'

'I have my suspicions.'

Pa's curiosity was aroused. 'Tell me more.'

Ma smiled. She seemed to be enjoying herself, playing a little game of cat and mouse. 'I'm too busy. I've got clothes to put through the wringer and supper to cook. I haven't got the time to just stand around gossiping. Ask that boy of yours. He'll tell you.'

When Pa started grilling me, I shut my mouth firmly and refused to open it, not for him, not for anyone, and stayed like that for the rest of the day.

'Sies tog, Jackie,' Ada said, passing me with a bucket of soapy water and a mop. She put the bucket down firmly so that the water slopped over the edge and formed a little pool of milky suds on the kitchen floor. 'Cat got your tongue? Can't you tell Ada what's the matter?'

I shrugged.

'Want a nice gobstopper from the jar?' she whispered.

I shook my head.

'Man, Jackie, something's really got to you bad. When a little boy doesn't want a gobstopper, things aren't looking so good.'

I turned away. I couldn't explain to her what I could hardly explain to myself, my terrible dread of saying something wrong. However careful I was, however sure I felt that I wasn't betraying or harming anyone, my words seemed to be fallen upon, devoured greedily, then spewed up in some distorted new form, used in some battle or other that made little sense to me. Safest to remain silent and not take any risks in the arguments between Ma and Pa, nor in the story of what was going on between Walter and Mrs Mostert, whatever that might be.

Later that evening, when I was supposed to be in bed and sound asleep, I woke up needing the toilet. I heard raised voices, so I crept down the stairs. Halfway down, in the darkness, I stopped and sat down, listening to the conversation between Ma and Pa in the kitchen.

'The boy shouldn't be too involved with that family,' Ma was saying, 'not if there's monkey business going on between her and him.'

'Is it so terrible, Sarah, what goes on between a man and a woman? Sad for Simey, yes, but these things happen.'

'Do they?' Ma said. I waited for Pa's reply but there was nothing.

'He's coloured,' Ma continued. 'Bad enough if she was just cheating on Simey, but with a non-white too. The hired man.'

'Does that make such a difference?' Pa said. 'A man's a man, after all. And Walter's a decent person, not a nishtikeit, a nothing. He's made something of himself and of that garage. It's impressive what he's done.'

There was silence. I felt a huge well of feeling surge up. This was Pa speaking, Pa, who wouldn't talk to me, who burnt my matchboxes, who hid money under the floor and lied to Ma about it, who loved Sauly more than he loved me. This was my father, standing up for Walter; Walter, who'd made me my toy garage and set me off with my matchboxes, who ate frikadells with us in the kitchen at the garage, and sat laughing and joking with Terence and me.

'That Walter does you a little favour with the car, no money to pay out, and now he can do no wrong,' Ma said. 'You won't hear a word said against him.'

'Just because you did your teaching exams, doesn't mean to say that a whole pile of nonsense doesn't come pouring out of that mouth of yours sometimes, Sarah. Book learning you may have, but brains, no! A big chochem you think you are! That garage would be closed and boarded up if it weren't for Walter. So what if he does a bit more than look after the cars? It's been a long time since Simey's been away you know and it's not such a crazy thing for May Mostert to turn to Walter.'

Ma's voice was full of scorn. 'Have you been walking around with your eyes shut or something?' she said. 'People don't like it, whites going with coloureds. Talk to Mrs van de Merwe or Arnie Fortune or just listen to the chitchat in the store. They don't like those coloureds thinking they can do whatever they like, forgetting who they are. Things are changing, Sam. We'll be branded kaffir-lovers if we're not careful and Jackie will too. He's still just a boy and he doesn't understand these things like we do. We have to protect him.'

'Tell me something. What if they start saying the same kind of things about Jews? Have you considered that possibility in amongst all your clever ideas? What if they don't want Jews doing this, or Jews doing that? What if they worry that the *Jews* are getting uppity, forgetting who they are? You shouldn't forget that, Sarah. Our parents, they came to this country to get away from all that kind of craziness, all that nonsense. A man's a man, at least in my book. So let the boy carry on playing with Terence – there's no harm being done.'

Ma didn't reply and I heard a chair scraping back and the sound of the kitchen tap being turned on. Quickly I got myself up from the step and tiptoed softly up the stairs and back into my bed, where I lay awake thinking and looking at the tired old gardenias on the wallpaper for quite some time before finally falling asleep.

*****

The next morning, Ada came to wake me for my breakfast and to say that Ma had gone off for the day to Ouma and Oupa's, taking Sauly and Mikey with her. My night-time wakefulness had taken its toll and I'd slept long and late, not even hearing the noise and the bustle of the family getting itself up and opening up the store, nor the excitement of the trip to my grandparents' house.

'She's gone to help your Ouma prepare for the Passover, cleaning the house ready for your Seder, and all that. So much to do, she says.'

'Cleaning up the chametz!' I wailed. 'I'll be missing them sweeping the bread up with a feather and a spoon! Mikey and Sauly are there doing it right now!'

I loved the rituals that surrounded Passover, everything from the cleaning out of the house of every single crumb of leavened bread from each nook and cranny, to the wonderful foods that only appeared at this festival time, my favourite being the charoset, a heady mix of grated apple, ground almonds and sweet wine, symbolising the mortar the Israelites used in their forced labour, when they built houses for the Egyptians. Passover was a special time, when Ma and Pa seemed to put their differences to one side and joined the rest of the family for the annual celebration. For once, the children were taken seriously, not just left to get on with things, but actually thrust into the limelight. Mikey was just coming up for two years old, so Sauly, as the next youngest, at six, would be asking the ritual questions, why on this night do we eat unleavened bread, why on this night do we eat bitter herbs, why do we recline in our chairs rather than sitting up straight, and, as his older brother, this year I would be able to join with the adults in supplying the answers that had become familiar to me. I'd help Sauly along – he'd need a bit of prompting and it would be a good chance to show him just how much his big brother knew. And then there would be the hunting of the afikomen, the piece of matzo, hidden for us children to find, and I would be best placed to find it, looking in the most likely hidey holes, in Oupa's workshop or Ouma's kitchen or out in the yard, while Sauly either whirled around like a mad thing, too young to know where to look, or trailed disconsolately after me, all too aware of the advantage of age that I had over him. A prize would follow, a few coins, or a bag of sweets from the store, and then, caught up in the spirit of Passover good will, perhaps for a change I'd choose to be gracious and hand over one or two to my younger brother, unasked.

'I want to go to Ouma and Oupa's,' I cried. 'I want to help sweep up the chametz with a feather and a spoon!'

'Not till this afternoon,' Ada replied. 'I've got to help your pa in the store. I'll take you there after lunch when things quieten down.'

'I can go myself. I know the way.'

I was growing up, getting to be quite confident, and thought myself perfectly capable of walking to my grandparents' house on my own.

'I'll ask your pa, see what he says. When I was your age I was doing all kinds of things – running down to the shops for my mother, selling mealies for her on the market, a good two miles walk away, looking after the little ones when she was busy. Once I even caught the bus into Cape Town to take my brother to a clinic for his skew eye. Boy, that was something. Scary as hell but lekker too. So walking to your Ouma and Oupa's house, why not? It should be a piece of cake for a big grown-up man like you.'

When Pa came back in, Ada asked him if I could do it. If I went soon, I'd get there in time for lunch.

'I know the way,' I said.

'I don't see why not,' Pa said. 'It'll get you out from under my feet and you can help them with the preparations for Passover. I suppose that's fun for a little kiddie like you. Your mother would object, maybe, but then she's not here is she? She worries too much about you, if you ask me! Wraps you up in cotton wool.'

I made a sudden dash towards him and hugged him round the waist as hard as I could. I wanted to thank him for letting me go. He looked down at me. Like a bag of nails, or a sack of rice, or a piece of dried biltong, he seemed to be examining me, weighing me up. With one hand, he finally patted me hesitantly on the head, then drew away.

CHAPTER 18

April 1958

It was the second night of Passover. Renee's parents were coming to them for the first time and Jack's mother was joining them too, along with Saul and Mikey, who, at fifteen, bore a striking and disconcerting resemblance to his father. Ouma was too frail to leave the nursing home to be there with them, so it made sense for Jack and Renee to host the Seder night for the small group of family who were left. It was just over a year since Sam's death, and Jack's mother was still rather lost – not exactly grieving but unsure of her role, wondering what her life was all about, what lay ahead. The Handyhouse had long been sold up, Oupa's cobbler's shop taken over by another Jewish family from the quarter and Sarah and the younger boys now lived in a small flat above Woolworths, which she had bought with the proceeds from the sale of the store.

'Of course, if there were a small child or two for Pesach, it would all be different,' she said, taking off her coat and settling herself into a comfy armchair. 'You need children at Pesach, for it to really mean something.'

They hadn't yet told Sarah Renee's news – it was a bit too soon – so it was hard for Jack not to catch Renee's eye and smile, and give the game away. His mother would be beyond excitement.

He couldn't help but think back to those Passovers at Ouma and Oupa's house, in the small living room behind the workshop, when he was a child himself; the year that his cousin Isidore threw up under the table from drinking too much sweet Passover wine, or the time when little Pearl, Isidore's younger sister, wet herself from excitement in the hunt for the afikomen. Or the wonderful Seder night when they left the wine goblet and food out for Elijah, according to custom, and opened the door to let him come in, only to see Uncle Solly, his mother's one and only keenly awaited brother, standing there at the door. He had driven all day to get there and arrived unexpectedly just at that moment. The children had all shrieked in terror and excitement and Pearl had burst into tears. It had been thrilling.

And then he remembered the year he'd first walked over to Ouma and Oupa's house on his own. He'd felt so proud, walking through the streets unaccompanied. He'd lingered on his journey, enjoying the sights and sounds of the neighbourhood in a way that he rarely had the chance to do, when Ma was hurrying him along with Sauly in tow and Mikey in the pram. Krapotkin's he knew well, but nevertheless he stopped to look at the banks of fat sausages, the piles of mince meat and thick slices of steak, sitting leaking little puddles of blood, seeing them afresh, as if through new eyes. He waved to Mr Krapotkin through the window and moved on, passing Dr Meller's surgery and the pharmacy next door, the bakery, the barber's shop with its stripy sign that looked like a lollipop, the Jewish Communal Hall and the flower shop, where he stopped to smell the musky rich scent of gardenias and admire the tall blue agapanthus plants in their buckets of water. He reached out to touch the tough-skinned protea sitting in a pot of sandy soil, then went on past the Victoria and Opal bioscope, stopping to look at the posters for the latest film, a western called *Stagecoach*, with John Wayne. At Mostert's Garage, he decided to go in and say hello to Terence. He thought he would ask him if he thought his mother might pay for them both to go and see the new film on Saturday afternoon.

'He's upstairs in his room,' Mrs Mostert said. 'Did you walk here all on your own Jackie?'

He'd nodded.

'Big boy now!' she'd said admiringly. 'Are you going to stay and play for a while?'

'Yes please,' he'd said, glad to have remembered his manners as Ma always told him he should.

A quick game of snap turned into a longer one, followed by an adventure with Tarzan and Jane and a Dinky car pile-up in a tunnel, and soon it was lunchtime. When Mrs Mostert's hot babotie was offered, he could not refuse.

Later that afternoon, he'd strolled down towards Ouma and Oupa's, still feeling very pleased with himself and his newfound independence. As he walked down the road, he could see in the distance, at the door to the workshop, the whole family, everyone except Pa, craning their heads, as if searching for something, scurrying around busily. Passover preparations, he thought. Getting closer, he saw that Ada was there too.

As he approached there was a shriek from Ma and the whole family started running towards him.

'The boy, the boy! Mein gott, thank the Lord, he's safe,' cried Ouma.

'Where have you been?' Ma shouted, through her sobs.

When the truth came out, Oupa whacked him hard across the legs with a strip of tanned leather and Ada was sternly admonished for ever imagining, in her wildest dreams, that he was old enough, or sensible enough, to be allowed to make the small journey through Parow from the Handyhouse to his grandparents. He'd missed the sweeping of the chametz, he'd suffered the stinging blow of Oupa's piece of leather on his skin and it was a long, long time before he was allowed the freedom he'd so enjoyed that day, to feel himself part of the street, to have his own individual encounter with the wider world around him.

*****

'You remember that Passover you went and spent the day with Terence Mostert and Oupa slapped your leg good and hard?' Sarah asked now, as if reading his thoughts.

'Funny, Ma! I was just thinking about that.'

'Pity about that family, the Mosterts,' she said. 'Something happened to them and they disappeared. And the garage shut down. But I can't really remember much about it. It's a good long time ago.'

Jack wondered whether she really couldn't remember or just didn't want to.

'The chicken soup's boiling and the kneidlach are ready to go into the pot, so we should get started on the readings and the whole rigmarole,' Renee said, coming in from the kitchen. 'Take your seats, everyone! My father's going to do the honours. He'll take us through the ceremony, with a bit of help from Jack maybe.'

The conversation moved on – there was the important business of the Seder night ahead – but Jack's thoughts kept coming back to that happy afternoon spent playing with Terence on the eve of Passover, and on the events that followed a few years later. He remembered the argument between his parents that night, when his mother had rounded on his father for allowing him to do the walk to his grandparents on his own. No harm had come to him that day, so maybe Pa had been right after all. Perhaps his mother had been over-protective? He would have to try to find a decent balance with his own child.

Renee squeezed his arm affectionately, and he shook himself out of his reverie to join in with the singing and the readings and the prayers, the sips of sweet wine and the tasting of salt water and egg, bitter herbs, matzo and his favourite, favourite charoset.

Later that evening, when everyone had gone and he and Renee were left clearing away the plates and washing the glasses, there was a loud ring on the doorbell.

'Who is it?' he called.

He didn't recognise the woman's voice coming from behind the door, with its strong accent; not Mrs Swanepoel from next door, not Vera, nor any of the other secretaries at the chambers. He was puzzled. Who could be ringing his doorbell at this late hour? A sudden thought struck him. Could it be Agnes Small?

'Hold on a moment. I'll open up for you.'

He went to get the keys from the hook, then turned to Renee.

'You go to bed. You must be tired. I think this may have something to do with the van Heerden case.'

Renee sighed.

She let her hand graze his arm. 'At least you're not having an affair, though sometimes, I must say, I think a mistress might be less competition. She wouldn't be in your thoughts every waking minute the way this trial is.'

'I know, I know,' he said. 'It's been taking up far too much of my time. You've been a saint, Renee, but I promise you, once it's over, I'll make more space for you and me.' He patted her stomach gently. 'And the baby.'

He waited till Renee had disappeared upstairs into the bathroom, then went to unlock the front door.

In his mind's eye, when the door opened, Agnes Small would be standing in front of him. She would be wearing a small felt hat and white gloves and a neat coat, buttoned up to the collar. She would be calm and composed but there would be signs of upset, the remnants of a few tears, dark rings beneath troubled eyes, suggesting sleepless nights, a slight trembling of the hands. He drew back the chain, unlocked the mortise and turned the doorknob.

Standing before him was a woman he had never seen before. She had fine blonde hair, pulled back into a bun, and a delicate, pale face from which startlingly blue eyes burned out. Her clothing was old-fashioned, a long brown skirt and a beige cardigan but it was a little dishevelled, as if she'd dressed in a hurry. She was an unusual combination of fresh, open-faced prettiness and rather staid conformity, as if a younger woman's frame had been placed in an older woman's clothing.

'I'm Laura van Heerden,' she said.

Jack took her arm. 'You'd better come in.'

He had been waiting a long time to meet this woman but had held off, hoping to interview her only when he had worked up his defence enough to be clear about whether he would have to use her as a witness or not. Clearly, with her health being so fragile, it would be better to avoid this if at all possible; an appearance in court was never easy, but in this particular case, feelings would be running high and the nature of the charge was likely to make it especially squalid and brutal.

Now here she stood, her face much as he had imagined it, with the exception of those startling blue eyes that seemed to look right into you.

He sat her down on the beige leatherette sofa, while he took the low armchair opposite her and pulled it up, to bring him a little closer to her. Even in the quiet of his house, speaking across the wide-open space of the large living room seemed too public, too distant. He felt all too aware that together they would be opening up the raw wounds of her marriage. He thought back to his own parents and their suffering, his suffering. For Laura van Heerden there could be nothing ahead but pain.

'Clara came to see me yesterday. She told me about that evening in Elsie's Fields. She said that she's sure that Johannes has been having an affair with that woman.'

Jack had been holding his breath. Slowly he released the air. So she knew about Clara. It would not be him who would have to tell her. 'I saw her myself a few days ago. She told me her story. I'm so sorry, Mrs van Heerden. This must be dreadful for you.'

'Oh yes, it is. But I'm strong, Mr Neuberger, can't you see? I have faith in God and in my husband. Johannes is a good, decent man.'

Jack realised that there had been no tears so far, no outward signs of distress. Even standing at his door she had appeared calm.

'Her account, if true, would make a defence case something of a challenge, especially if she agrees to be a witness for the prosecution,' he said.

'She has already agreed to that.'

Jack sat bolt upright. 'How do you know?'

'She told me. She's been coming under pressure, from Dirk Fourie and the others. She says she saw what she saw and there's no getting away from it.'

'This is a blow.'

'Yes, if you believe her story.'

Another surprise. Laura did not trust Clara, yet Clara Joubert was her closest friend. Surely Clara wouldn't be making this up, as a wilful act of mischief? She would be well aware of the distress she would cause.

'You don't believe what Clara told you?' he asked.

'Of course not,' she said emphatically. 'And that's why I've come to see you, Mr Neuberger, because I want to help Johannes. I want you to know that Johannes is entirely innocent.'

'I see.'

She had clearly thought hard about what she was going to say and needed no prompts or cues to proceed.

'First, Mr Neuberger, let me tell you that Johannes is not the kind of man to have an affair. He has been faithful to me all our married life. He took a vow of fidelity in church and he would never break that, never falter or swerve from the path of righteousness. He is a strong man, stronger than most. During our courtship he was firm in his commitment to abstinence and the sacredness of love in marriage. I know all of this and I trust him to abide by his true beliefs.'

'I understand that, Mrs van Heerden, but –'

'Second, I want to tell you that there are people in the community who are not fond of my husband and who do not like our work with the coloured families in Elsie's River. There are some who believe that all our charity should go to our own kind. "Leave the coloured churches to look after their own people," they say, "or the mosques for the infidels." Dirk Fourie, Jan van Zyl and even, more recently, Francois de Klerk, have questioned my husband's views. There have been stirrings and rumblings and even talk of going to the archdiocese. Some people want my husband to go.'

'I see. And Clara?'

'Clara comes from an old Afrikaner family, with a long past. Their ancestors, the Voortrekkers, fought the Zulu; her great-grandfather had a farm and great estate in Natal. Clara has been my dearest friend but recently I have become more aware of differences between us. We have not been so close. She sways with the breeze and the breeze that's blowing her way at the moment isn't taking her in our direction. Johannes and Clara have argued.'

'But she is one of the Elsie's River group. She dedicates time to working with the poor there, no matter what their colour, doesn't she?'

'That's true, Mr Neuberger, and the same could be said of her aunt as well. But there's always been a certain hesitation, a questioning about who we help and how. Her parents do not think the same way that we do. They are Afrikaners first and foremost; their God speaks only Afrikaans. They have recently threatened to go to a different church if things don't change, and she has been caught up in that.'

'I see.'

'You may have been told of my fragile health, Mr Neuberger.'

'Something has been said of it.'

'Well, in part it is to do with the birth of my daughter Beatrice – I was very ill, as you have probably heard and the child was taken from me too soon. I've struggled to get back on my feet and look after my family, as a woman should. But I have also been sick with worry about our small community. My father entrusted his church to Johannes and me and I don't want to let him down. All the bickering and arguing has left me exhausted, drained. And now this!'

'Let me get this straight, Mrs van Heerden. You believe that Clara is lying about what she saw that evening at Elsie's River?'

'I do. There was no one else who witnessed what she claims to have seen. It's her word against my husband's.'

'You feel that she's part of a campaign against him?'

'Indeed. Perhaps she didn't set out with that in mind but she's got caught up in it and it's got out of control. People like Dirk Fourie, like her own father, they're hard to resist.'

'A pure lie that she now has to sustain? Is that what you're telling me?'

'If it's not barefaced lies, then perhaps a misunderstanding that's turned into something else. Maybe she saw my husband comforting the woman, praying with her. Maybe his arm was round her shoulder in an act of Christian kindness. Perhaps she allowed her imagination to run wild and now has been shocked by the impact of her little fabrications. I do not believe Clara to be a bad person, just a weak one. All I know is that she is no longer a good friend to Johannes and me.'

'Will she go through with it, and speak out in court against your husband, do you think?'

'Who knows? On her own, perhaps not. But with Dirk Fourie behind her, I think she'll find it hard to back down.'

Jack's thoughts were racing. He had heard many of the main protagonists – Johannes and Agnes, Francois de Klerk and Clara Joubert and now Laura van Heerden, the wife in the shadows, who was turning out to be more robust and more sure of herself than he could ever have imagined, not the frail, wilting plant that had been described to him. She was convincing and her story made sense to him, but then so did that of Clara. Each person he saw seemed to speak honestly to him, yet their stories couldn't *all* be true. A man commits adultery, plain and simple, or a church splits in acrimony and turns viciously against its leader, or a misunderstood embrace becomes blown up out of all proportion. What was the truth of it all?

'One thing, though, Mrs van Heerden. I'm not sure what the urgency is for you to have come all this way to see me at this time of night.'

'Johannes is planning to come to see you in the morning. I wanted to speak to you first, to tell you about Clara, Fourie and the others, to explain to you what I know. He will not tell you himself. He couldn't bear the thought that the difficulties and arguments in our church will be brought into this and its reputation sullied. He doesn't know that I'm here and I'd rather that you keep it that way.'

'I may have to tell him,' Jack said. 'If I'm to make good use of what you've told me, he'll need to know where I've got this information from. But I promise I'll use my discretion. I'll make sure he understands that you've come to me to help him – that I need to know everything if I'm to mount the best defence for him.'

He hoped that she would accept this – her words were of no use to him if they could not be repeated to her husband, or indeed later, in court, where discrediting Clara Joubert's claims would be of the utmost importance. He thought she was clever enough to see that, and he was right; after a moment's hesitation, she nodded. It was only then, after all of this, that she finally broke down, not sobbing or weeping but allowing a few small whimpers to escape her lips and succumbing to little shudders that, to Jack, seemed all the more affecting for their quiet restraint. Not for the first time in this case he found himself promising that he would do all he could to ensure an acquittal for Johannes van Heerden.

When Jack had finally called for a taxi, seen Mrs van Heerden into it and locked up, he came back into the living room and sat down. Around him, there was still some of the debris of the Seder night that he and Renee hadn't finished clearing up - a few half-empty wine glasses, paper napkins, little depleted bowls of peanuts and matzo crumbs on the floor. He was too tired to do anything more; he would leave it for the maid to do in the morning.

He tiptoed quietly into the bedroom so as not to wake his sleeping wife.

'Was that Agnes Small?'

'Ah, you're still awake. No, a bit of a surprise really, Laura van Heerden.'

'Oh my!'

'Go to sleep my love. I'll tell you all about it in the morning.'

Jackie comes downstairs. It is dark on the stairs. He feels for each step with his bare feet. Now he is in the dark kitchen, opening the door into the store. Someone is there with him in the kitchen. Someone is watching everything that he does. It's Ma, he thinks. No, it's his grandmother, his dear old Ouma. Or is it Renee? But he's only seven. He hasn't got a wife. Why yes, it is. It's Renee.

'Come to bed why don't you? It's late. You must be tired.'

'Yes Laura,' he says. And he looks at her blonde hair, lying unpinned on her shoulders and sees her burning blue eyes gazing at him.

Light floods the doorway. He looks into the shop. Pa is behind the counter. He is counting out pound notes. He turns to look at Jackie. Yes, it's Pa. It's Pa but it's also Jackie. It's himself, Little Jackie, counting out pound notes behind the counter in the store. There is sawdust on the floor and strips of biltong hang from a hook. He tries to cut them down but the string is tough and the knife blunt. He saws away at the string but it will not break. Pa looks at him and frowns. He wags a finger at Jackie and kneels down under the counter. He opens up a floorboard and pound notes tumble out. They scatter across the floorboards and drift up into the air like pieces of burnt newspaper, ashy fragments, floating towards him. Pa places a single finger to his lips and stares at Jackie.

'No, Pa. No.'

He hears his voice. It is a surprise. He is speaking. 'I didn't think I could speak,' he thinks. 'But I am speaking.'

Laura looks at him. Her face, which is perhaps Ouma's face, is angry. Her face, which is perhaps Renee's face, is sad. Her face, which is now Ma's face, crumples into a grimace of grief, like a tragic mask, a howl of pain.

'Why did you speak?' she says, 'Why didn't you stay silent?'

Jack woke up. His pyjamas were soaked in sweat; his forehead felt cold and clammy. Renee was asleep beside him. He heard the soft bubble of her breathing. He went down to the kitchen to get a glass of water. It was dark on the stairs. He felt for each carpeted step with his bare feet.

He sat down for a few moments at the kitchen table and sipped at his water. Then he swallowed the rest down in one gulp. He needed some sleep; van Heerden would be coming to see him in the morning and tomorrow was going to be an important day. He rinsed the glass, then quietly made his way back to bed.

CHAPTER 19

1948

I lay in bed looking up at the gardenias on the wallpaper, trying to persuade myself into a sleep that was looking increasingly unlikely, as the first light of day began to filter through the thin curtains of my room.

In the bed across from me, Saul was sound asleep, his face turned towards the wall. And my younger brother Mikey too, tucked up in the sheets of his smaller cot-bed, was breathing loudly and peacefully. Though both had witnessed the scene of the night before, they seemed oblivious to its full significance. It would have had little impact on either of them, young as they were, and not yet ready to think of such things, but for me they were a devastating blow. At twelve years old I knew what this would mean for me and for my future. Pa had refused to pay for my bar mitzvah, for the teaching, for the ceremony, for the celebration. He had rowed with the rabbi, refused to make the customary donations and ended up angrily proclaiming that he would leave the synagogue altogether.

'Why do we need the synagogue? We're not frum or anything; we don't even keep a proper kosher home. They just take our money and run. And we're not really part of the community anyway. What do we get from them? Nothing. Not a thing. We're Jews, of course we are, but we don't need some know-it-all rabbi telling us what to do and taking all our money, with nothing in return. When it comes to it, let them bury me in the public cemetery too. I don't need to go on paying for a Jewish burial plot for the sake of a load of old mumbo jumbo said over my grave. We'll just stop paying them altogether and be done with it. No burial, no bar mitzvah, no stuck-up rabbi telling me what I should and shouldn't do and putting his hand in my trouser pocket to extract money for the privilege.'

I had begged him to change his mind. All Jewish boys had a bar mitzvah at thirteen, where they were welcomed into the adult community of men. The Jewish boys at my school were all talking about it, planning for it, complaining about the work involved in learning the Hebrew section of the Torah that they would have to read aloud, in front of the whole congregation, but secretly fiercely proud of their new status in their families and among their friends.

'I must have a bar mitzvah,' I said to Pa.

'Must? Must? What's must? Why *must* you? I didn't. Am I not still a Jew?'

'Everyone else is having one.'

'You're not everyone else and the sooner you learn that the better. You must carve your own path in the world, plough your own furrow, not look left and right all the time to see what other people are doing. Learning all that ancient Hebrew, where's that going to get you? Better to spend your time helping me in the store.'

My fury overflowed.

'If it's to do with the money,' I said, 'you have enough to pay for it. I know that. I've seen it.'

Pa flushed red, the veins standing out on his forehead and in his neck. Ma rushed over to him.

'Don't hurt the boy,' she cried. 'He's only asking for what he should be entitled to.'

'What? Do you think I'm going to hit him? Do you think I'm going to hurt him? What do you take me for, Sarah? You and your son, you're both the same. You think the worst of me, when all I have done has been for you, all my efforts have been to build up the store and make it a success. And who for? For you.'

'But the boy needs to become a man, a Jewish man. Don't shame him like this, Sam.'

'The shame comes on me, if I continue to bow my head to that rabbi of yours, that big brains scholar, who doesn't know the first thing about anything. Put that man in front of a handsaw or a plane and he wouldn't know what to do with it. No. Jackie will survive without a bar mitzvah, I promise you. And what little money I've managed to save can be put to better use.'

'Like what?' Ma said. 'Like giving money to that –' She looked at me and stopped short.

'Whatever you're insinuating, Sarah, it's all lies. You know that and you've always really known it, whatever you may say, whatever meshugas you've got swimming around in that head of yours. I keep something back for emergencies, that's all. A man's entitled to do that, isn't he, when he has a wife who fritters away his money, who thinks that it falls like manna from the trees, rather than being the product of hard work?'

The row had gone on and on, circling and circling round the same old arguments, but this time with me and my bar mitzvah right in the middle of it. Once Ma had come out on my side, Pa was never going to budge. So I left them to it and went up to my room, to shut it all out and try to come to terms with the hurt, the sense of lack, the shame that I believed I would carry around with me for the rest of my life. What decent Jewish woman would want to marry a man who was not fully accepted into the faith? And if I did ever find someone who would marry me, what would I say to my own son, when he asked me to tell him the stories of the big day when I became a man?

Now waking in the morning, dull-eyed from lack of sleep, I lay in bed as long as I possibly could, wanting to avoid my parents, hoping that Pa would be too busy to make reference to the discussions of the night before. I ate my breakfast in silence and went to school without having said a word to either of my parents. When the school bell went at the end of the day, I hurried out and rather than going straight home as usual, I stopped off at the garage to see Terence.

Terence and I had gone to different high schools, his the rough one on the other side of Main Road, mine the more desirable one, which I was only able to attend because I had won a hard-fought battle with my classmates for the single full scholarship available. Terence wasn't back yet, but Walter was there, in the garage, taking a break from his work. I sat down on a stool in the workshop and he offered me a cup of strong tea.

I had got to know Walter well by now and felt comfortable in his presence. I knew that my parents had doubts about him and, in particular, about his relationship with Mrs Mostert, but to me it wasn't an issue. Though I knew he was coloured and that Terence and May were not, and I was quite aware of the mutterings of the people around me, I'd got so used to seeing them all together and enjoying their company that, when I was with them, thoughts about his colour never entered my mind.

He wiped his hands on his overalls and opened a drawer of the big cupboard that stocked the nuts and bolts and spare parts, and took out a packet of Marie biscuits, which he offered to me, pulling open the wrapping with his teeth to avoid staining them with grease and car oil.

'Looking glum, Jackie,' he said. 'Something wrong?'

I told him that I'd had a row with Pa, but didn't tell him what it was all about. I wasn't sure that Walter, even with all his powers of empathy, would be able to fathom the complexities of my family life, nor the significance of a bar mitzvah to a Jewish boy like me. And anyway, I was ashamed. What would a man like Walter make of my parents, constantly carping and bickering, when he and Terence's mother were so very different? They seemed to actually like each other, where my parents so clearly did not.

With Terence, though, it was a different story; I could tell him everything. So when he finally came home, slung his satchel down in the workshop, peeled off his jacket and helped himself to the remaining biscuits, we disappeared up into his bedroom to talk and I told him all that had happened. He couldn't do anything to help but he just listened and nodded sympathetically. Then we got out his Spiderman comics and his Superman annual and read them happily till, for a brief time, my problems were forgotten.

Shame is a funny thing. Pa felt shamed by the rabbi, I felt shamed by my family and by my failure to join my community as a fully-grown man. Terence felt shamed by something else, and in my preoccupation with my own worries, I scarcely noticed it. For me, Terence's family was everything I could have wished for. There was harmony in the house, no raised voices, meals eaten together, thoughtful conversation, laughter. Often May would rest a hand on Walter's shoulder, or Walter would ruffle Terence's hair. The physical expression of their feelings was something I had experienced, in some measure, in Ouma and Oupa's affection, in Ada's love, even in Ma's occasional brusque kisses, but it was always tinged with anxiety, always half in shadow rather than full sunlight.

I wasn't really aware of the shadows in Terence's world, or if I was, I chose not to let them trouble me too much. I occasionally wondered why Simey was never mentioned and I sometimes thought about what it felt like to have your father stuck in a sanatorium for years and only get to see him on visiting days, but I never asked Terence about it. If Terence had troubles, they paled into insignificance against my own, more urgent ones and I scarcely noticed even the worrying signs that stuck out right in front of my nose. Maybe I didn't *want* to see them, because seeing them would have disturbed the lovely safe world of the garage that I could escape to, away from the arguments and conflicts of my own home. Afterwards, from a distance, and with the benefit of hindsight and growing maturity, it all became much clearer; I understood more about it and about my own blinkered vision, but at the time I was like a mole burrowing furiously into my own dark hole, unable to see anything of what was going on around me.

Later that afternoon, I left Terence's and walked back down Main Street to be home in time for my supper; after the fiasco of the Passover afternoon spent at the garage, I was careful not to worry my parents by staying out too late or too long.

Nevertheless, walking down Main Street, I was in no particular hurry to get back to the store. Facing Pa after the arguments of the night before was not going to be easy; he would be certain to have something to say to me, and I would have to bite my lip, to avoid yet another angry confrontation that I knew I could never win.

I dawdled as I passed the florist's in the hope that Rita, the pretty young florist's assistant, might be visible, cutting up flowers or gathering them up in their Cellophane wrapping and tying them with fancy knots and curls of glossy red ribbon. She was in her early twenties but that didn't stop me from hoping that one day she might take a shine to me despite the depressingly large age gap between us. To kiss her on her full lips, or unbutton her blouse and touch her breasts, seemed like impossibly exciting and desirable aims that kept me awake on many nights. If she saw me passing and gave me a friendly wave, I was filled with embarrassment and shame. What if she knew what I was thinking about in the secret darkness of my bedroom?

Further along the road, outside the Jewish Community Hall, there was a small cluster of boys just coming out after their Hebrew classes, some wearing their prayer shawls, others having already folded them away. Several of them nodded to me, or raised a hand in recognition – they were often in the store with their parents and knew me well, if only to say hello to, and one or two of them went to my school. I speeded up to get past quickly; I was in no mood to be reminded of the differences between these boys and me. A few yards further down, I stopped at the little sweet shop that had opened just a year or two before, and stared at the tempting array of confectionary in the window: sherbet lemons and aniseed balls, gobstoppers, toffees, Parma violets and chocolate nut clusters, sugar mice and, my favourite of all, peanut brittle. If I waited long enough, I knew that Mr Weinstock, the owner, would beckon me into the shop, with the same words that he repeated each time he called me in: 'Jack Neuberger, you'll be the ruin of me one day. Come, I'll give you just a handful of broken sweets and then maybe you'll leave me in peace.'

Sucking a broken humbug, I wandered on. As I got closer to the Handyhouse, I noticed, on the other side of the road, a large group of men standing on the corner. In among them I could see a few people I recognised, among them Piet du Plessis' father Cornelius, and Mr van de Merwe, as well as a few of our other regular customers from the store. I waved to Mr van de Merwe but he didn't seem to see me; he was too busy tying a large piece of cardboard to a wooden stick. There was movement, men scuffing up the dirt from the road or pacing back and forth, groups amassing to talk among themselves and then separating again. An old open-topped van was parked beside the road, and some of the men were taking placards and fat piles of flapping leaflets from the back of it.

I went to cross over the road to see from closer up what was happening but someone pulled me back. It was Mr Choudhary.

'No, Jackie. Don't go over there. That's not for a young boy like you to see. Go into the store – go back to your ma and your pa now.'

'But what's happening, Mr Choudhary? What are they doing?'

'It's the Nats,' he said. 'They're drumming up support. They're hoping to win out and out this time round, no coalitions or anything, just National Party pure and simple, with a mandate to do what the hell they like.'

'Why can't I watch though? I want to know what's going on.' I had begun to get interested in the conversations I overheard in the store, in Pa's animated talk with customers and in his arguments with Ma about the United Party, led by Smuts, our prime minister. Neither Ma nor Pa liked D. F. Malan, the leader of the Nats – 'He's not a good man,' Ma complained, and 'He's taking the country into dangerous waters,' said

Pa – but still they managed to find something to argue about. Ma had always had a soft spot for Hertzog and thought he should still be leader, while Pa was a Smuts man, despite his constant gripes and grumbles about his failure to turn the economy round. I'd heard them talking about the coming election and the growing support for the Nationalists across the country and now, here it was, before my eyes, the nervous excitement of a campaign on the streets of my very own neighbourhood.

'Go home, Jack. It could easily turn nasty like it did when they went to Elsie's River. There were fistfights there and the police were called. Just look what they've got on their signs – if someone challenges them, there could be a fight here too. I'm not hanging around myself – I don't want to get caught up in any trouble.'

I looked across at the placards, being raised up now by the men. Cornelius du Plessis held one that said 'DIE KAFFIR OP SY PLEK'. Another man held aloft a sign saying, 'DIE KOELIES UIT DIE LAND'.

'What do they mean?' I asked Mr Choudhary.

'"The kaffir in his place" and "Coolies out of the country".' He spat onto the ground. 'Bad times,' he said. 'Bad times ahead.'

'And what about that one?'

'Which one?'

I pointed to a sign being waved around enthusiastically by Mr van de Merwe.

'"APARTHEID,"' he said. 'That means "separateness". I've not heard that one before, but I suppose it means blacks and whites apart, like on all the signs they're talking about putting up around the place, "Net Blankes", only whites, or "Net-Nie Blankes", non-whites only. I think it's going to be more than just toilets and park benches and buses and beaches though. There's talk that they'll take it a whole lot further than that, the Nats, if they get in. Who knows, maybe I won't even be able to walk on this pavement any more, if they have their way. I won't be able to come and talk to your Pa, or even warn a curious young man like you to stay out of trouble.' He laughed. 'I don't think it'll happen though, so don't you worry about it. The United Party'll hold strong, I'm sure. There's too many decent people in this country to let the Nats in. And anyway, I'll pray to Allah for them to lose, and that can't fail!'

He took my arm, laughing wryly at his joke. 'Now, I'm going to escort you safely home before this rabble start all their shouting and other nonsense.'

He dragged me, somewhat reluctantly, towards the store, where I could see Ma, Pa and Ada all peering out through the window to see what was going on across the street. Some of the customers were out on the pavement watching and talking. Mrs van de Merwe seemed to be arguing with another woman, defending her husband against her angry complaints, while Mrs Levy, her face furrowed in an anxious frown, was talking to Mr Rabinovitz in hushed tones. Billy and Maisie Edwards were there, but standing well apart from each other, on either side of the door, Maisie next to the wooden bucket filled with mops and brooms, Billy, in front of the sleek rolls of linoleum.

'Just brought him back to you, before he gets caught up in any of that nonsense going on over there,' Mr Choudhary said and Ma thanked him brusquely. 'I'll be straight off home now, I think. I'll come back and see you another day, Sam, when things are a bit quieter round here.'

Pa shook his hand firmly and then returned to his place at the window to watch the scene across the road. There was a sudden swell of noise, chanting of slogans and waving of banners, and a big crowd formed around the group of men. On our side of the street, people started coming into the store, to watch from the safety of our shop window. I swung myself up to sit on the counter, so I could see over everyone's heads.

A man with a loudhailer, who I didn't recognise, started talking, announcing a meeting at the Town Hall in a few days' time. He was dressed in a grey suit and tie and looked out of place among the men around him, working men in their everyday clothes or farmers in their khaki shorts and short-sleeved cotton shirts.

'Who's he?' I asked Mr Edwards, who was standing in front of me.

'The candidate,' he said. 'Bertie Barnard. They call him Battling Bertie or Bertie the Bully, depending on what they think of him.'

'What do *you* think of him?'

'I keep my head down, Jackie – I don't voice any opinions, not a word. That way you stay out of trouble. You never know who's going to win and if you've been shooting you mouth off in favour of the wrong man, then word may get out and they might start making your life a bit difficult. No planning permission for that building, up at the Town Hall, or not getting that contract you thought was safe, maybe telling their friends in the police to pull you in for a driving ticket or some other rubbish like that. Our Maisie, though, she's got herself in with that friend of hers, Toinette, whose family's mad keen on them – hardliners, Afrikaans speaking, crazy about Malan and what he'll do for our country – and now there's rows between her and Billy, morning, noon and night, 'cause he says she's always on about the Nats this and the Nats that and he says he's sick to death of it. Soon as the election's over, she'll lose interest I hope, or find herself a new best friend. Me, I keep out of it all, get on with my own business. That's the best policy.'

I looked out over his head. The crowd of men was now beginning to move away, as one big group, with the placards held high in front of them. They were starting to walk slowly down the centre of Main Road, in the direction I had just come from, past the Jewish Community Hall, Mr Weinstock's, the barber's, the florist, the bioscope and the garage, handing out leaflets as they went. Some people took the leaflets politely; others threw them straight to the ground.

The people in the store hurried out into the road now, to watch them go. I ran out with them, and stooped down to pick up one of the leaflets. One side was in Afrikaans, the other in English. I started to read the English words:

THE KAFFIR IN HIS PLACE

Vote Bertie Barnard, National Party

Come to a meeting on Sunday 8th April at Parow Scouts Hall to find out more about what we stand for:

•   APARTHEID – separate development for blacks and whites. No more racial integration.

•   New laws to stop blacks from moving into our cities.

•   Immorality laws, to stop mixing between natives and Europeans – no more interracial intercourse!

MAKE A STAND AGAINST THE RED PERIL, IF YOU DON'T WANT TO BE TAKEN OVER BY BLACKS AND COMMUNISTS!

I went back into the store to show it to Pa. He took one look at it, then screwed it up tightly into his fist and threw it across the store, aiming for the rubbish bin.

'Be careful, Sam,' Ma said quietly. 'There are plenty of our customers who're supporting the Nats. Some are even members of the party. You don't want to lose them, do you?'

'You're right, Sarah,' Pa said. 'We *should* be careful, we should keep shtum. Who knows what it'll be like if these people get in, but we've got a store to run and a living to make. We can't afford to take sides. Just get on with it and keep our mouths shut.'

Like Mr Edwards, they both seemed a little nervous, edgy, this noisy gathering across the street having disturbed the normal run of their lives. Pa placed an arm on Ma's shoulder. 'We're together on this,' he said and she seemed, for once, to agree.

Chapter 20

April 1958

Despite the Passover meal, the unexpectedly late night and the lack of sleep, Jack was in chambers early, planning to read through his papers and make notes on the case before his meeting with van Heerden. Only the caretaker was there, sorting through the early-morning mail.

'Got a few letters here for you, Mr Neuberger.'

'Thanks, Charlie.'

'Oh and there were two men here earlier, come looking for you.'

'Really? What did they look like?'

'A big beefy one with a gap in his teeth and a thinner one – had a bad face, all rough and bumpy, like the surface of the moon. Acne or something.'

The two Special Branch officers, thought Jack.

'Asked me a few questions. Wanted to know about your friends, that's what they said. Wanted to know who you 'associate' with. Threw out a few names I'd never heard of. Asked if these people came to see you. Asked if I thought you were a communist sympathizer. I just laughed. 'I'm the doorman, I said, 'What the hell do I know about these things?' So they said they'd be back another time. Special Branch, I reckon,' Charlie said. 'Looked the types.'

Jack climbed the stairs to his office two at a time. Inside, he sat for a while, thinking, then unlocked the wooden cabinet, pulled out the van Heerden files and began sifting through his notes and papers. Time was moving on, the date of the trial was approaching and he needed to start to put together a plan of action, identify his main witnesses, organise his thoughts into a clear line of defence. But it was proving harder than he expected. Most of the advocates in the chambers wouldn't have taken it all so seriously, he knew that; they'd have interviewed a few people, read all the papers and then gone home and spent a night or two hammering out an approach that would do a decent enough job for their client. If it didn't work out in court, so be it. They'd have given it their best shot and been satisfied with that. Putting too much time into a single case wasn't good business, nor did it necessarily help; the more you got sucked into the detail, the harder it could be to get a sense of the whole, to carve out a clear path through the undergrowth.

Jack sat with the papers spread out in front of him. Truthfully, if it had been any other case, he would probably have done the same; he would not have allowed himself to become quite so involved. He knew that he'd begun to let it get to him, in a way that risked clouding his judgment, turning him into a moral detective, a seeker of the truth, rather than a straightforward advocate who puts forward the best defence he can, given the inevitably partial facts available to him.

If only it were all more clear-cut – rock-solid character witnesses, alibis, people whose testimony was patently robust and reliable – but he was beginning to feel that everyone he spoke to couldn't quite be trusted; each one seemed to have their own motives, their own axe to grind. Even the gentle, decent woman who had come to see him the night before, Laura van Heerden, was not quite what he'd expected, and though he felt persuaded by her story and by her dignity, now, in the cold light of day, he had one or two little worrying doubts. She had given her reasons for coming to see him late at night, wanting to prevent her husband from knowing, but why the hurry? Why not wait and come and see him in his office? And surely her husband would have noticed her absence and her late return in a licensed taxi? What's more, he felt uneasy about the Clara Joubert aspect of the case – why were Clara and Laura no longer close, when they had been such devoted friends, with Clara being godmother to two of her daughters? Was it likely that she would so easily be persuaded to become a prosecution witness? Laura was quick to dismiss her evidence as untrustworthy.

'It doesn't add up,' he said out loud. 'There must be something I'm missing here.'

There was a knock on the door. Still much too early for the van Heerden interview, or indeed for anything else, as the building had not yet come to life. Vera poked her head round the door. What was she doing in so early?

'Can I fetch you a coffee and slice of strudel from the café?' she said.

'That's kind. I'll take you up on the coffee but Renee tells me I've got to watch my waistline, so I'll say no to the strudel thanks. You're in very early, aren't you?'

'Ja, I woke up at six and couldn't get back to sleep, so thought I might as well come in and tidy up a bit, do some filing. I was thinking about our case, lying in bed, churning it all over.'

'*Our* case?'

She laughed. 'It's kind of got to me, Mr Neuberger. It's an interesting one.'

'Certainly is!'

'Thing is, I've been sitting in on some of these here interviews of yours, and wondering what really went on with Mr van Heerden and that woman, Agnes Small.'

'You think there's more to it than meets the eye?'

'Maybe. Depends who you believe.'

'And who do you believe, Vera?'

'I don't believe Agnes Small,' she said.

'What makes you say that?'

'I dunno, Mr Neuberger. I can't really say. Something about her face when she was telling you things. She seemed uncomfortable, edgy.'

'Perhaps she was just nervous about meeting me – this is a worrying time for her.'

'Maybe.'

'And Johannes?'

'Not sure. He seems like a good, decent man to me. But you can't always tell. The best of men can do the stupidest of things when it comes to women.'

Yes, thought Jack, she's right about that.

'How about Clara Joubert?'

'Not so fond of Mr and Mrs van Heerden as she makes out she is. Otherwise what's she doing, saying all the stuff she's been saying and talking to all those people behind their backs? If she was worried she should have gone to them first, not stirred things up with nasty gossip with Mr Fourie and Francois de Klerk and all those other men, who she should have known better than to talk to. Whatever she says, she's put herself on their side now and that's a fact.'

'So what do you suggest, Vera?'

Her hesitation indicated a pause for thought but it soon became obvious to Jack that she'd already decided on what she considered to be a good course of action and was keen to let him know.

'Oh my God, Mr Neuberger, I'm no expert in these things you know. But how about talking to Agnes Small again and maybe her neighbours too?'

Her neighbours. Of course. Why hadn't he thought about that before? Maybe there would be someone who knew something, a neighbour who had witnessed the comings and goings of Johannes van Heerden. If so, his adversary, du Toit, would undoubtedly have already talked to them and lined them up for the prosecution if they had a story to tell. He could kick himself for missing something so obvious.

'Thank you, Vera. I think I'll do that, just as soon as I've had my meeting with van Heerden this morning.'

'Oh, did I not say? There was a phone call that Charlie took for you just now – he handed me a note as I was coming up. Apparently Mr van Heerden's had to cancel. He wants to rearrange the interview for tomorrow instead.'

'I wonder why? He's usually pretty reliable. Well, that gives me a spare morning anyway.' Working through the papers again wasn't going to get him any further though, and time was moving on, the date of the trial fast approaching. 'Forget the coffee and grab your coat, Vera. I'm going to follow your advice. We're going back to Elsie's River to see what more we can find out.'

He picked up the Ford from the car park round the back of the chambers and collected Vera from the front, beeping the horn to let her know he was there. In the car driving out to Elsie's River, both of them were silent, absorbed in their own thoughts. Jack was thinking about Agnes Small. He realised that, during that first interview, he hadn't really asked her all that much; he'd been so strongly affected by her discomfort, so wary of probing too deeply, that perhaps he'd failed to get the full story. He'd seen her at an early stage, before he really knew what he was looking for. He wondered how her own defence was progressing and remembered his promise to her to make sure that he would co-ordinate his efforts with that of her defence counsel. Soon after seeing her he'd done just that. He'd had one or two brief conversations with the advocate – a hardened, middle-aged man in a small lower-ranking chambers the other side of the city. He had not been impressed with him; he had found him both uncommunicative and dismissive – he hadn't really got going on the case yet, he'd said, but would be happy to chat when the date of the trial was announced and he'd got properly stuck in to reading all the papers and planning his defence. A third conversation after the date was finally set hadn't got him much further.

Jack found himself thinking again about all three of the women he had met: Agnes, Clara and Laura. Of the three, Clara had been the most vocal and articulate, telling him her story in great detail, anticipating the possible questions he might have and filling in all the gaps. She had been entirely plausible, though her motivation had seemed unclear and her switching of sides was worrying. She had appeared level-headed and yet both Johannes and Laura had accused her of fickleness and instability. If Johannes was to be believed, she was easily swayed and subject to flights of the imagination. Yet that was not how she had appeared to him. But nevertheless he could well imagine the pressure that she might be coming under from some of the church elders, Fourie, van Zyl and even her own parents.

What of Agnes? He had been impressed by her quiet calm. She did not seem like a woman who would be swayed by passion. He had liked her and felt sympathy for her plight. Her clean, well-kept, simple home, her well-behaved, well-looked-after children, the treasured photograph of her dead husband all spoke of a woman managing to cope in difficult circumstances, whose behaviour was entirely consistent with an honest struggle to keep her life on track. She may have been nervous, as Vera suggested, but there were perfectly justifiable reasons for that; the woman was facing legal action and the most dire of consequences if found guilty. He felt that he could trust her.

With Laura van Heerden, he had been surprised by her strength and determination, in circumstances that could have both shaken her faith in her husband and sent her spiralling into deep despair; though all around her described her as frail, that was not the view he had taken away of this woman. He was puzzled by the discrepancy between people's accounts of her and the woman as he saw her. Her life had been turned upside down, her husband was facing disgrace and possible imprisonment and yet she seemed utterly certain that good would prevail. Perhaps it was her faith in God that gave her this courage? For a woman in such difficulties, her strength of character and her willingness to stand by her husband were impressive.

Would his own mother have stood by his father in similar circumstances? Ma and Pa's problems had been different ones – financial worries, the ups and downs of the store and what he now saw as some deep incompatibilities – Pa's practicality and pride in his work, Ma's scorn for her life as a shopkeeper's wife when she thought she could be doing so much more. As a boy, he'd taken her side more often than his father's but, looking back, he could see that his mother had also played her part in their difficulties; she had not been blameless.

Jack had picked up from hints, over the years, Ma's suspicions about a woman but he'd never found out whether they were well founded or not. Pa was adamant that it was all a figment of her imagination but, for Ma, there was always that uncertainty. When Sam went out to Stellenbosch or Paarl and came back late, was he really meeting wholesalers and buying corn, chicken feed or flour, or was there something else going on? Jack liked to think that, for all of Pa's flaws, womanising was not one of them. He desperately hoped so, though Vera's words were ones he couldn't deny: the most decent of men could stumble where women were concerned.

But then women could stumble too. May Mostert had betrayed her husband hadn't she? She'd allowed him to languish in a hospital, while behind his back, she conducted an affair with the mechanic who worked on the cars. Jack had often thought of her over the years. He saw her, standing in the garage talking to customers, a thick stub of a pencil in her hand, noting down their details and the number plate of their car, always good-humoured and ready to share a story or enjoy a joke, at ease with the men in their conversation. Or cooking babotie in the kitchen, surrounded by steaming pots on the stove and the rich smells of spice and meat and warm egg, her hair swept up in a neat knot, her face pink and moist, humming a traditional Afrikaans song. He saw her sitting at the kitchen table, with him and Terence and Walter, playing a raucously competitive game of rummy, or standing next to Walter by the sink, washing up the dishes together, their bodies close up against each other.

He remembered that time on the beach, the drive back in the car, with Mrs Mostert asking him whether he'd rather go back home to Ma and his fiercely loyal decision to stay the night with Terence and Walter and her, not to abandon them, despite the upset of what had happened. He remembered his attempt to keep what had happened secret from Ma.

And then another memory surfaced. Driving out to Elsie's River, with Vera sitting quietly beside him and the car almost taking charge of itself on the clear, empty road, try as he might, he could not shut it out.

He had not had an easy childhood, not what you might call a happy one, yet most of the difficulties he had come to terms with in one way or another. Here he was, after all, making his way at the Bar, putting all of the obstacles behind him. Despite it all, he'd worked hard, won a scholarship to a good school, ended up winning a bursary to see him through his studies at varsity, which Pa had refused to fund, and then finally qualified with top marks. Ma had been proud of him, he'd brought her naches, the joy that only a child or a grandchild can bring, she said, and even Pa had grudgingly shown some pleasure in his successes. And yet…

That late autumn of 1948, when the Nats were campaigning hard in Parow, when they won the election and took the reins of power. There'd been the demonstration, men marching down Main Road, now Voortrekker Road, with placards, handing out leaflets about reds and kaffirs and the big new idea for segregation. And a public meeting, calling on people to come and listen to their election platform. There was a lot of talk in the store, strong words and worried looks. Some of the customers were already supporters, Mr van de Merwe and Mr du Plessis and a few others; some had decided to go along, just to see what these National Party people were all about, so they said. Ouma and Oupa, Ma and Pa and most of the Jewish customers were anti, but they kept their views to themselves, fearful perhaps of being labelled communists or conspirators.

The day of the meeting, Jack had gone over in the morning to see Terence and then come back for lunch. He'd spent the afternoon studying for his History exam the next day. At 7 p.m., Pa locked the store and Ada packed up her things and headed off to her home in Athlone. Ma made lokshen soup and boiled wiener sausages and cabbage for supper, then went up early to bed, along with Saul and Mikey. At around 9 p.m. there was a sudden burst of noise out on Main Road, a small group of people running past, followed by a larger, ragged band of men and women following on behind. Pa unlocked the store door to find out what was happening and Jack joined him.

'What is all of this?' Pa called to Cornelius du Plessis, who was hurrying past.

He shouted as he ran. 'Showing that the Nats mean business! Giving all those kaffir-lovers a bit of a taste of what's to come.'

'Come inside, Jackie,' Pa said, pushing Jack back into the store and locking the door behind him. He put on the extra bolt that was rarely used and pulled the blinds down over the windows, leaving just the glass in the door uncovered so that they could see out.

'What's happening, Pa?'

'Trouble,' he said.

Jack sat at the kitchen table reading his History notebook, memorising the dates of the great Voortrekker campaigns, the Battle of Blood River and the founding of Cape Town by Jan van Riebeeck. He was determined to do well and concentrated as best he could on his revision, despite the noise outside. Already he was aiming for that bursary to university, though he knew he had many years to go. Pa was busy in the store, sorting out his paperwork and tidying up for the next day.

About half an hour later there was a banging on the door. Jack went through into the store to see what it was. Ma was moving around upstairs; she came down to join them, dressed in her nightdress.

'Shhh!' Pa whispered. 'Be quiet.'

They stood in the darkness at the back of the store watching.

At the door were May Mostert and Terence. Mrs Mostert was banging frantically on the glass, shouting out to ask them to open up and let them in.

'For God's sake, help us. I beg of you. They're at the garage. We need to find somewhere to hide.'

That was Jack's last memory of Terence, seeing him standing in front of the locked door of the Handyhouse, next to May, as she stood knocking and knocking, her eyes peering through the glass window of the shop door, desperately searching the darkness in the hope that someone was there to help her. Terence had no coat on and he seemed to be shivering. He was just wearing his school jumper and his khaki shorts, a pair of long woollen socks held up with elastics and his brown sandals. He carried a little suitcase in one hand, a scuffed brown cardboard case that Jack recognised as the one that usually sat empty on a shelf in his toy cupboard. They'd often used it in make-believe games, filling it with clothes and toys when they pretended that they were leaving home, or going on adventures, in the jungles of Borneo, along with Tarzan and Jane, or seeking their fortunes on the streets of London, England or New York. Terence held the suitcase tightly, and shifted from one foot to another, looking this way and that, while his mother banged and banged on the door. Ma and Pa stood stock still at the back of the store. They made no moves to go and open up. Jack edged forward but Ma pulled him away. 'Don't do a thing,' she hissed. 'Do you want those men to come after us as well?' Pa said nothing, his silence a tacit agreement.

Jack had buried his head in his hands. He couldn't bear to watch. After a while, the banging on the door stopped and when he looked up into the street again, they had gone.

The next day, Jack had gone off to school to sit his History exam. He shut out the events of the night before; he wanted to come first in his favourite subject and beat off the competition from the other boys. If he got the highest mark, he would win the History prize, a book of his own choice and he'd put himself in line for the prize of all prizes, top of the class. First step towards the final prize, the bursary. He was pleased with how straightforward the exam had been and came back home glad to have answered all the questions with such ease. He'd thought of going past the garage to see Terence but decided against; he would come straight home to tell Ma about the exam and how well it had gone. Perhaps he was also afraid to go there, fearful of what he might find?

In the store, Ada was looking glum and Ma wasn't speaking. Pa had gone off to Paarl on business. Jack had asked what was wrong but Ma refused to say, so Ada had taken him into the kitchen and told him everything she'd heard from the talk in the store.

Arnie Fortune had come in first, with the news. He'd gone along to the meeting just to see what was happening. It had been packed with people, with no room to sit and people standing in the doorways, pushing to get in. The candidate, Bertie Bertrand, had whipped up the crowd with talk about the neighbourhood going to the dogs, the coloureds and blacks coming in and taking white housing and jobs, and the threat of communists, insinuating their way in and damaging the very fabric of the community. 'Who knows, there may be communists right here in this meeting, taking notes on what we're doing and sending it all back to their masters in Russia,' he'd said.

There had been groans and cheers. But he'd saved his most powerful message for the end. There was too much mixing of whites and blacks. It wasn't natural. One race was superior to the other, and if this continued unchecked, the purity of the whites would be contaminated. Blacks were closer to the monkeys and apes than whites; that was scientifically proven. Soon the whole history of South Africa, the glorious achievements of their forefathers, the Voortrekkers and the Boers, their pioneering ancestors, would come to nothing, lost for ever, as the whole country turned muddy brown, with the dark stain of intermarriage and miscegenation. There were cheers from the crowd in the hall.

'We'll introduce new laws against this kind of immorality, this flouting of what's natural. But why wait for the election?' he said. 'Let's take action now, here in our own community. In among us there are people who think it's fine to do the sexual act with kaffirs. There are others who have even set up home together, living as man and wife. It's the thin end of the wedge; once we accept this as normal, it'll *become* normal. Before you know it, your daughters and sons will be giving you little black grandchildren, little piccaninnies to inherit your money and your homes!'

A howl went up from the audience and the meeting drew to an end with emotions running high. A group of men gathered around the National Party stewards. Someone suggested striking while the iron was hot. They shouted out names of neighbours, gave out rumours as facts and before anyone could even pause to question the wisdom of it all, they were off out into the street, in a boiling mass, on their way to teach these people a lesson they wouldn't forget.

Ada told Jack that the Mostert Garage was the first place on their route. Stones were thrown, windows smashed and Walter was forced to flee for his life. Terence and Mrs Mostert were unharmed but when the crowd moved on, they left the garage to seek shelter, fearful that at any moment the crowd would be back to threaten them once more.

Jack thought of Terence and May standing in front of the store, begging to be let in, the one place where they thought they might get help.

In the following few days, he asked repeatedly if he could go and visit the garage but Ma said no. It was too dangerous; they'd be labelled kaffir-lovers and then the Handyhouse might be subject to similar treatment. Jews had to be extra careful, she said, or the finger of blame would be directed towards them. Hadn't they suffered enough? Hadn't they been ostracised and persecuted, wherever they went, blamed for all the ills of the countries in which they lived, scapegoated and hounded out of their homes? No, they needed to keep their heads down and stay shtum or God only knows what problems they'd bring on themselves.

He could, of course, have just slipped out unnoticed and run down the road to see Terence, or made a detour on his way back from school, or even walked across from his school to Terence's in the lunch hour, to find him and talk to him, but he didn't; he was afraid and ashamed.

Some days later, Pa asked him whether he wanted to come with him into the town centre on an errand and he agreed. Sitting in the Ford next to his father, they drove along Main Road, past the sweet shop, the Jewish Community Hall, the florist's, the bioscope, the garage. Jack hoped to catch a glimpse of Terence, or Walter, working on the cars, or Mrs Mostert helping a customer at the petrol pump, but the windows were all boarded up and there was a 'For sale' sign on a wooden stake that had been driven into the patch of hard earth and dry grass on the corner. All the cars that usually sat on the road outside and in the workshop had disappeared and the petrol pump was locked. The forecourt was deserted. They had gone.

When Mrs van de Merwe talked about the events with Ma the next day, she folded her arms firmly and said, 'Good riddance. That Walter, her coloured fancy man, he's gone too. That'll clean up the area, keep it safe for decent people like us, Mrs Neuberger. It wasn't right what was going on. Shame for the boy having a mother like her, sies tog, up to no good with a kaffir, and for that poor man Simey, her husband, stuck in the sanatorium not knowing anything about the goings on while his back was turned.' She paused, waiting for a response that did not come, then continued: 'I always thought that garage overcharged anyway. That boy Walter did a lousy job on our car. Did things that weren't needed, my husband reckons, then piled them onto the bill.'

Jack said nothing, too bewildered and frightened to speak. Though it made him feel sick to the stomach to hear Walter described in that way and to discover that Terence was gone for good, worst of all was the knowledge that he and his family had let them down. They had liked May Mostert, all of them had. They had admired Walter; even Pa had thought he was good for the garage and for Mrs Mostert; and Terence was the best friend he would ever have. Yet when the Nats came for them, they hadn't done what was right, what was decent. They'd stayed silent and kept their door closed.

A mensch, Jack had thought. Ma talked so often about menschlichkeit, the properties that make one a decent human being. What would a mensch do in these circumstances? He knew that whatever high standards they had set themselves, or pretended to set themselves, he and his parents had failed to live up to them. They had escaped the fate of their own forefathers, the pograms and burning of synagogues, the hostile treatment at the hands of Russian peasants and soldiers, the later atrocities of war and genocide in Europe, and now they watched others suffering in the same way, without saying a word. He too had failed.

He had not had a bar mitzvah – Pa had not relented – but, for all his bitter tears and anger at the time, it *hadn't* ruined his life. Far from it. It was still a source of regret but now he had to acknowledge that it was not so very important after all. When he met Renee she had shown little concern, other than sympathy for him, and when he thought of the son he might have, he had no qualms in imagining himself explaining to him honestly why he had been denied it. Being bar mitzvahed or not had neither defined him, nor changed his life. But the memory of Terence and that night in 1948 was different. He had been marked by it, and the joys of that earlier time spent at the Mostert Garage were tainted; he could never think of Terence and Walter and May without shame, or without fearing for what had become of them.

'You're very quiet, Mr Neuberger,' Vera said.

'Just thinking,' he said.

'About the case?'

'In a way. Just remembering something.'

They were approaching Elsie's River and he needed to prepare himself for what was to come.

'I think we'll try the neighbours first, then go to Mrs Small's. I'll do what I did last time and park the car round the corner. That way we won't announce ourselves too loudly.'

'Are you nervous, Mr Neuberger?'

'A little. Not so much about asking the questions, more about what we're going to find out. If there's more evidence against Van Heerden, it's going to be hard to get him off. I've come to like the man, whatever he's done.'

'What do you make of this law, Mr Neuberger?'

Jack was slowing down, ready to park. He manoeuvred into a space, pulled on the break and switched off the engine. He looked hard at Vera.

'What do *you* make of it, Vera?'

'I think it stinks.'

'Me too.'

'Thought so,' Vera said. There was a moment's pause. 'So if he were guilty, you'd still try to get him off? Would you think any less of him for what he'd done, if it weren't a coloured woman?'

Jack paused. It was complicated. There was the question of legality and the rights and wrongs of the law, the issue of adultery and the betrayal of Laura, and then the additional question of race. Murky areas that were hard to disentangle. How to explain how he felt to Vera, when he was struggling to understand it himself?

'I know it's my duty to mount the best defence for him come what may. I'll try as hard as I can for him as an individual, as his advocate. That's my job. But it's also a law that should never have been passed; it makes me ashamed to be South African. So regardless of whether he's guilty or not, I'd like to do my damnedest to get him off. I want to see him walking out of that courtroom a free man, not just for him but for all of us. There's a history of juries acquitting on bad laws and if there's that kind of reluctance to convict, it can sometimes bring about change. The law's the law, but it has to be by consensus. It can't flout the will of the people forever. So getting him off would be a way of standing up for a principle that's been lost. I'd feel proud of that, if it could be done, and if I had the strength to do it. Both big ifs though.'

'And what about Laura?'

'Ah, Laura.' He knew what Vera meant. It was painful to think that Van Heerden might have betrayed her with another woman, regardless of her colour. Adultery itself wasn't a crime, but it caused hurt to someone you were supposed to love and respect more than anyone else, your wife or husband. You'd taken vows of love and loyalty. He thought of himself and Renee. There was a different kind of decency at stake to the one that this law had been designed to uphold.

'I don't think anything short of an acquittal's going to help Laura van Heerden. And even then, I'm not sure what will happen to her and Johannes. Their whole community's been torn apart. I don't think the van Heerdens are going to find this easy, whatever the verdict. She seems strong to me, though, despite what everyone says, so who knows? She trusts her husband and she has unswerving faith in God, so maybe that gives her the kind of bravery that others don't have.'

Vera nodded. 'And do you think he did it, Mr Neuberger? Do you think he *did* commit adultery with Mrs Small?'

He smiled. 'Who knows? The crunch question. Let's see what we find out today.'

His gut reaction was to say no. The way Clara had described Johannes as a young man, the accounts of the character witnesses that Jack had interviewed, Laura's description of him and their courtship, his reputation in the community, everything pointed towards a man of supreme self-discipline and control. Yes, his views were more liberal than some in his church, and he had perhaps shown some naivety in visiting Agnes Small on his own, but it seemed so unlikely that he would do anything to jeopardise his position and his marriage; he was such an upright man. Clara's testimony was troubling, very much so, both for its content and for the fact of her having abandoned her loyalty to her close friends, but then Laura had given him plausible enough motives for that. Clara was in the thrall of her illiberal parents, afraid of Dirk Fourie and his faction. He didn't doubt that she had seen something that day in Elsie's River, but surely she had mistaken a brotherly gesture of compassion for something else? It had all then got out of hand and retracting had become impossible. She was swept along by the tide of scandal and the pressure from the reverend's detractors and she couldn't row back from it. He could make a plausible enough case for himself for Clara's story not being entirely trustworthy. Most of all, though, he felt that Johannes Van Heerden just wasn't that kind of man and nor did he believe that

Agnes Small would be swept off her feet by him. Neither seemed to him to be likely candidates for a passionate, risky affair.

'Let's go and see if we can talk to any of the neighbours,' he said.

He locked up the car and they walked round the corner. The grocery store was just opening up; the owner was drawing back the shutters and pulling down the blind for the day. He was a coloured man, thin-faced, with gaps in his teeth and a stubbled chin, wearing just a white cotton vest and shorts. His arms were strongly muscled from carting crates of bottles around and bore large tattoos: a woman's name, a naked female body, a lizard, a wreath of flowers.

'Can I buy a cooldrink?' Jack said.

'Ice-cold ginger beer, lemonade, Coca-Cola. Take your pick, baas.'

'Ginger beer for me and the lady'll have something as well.'

He paid for the drinks and they stood beside him drinking them down with straws.

'Know the woman who lives across from here, Mrs Small?'

'Yes, baas. Her kiddies come over here sometimes to buy drinks or ice pops. Good-looking woman.'

'No husband?'

'No, baas. He died some time back. Struck down with something bad. Not sure what it was.'

'On her own then?'

'Yes, baas. Her and the children. Nice kids. Well brought up. Polite. Always neat and tidy.'

'Must be hard for her with no husband? Does she have men visiting?'

The man hesitated. He narrowed his eyes. 'I run a grocery store, baas! I mind my own business. Keep your eyes fixed on your own affairs, I say, that way you don't get into no trouble or anything.'

'Just wondering if you happened to know whether a particular man visits a lot, a man of the church, dark-haired, greying at the front, heavily built?'

'Couldn't say. Too busy making a living to worry about other people and their lives. If I had time to sit on my backside watching what other people are up to, I wouldn't be here selling groceries in Elsie's River. I'd be off somewhere else, having a fine old time, living the high life!' He turned away, opened the icebox and started filling it with bottles.

'Thanks anyway.' Jack put his bottle into the crate of empties and walked away, Vera following on behind.

'That approach didn't work too well. Maybe I was a bit too direct – he clammed up pretty quickly once I mentioned a man. Can't be sure whether it's because he genuinely hasn't got anything to tell, or just isn't saying.'

'I'd be prepared to bet he knows all about the comings and goings. Her house is right across from here and he's out there on the street all day long, at the front of the store, so he must see everything. Maybe he thinks you're a policeman, or Special Branch or something?'

'Pity he's not more forthcoming. Let's try the bungalow on the right.'

It was a small, squat house, with peeling paintwork and a garden that had grown out of control, weeds fighting with overlong, scrubby grass, and an old chipped sink sitting right next to the front door. A heap of tyres, a broken children's trike, a flattened, orange-stained paddling pool and a rusty old barbecue stood on the other side, piled up against the wall, in a disorderly jumble.

As Jack got closer, he realised that the house was uninhabited. The curtains were drawn; letters and circulars were crammed into the letterbox and lay strewn on the front mat. There were no signs of life.

'Empty,' he said. 'Just our luck.'

'What about on the other side?'

'That's a lock-up or something. A garage or a barn for storage. All closed and padlocked. Nobody there to ask, I reckon. Let's go back over the road and try the house next to the grocery store. Maybe someone there knows something.'

They crossed over to the neat little house, with its small patch of lawn. He was just about to knock on the green-netted outer door, when Vera tugged at his arm and pulled him quickly round to the side of the house, behind a large leafy buddleia.

'Look,' she whispered. 'Over there.'

He peered out from behind the shrub. Across the road, a man was leaving Agnes Small's home. He stood on the doorstep for several minutes talking to her. She looked around nervously, then continued the conversation, her face strained. She folded her arms; the discussion seemed to be over and the man looked as if he was about to go. He started to move but then hesitated, stopping for a moment to say one more thing. Finally, as he moved back a little, as if ready to step down from the porch, he touched her arm. Then he turned quickly and hurried down the path.

'Oh my God,' said Jack.

It was Johannes van Heerden.

'That's it, then,' said Vera. 'He's guilty.'

A series of looks, a conversation that couldn't be heard, a tiny gesture of his hand on her arm, a little pressure on the soft flesh above her elbow, and there could be little doubt about it. Jack's heart sank. It seemed that Agnes Small and Johannes van Heerden had been having an affair.

Chapter 21

The following morning, Johannes van Heerden came into the chambers to see Jack.

Jack had spent a sleepless night churning over the trip to Elsie's River and what he had seen. Could he, like Clara, have simply misunderstood the gesture? Was he reading too much in to it? He thought not. Both he and Vera had had the same reaction, responding to the scene in exactly the same way. On the drive back into the office, they'd talked about it.

'There was something so intimate about it,' Vera said. 'The way she looked at him, the way he touched her arm. I can't explain it really, Mr Neuberger, but it was like they knew each other really, really well.'

'I know what you mean,' Jack said. 'Something about the distance between them – they stood so close to each other – the lack of a formal goodbye, a shake of the hand or a wave. And that squeeze of her arm. You wouldn't do that if you were just offering her support. And anyway, what's he doing back there, talking to her on his own, after everything that's happened? It's madness. He must know that if he were seen it would be disastrous.'

He'd talked to Renee about it when he got back in the evening. 'I can't really believe it,' he said. 'I'd been feeling pretty optimistic that we could cast serious doubt on Clara's testimony. If Laura took the stand in support of Johannes, she would be so completely convincing – it would take a hard-hearted jury not to feel sympathy for her. And all those character witnesses would have counted for a lot. But now, I'm not sure. If he really is guilty, there's bound to be more coming out at the trial that I don't even know about, maybe even other witnesses waiting in the wings. The prosecution have Clara as their biggest piece of ammunition and if she saw a lot more than Vera and I did that day, she's going to make the case against him hard to refute.'

'Could you acknowledge some kind of relationship, but suggest it fell short of a full-blown affair? You know, they were close, they'd developed a friendship, he was showing brotherly concern for her well-being, that kind of thing.'

'I've thought of that. This new law, though, it's not just about intercourse, it's about other sexual activity too – "immoral and indecent acts" is the phrase used. What does that mean? It hasn't been tested yet in a court of law. In the end it'll all be down to interpretation. A kiss, a touch, an embrace? Clothes on? Clothes off? In a bedroom, or a living room, in a garage or on a darkly lit street? All these things will be really significant. I heard of one case, under the previous law, where an advocate was defending a man accused of having sex with a coloured woman. The advocate sought to prove that it was too dark in the alley for the man to know whether she was white or not. He got the man off. Good for him, and for the man, but what a comment on this society of ours! My case may well hinge on what Clara describes and the precise words she uses, and whether there can be any doubt at all about the nature of the encounter being a sexual one. And you can be pretty sure that Willem du Toit and the prosecution team will have thought hard about that and will have schooled her well.'

'Poor man,' Renee said. 'It looks bad for him.'

'And for his wife. God only knows what'll happen to her. If he goes to jail, then what? Will the community support her? Or will they turn their backs on her, after all that has happened? The woman has four children! It doesn't bear thinking about. But even if I manage to get a good verdict for him, and he gets off, or has his sentence suspended, I wonder whether she'd stay with him? I doubt that they'd be able to remain at the church – there's too much feeling against him for them to just forgive and forget.'

'You mustn't eat yourself up about it, though. You can only do your best, after all. You're an advocate, not a miracle worker.'

He'd nodded; she was right, of course, but that didn't stop waves of anxiety from engulfing him. The arguments for the defence were draining away quickly and his options were becoming increasingly limited. In just a few weeks' time he'd be standing up in court, desperately trying to succeed for his client, but with all the odds now stacked against him.

'I hope when the baby comes you're not going to be stuck with a case that swallows you up like this one has! We hardly talk about anything else these days. You'll have another little person to think about then, you know. I realise how important your work is to you and I don't usually complain – I'm an absolute angel – but *she's* going to want a bit of your time, you know! She might be more demanding on you than I am! I reckon she's going to be a tough little cookie, given all the kicking she's been doing.'

He smiled. '*He's* going to get lots of my time, I promise you. But, as my father never ceased to say, I do have a living to make, and this particular path I've chosen doesn't happen to be one that you can easily forget about the minute you turn the key in the lock and say, "I'm home!" But you're right, my darling, you *are* an angel. Why do you think I married you?'

He came over and kissed her tenderly, then placed his hand on the swelling shape under her dress and patted it softly.

'I want him to have a father he can be proud of.'

'Whatever it is, a boy or a girl, they couldn't fail to be proud of you, Jack. Our child will learn all her menschishkeit from you.'

He didn't reply. He wondered whether Renee realised what was at stake in this trial, when she showed such support for his principles, such trust in his basic decency. Had she really understood the possible consequences for them? Soon they would not just be a couple; they'd have a child to think of as well and the thought of watching his budding career wither on the stem was a difficult one to contemplate. He felt he was moving into unknown territory. With the Special Branch already paying the occasional 'friendly' visit, life could get difficult, but how difficult wasn't clear. He'd heard about one or two people he'd known as acquaintances at varsity, men a few years older, who'd got involved with black activist groups. One in particular, Sol Levine, had been quite a close friend. While doing his medical training, he had been recruited to work with a banned group, which had been threatening to blow up government buildings and installations. Sol's wife, Thelma, had been given a tip-off that the Special Branch were coming for him, so he fled one night, crossing the border into Botswana, leaving her and the family behind. Jack didn't think he was at risk from the Special Branch in that way – he wasn't a terrorist after all – but nevertheless, life could become uncomfortable. He would almost certainly be watched, and a successful career as an advocate might well be put at risk.

Jack was thinking of Renee and the baby and this conversation when Vera announced van Heerden's arrival through the intercom and then ushered him into the office. He was looking ashen-faced. He had clearly lost some weight and his suit was hanging loose on him. There were dark rings under his eyes and a weariness about his whole demeanour that suggested a man in despair. But nevertheless he came up to Jack with a quick stride, shook his hand strongly and greeted him with an attempt at a cheery smile. Trying to keep up the appearance of confidence, thought Jack. Trying not to give too much away.

'Well, Mr Neuberger, I expect by now you've talked to all the people you need to. They're going to speak up for me in court, ja? All going OK with the case, ja?'

Jack hesitated. He'd been planning on getting pretty much straight to the point, letting him know that he'd seen him with Mrs Small the previous evening. That way he might catch him unawares, before his defences were up; he'd stand a chance of breaking down the fortress that he'd so carefully constructed for himself. They could then start all over again, begin to search the rubble and see if there was any way of salvaging something from the debris. He wanted to just get it over with, rather than tiptoe around. But van Heerden's wan face and his wishful, optimistic words left Jack floundering. It was too hard to brutally come out with it, just like that, though he knew he'd be forced to sooner or later.

'Not so good, Mr van Heerden, I'm afraid. Some really nice people from your church that I've talked to and I think they'll speak up for you in court – they'll vouch for your good character. But Clara Joubert, that's a real blow.'

'Ah, yes, Clara Joubert.'

'Your wife's talked to you about coming to see me, I'm sure. She gave me some of the background to the whole thing. She gave me her view of it and her thoughts on why Clara's saying what she is. But it's still a problem for us.'

'Ja, of course. Clara's a problem, I see that. But you know she's not so stable, Mr Neuberger. She's got a vivid imagination, gets things out of proportion, exaggerates a bit. She's known for that. Everyone says so. And she sways with the tide. What's that phrase from Shakespeare again? "Like to a vagabond flag upon the stream, Goes to and back, lackeying the varying tide, To rot itself with motion." *Antony and Cleopatra*. I studied that speech at school. Clara's like that. A vagabond flag. That's a reed, you know, Mr Neuberger, a flag. A reed, floating this way and that in the breeze. But why am I telling you all this? I'm getting off the point. Clara, she's been Laura's closest friend since they were girls but, to be honest, I've always wondered why. She's easily led, that girl. She's obviously got persuaded by Dirk Fourie and his lot, and by those parents of hers of course. They've got it in for me for some reason and they've been looking for an excuse to get rid of me, oust me from the church. I'm sure Laura told you that too. So we can say all that in court, can't we? We can say about her being easily led, about her parents and so on. Her evidence won't be believed, will it, if we tell them what she's like? Not a reliable witness.'

'I'm not sure it's quite as simple as that, Mr van Heerden.'

'I can get other people to back that up, if you like. There's others will say just the same. They'll tell you a similar story about her.'

'Like who?'

He hesitated. 'Laura has agreed to speak. She'll tell the court what she thinks of Clara's behaviour. It'll be tough on her, I know, but she's willing to do it for me.'

'That will be very helpful, Mr van Heerden. I'm sure your wife will be a great asset.' He pulled his chair forward and swept his hand through his hair. This was it. It had to be done. 'Look, Mr van Heerden, something else has happened that I need to talk to you about.' He paused. 'I need to know the truth now, Johannes, so I have to tell you something that's been worrying me about your case.'

Van Heerden flushed. Beads of sweat seemed to suddenly appear from nowhere on his brow. He wiped his face with his hand and sat forward in his chair, his legs wide in front of him, planted firmly on the floor, as if keeping him in place.

'I was in Elsie's River yesterday. I saw you coming out of Agnes Small's house.'

There was a long silence. The man sat completely still, as if turned to stone, his face chalky pale, his eyes intently focused on Jack. For what seemed like an interminable time, he said nothing. Then, all at once, his words came out in a sudden rush. 'I went to talk to her about the case. I wanted to tell her how it was going and find out what her advocate is doing, what line he's taking. I wanted to reassure her. It was innocent, Mr Neuberger, perfectly harmless. I felt concerned for the poor woman.'

'Not very sensible, going to her house alone, though, given the nature of the case, surely?'

'I couldn't help myself. I was worried about her.'

'Wanting to make sure your stories tallied? Share with her the fact that Clara Joubert had seen you together?'

'No, Mr Neuberger.'

'Wanting to ask her advice on what to do?'

'No.'

'Just wanting to see her again, perhaps? You've not been able to visit since all this blew up and you've been missing her.'

'No.'

'Johannes, I saw the two of you on the stoep, talking.'

There was silence.

'I saw enough to know that there's more to this story than what you've told me so far.' He said it gently, speaking quietly, wanting to soften the blow.

The man looked up at him, as if weighing his words carefully. He was perfectly still, his only movement a nervous pulling at his lip with his top teeth.

Then suddenly, with no prior warning, he collapsed into a flood of tears. His cries brought Vera running in from the outside office.

'Is everything OK? Can I – Oh, sorry...' She took in the scene, realised her mistake, then backed out quickly, shutting the door behind her.

Jack reached into his desk drawer and found a clean linen handkerchief. He handed it to van Heerden.

'I think we'd better start from the beginning, Mr van Heerden. If I'm really going to be able to help you, I need to know exactly what I'm dealing with here. I can't be worrying about all kinds of unexpected things suddenly being hurled my way when I'm standing in that courtroom trying to defend you. You need to be straight with me. I need you to tell me everything.'

'I understand,' van Heerden said.

Chapter 21

1957

The day that his father was taken into hospital Jack was out at a small court in Stellenbosch, with his pupil-master, Louis Abrams. It was his first time speaking in court, acting on his own, and Louis had accompanied him, agreeing that he would listen, observe and later give him his comments on how it had gone but wouldn't intervene in court unless absolutely necessary.

The trial was a case of arson, where a young white man was accused of burning down a farm building in an act of revenge against the employer who had given him the sack. Jack emerged from the courtroom elated. After a shaky start he had managed to put across the case tolerably well and in the end all the evidence of reasonable doubt that they had marshalled had convinced the judge; the man was acquitted.

Louis had suggested lunch in a small restaurant nearby to celebrate, over a steak and a glass of wine. But just as they were leaving the court building an usher came hurrying up.

'Mr Abrams? Mr Neuberger? We've had a phone message from Cape Town. I'm sorry, Mr Neuberger, your father has been taken to Groote Schuur hospital and your mother has been trying to get hold of you. She wants you to meet her there as soon as you can.'

Louis had driven him straight to the hospital. At first during the long car journey they talked, both men's shock and worry bringing an outpouring of anxious speculation about what might have happened and how best to deal with it. But soon Louis went quiet, concentrating on getting them there as fast as he could, and Jack was left to his own thoughts.

In the previous few years, now that he'd started his career and met Renee, he'd hoped for a rapprochement with his father; some of the anger of the early years had faded and he realised that there were more things that perhaps he'd like to know about him, that might allow him to see his behaviour in a different light. It had been hard to feel so little respect for one's father; he would have preferred to find a way of redeeming him from the role of villain he had seemed to play when Jack was a boy. And, as he'd grown older, Jack had also gradually become more aware of his mother's part in the problems of his childhood. Difficult though it had been to acknowledge it at first, he had begun to see how easily and willingly she had inflamed his father's fury. If he had been a difficult husband and father, perhaps she had helped him towards this, in being an ungiving and unsupportive wife.

Renee coming into his life had been the start of the change in his feelings about his father, the catalyst for going back through it all, remembering and re-evaluating Ma and Pa's marriage. It was partly that he suddenly understood what a woman could bring to a relationship if she genuinely loved and respected a man; the joy of their first year together was something he could scarcely believe or make any sense of. It was amazing, staggering, to spend time in her company without the kind of bickering and simmering resentment that had characterised his parents' everyday lives. So that's what love is, he thought. So that's what a marriage can be.

But it was also Renee's relationship with his parents that was an eye-opener. Renee actually liked his father. Once Pa had got over the irritable grumblings about the foolishness of getting married so young, the preoccupation with how much money Renee was bringing to the marriage and the ridiculous cost of setting up home together, he soon became a model of politeness towards Renee. He seemed to positively look forward to her visits. And when she started to show a willingness to help out in the store if they were short-handed, Pa was completely won over. Ma had been nothing but a hindrance in the business, as far as he was concerned, Jack hadn't been remotely interested, and Sauly, for all his early enthusiasm for practical things, had ended up following the same path as Jack into a university education, opting for dentistry as his career. By the time Mikey hit high school, Pa had given up the ghost and allowed him to continue his academic studies without a fight. None of them had wanted anything to do with the one thing that meant something to Pa, his whole life, his raison d'être, the Handyhouse that bore his name. But here was practical, down-to-earth, head-screwed-on Renee, happily joining him in slicing biltong, sorting nails and scooping measures of chicken feed out for customers.

By contrast, Renee found Sarah quite tricky. Jack was her boy, her firstborn, and she didn't take well to having to share him with another woman. She also seemed to resent the growing closeness between Renee and Pa. So, while Renee could see all his flaws and his foibles, his obsessions about money and his flaming temper, she could also identify the way in which Ma's behaviour only confirmed and exaggerated Pa's worst sides.

Jack had never had a conversation with his father about any of this. They'd never talked about anything important. Coming to visit him with Renee, they could make friendly small talk, ask about each other's daily lives and avoid areas of possible disagreement; he could reach out to his father by discussing a troublesome wholesaler, or enquiring about the price of wood, and his father could engage in conversation about the outcome of a case or advocates' fees. But talking about the past was forbidden territory for both of them. It was too dangerous to start on that path, with no map and no equipment and the risk of getting lost in the dark and dangerous undergrowth.

But now Pa was in hospital. If Ma was asking Jack to come, it must be serious. He realised that perhaps he'd left it too late, that it was very important to him, after all, to turn back to that past and make a rough, dirty, ugly little track through it, however difficult and treacherous it might turn out to be. He wanted Pa to be straight with him. There were things he wanted to know: why Pa had burnt down the shed and what he'd been doing with that money under the floor; what he'd felt about his relationship with Ma; whether, as Ma suspected, he'd had a relationship with another woman; why, when he'd clearly liked and admired Walter and when his views had been broadly liberal ones, he had failed to stand up for Terence and his family when they were in trouble. Finally, and perhaps most important of all, he wanted to know whether his father had ever forgiven him for being who he was and for what he saw as the betrayals of his childhood. Did he still feel disappointed in him, still wish for a son to stand beside him in the store, rather than having to make do with this too-clever-by-half young man, who had become educated beyond him and his world?

If his father could be straight with him, he too could try to explain things, as he saw them. Most of all, he wanted to now tell his father about the things that had been said, and the things that were left unsaid. In the world of his boyhood, speech had been dangerous, silence safe.

'Yet here I am, Pa, talking for my job,' he heard himself saying. 'Being an advocate for other people. Isn't that funny? Isn't that absurd? I started out as that little silent boy who wouldn't say a word. You worried about me, didn't you? You thought I'd be mute forever. And then when I spoke, all hell broke loose. I seemed to say all the wrong things. Funny, isn't it? Crazy. Stupid. And very, very sad.'

'How much further?' he asked Louis.

'Not far now.'

'I feel like I need to get there. I need to talk to him.'

'I know.'

When they arrived at the hospital, Ma was waiting in the lobby. He could see straightaway that it was over. She shook her head. His father had died soon after the phone call to the courtroom. There was nothing more to be said.

Chapter 22

1958

The day after his interview with van Heerden, Jack was sitting in the chambers library, leafing through one of the books, checking a small detail, when Vera knocked on the door.

'Your wife's on the phone, Mr Neuberger. She says it's urgent. She needs to talk to you. I said I'd come and get you.'

'The baby?' His first reaction was the panicky terror that a phone call like this induced in him, flashing past like still frames from a film.

'Oh no. She said to tell you she's fine but she needs to talk to you straightaway.'

He hurried down the corridor. 'I'll take it in my office,' he said.

'Listen, Jackie, something's happened. I'm absolutely fine but I want you to come home.'

'What is it? Are you OK?'

'Don't worry about me, that's not it. But I don't want to talk on the phone. I think it's best if you come home.'

Jack put down the phone, grabbed his jacket and left the office.

Vera looked up anxiously.

'You'll need to postpone my meeting with Agnes Small's counsel. Oh and can you ring my brother and cancel my lunch with him? And please tell Mr Cohen that I've been called home urgently, just in case he needs to talk to me. I don't know what it is, but Renee wants me there.'

'Fine, Mr Neuberger. I hope it's nothing serious.'

'So do I.'

Later that day, Jack returned to his chambers. He dropped his briefcase by his desk, then looked round the room, surveying the row of law books on the bookcase, his desk, crowded with papers, his filing cabinet, the hook on the door with his coat, the second hook next to the door with his gown, his table, with its glass ashtray, jug of water and pile of *Cape Argus*es, the lamp stand and the single light fixture in the middle of the ceiling. He looked at the cream walls of the room, and the single painting by Boonzaier of a District 6 street, vibrant with colour, which he'd bought with the proceeds of his first big case. He looked at the faded Persian rug on the floor, its weave breaking down in places, unravelling its threads of wool.

He called Vera in. 'Can you spare ten minutes? I want to take a little walk with you, out in the Company Gardens.' He spoke quietly, almost in a whisper.

Vera looked puzzled. 'Of course, Mr Neuberger.'

Walking in the park he told her what had happened. Renee had been sorting linen with the maid when the doorbell had rung. She'd opened it, thinking it was the laundry van, and two men had been standing there. They'd politely but firmly asked to be let in. She'd said that she wanted to phone her husband but they said that wouldn't be necessary and she had been persuaded to let them come inside.

They walked straight into the living room. Without asking permission, they sat themselves down and started to question her, politely enough, it was true, but nevertheless with singular determination, about Jack's past, about how they'd met, his political persuasions, his friendships and his contacts. They wanted to know whether he'd ever been a member of a Zionist group, or the Communist Party. Perhaps he was just a fellow traveller? They questioned whether he'd associated with members of the African Nationalist Congress, or with known enemies of the Republic of South Africa. They mentioned names, Ruth First, Albie Sachs, Sam Kahn, Walter Sisulu, Nelson Mandela and others, a few of which she recognised. In among the names were a few old university friends and members of the university debating society that Jack had chaired, including Sol Levine, of course. It came as no surprise to her that his name was there, given his notoriety. They looked her in the eye when they asked if Jack had known Sol. She tried hard to keep her face blank, so that no flicker of a change of expression would pass over it when she heard his name. She claimed ignorance of Jack's previous friends from the time before he knew her. There was a long pause before the questions continued. Had Jack ever travelled to Russia? Had he been out of Cape Town, on visits to Kwazulu, or Niasaland, to the African homelands, to Rhodesia? Did he consort with natives, or coloureds, with Malays or Indians?

Renee had refused to answer any more of their questions. 'I think you need to speak to my husband,' she'd said. 'I'm tired now and need to lie down.' They flipped over their notebooks, put them back in their pockets, and got up to leave.

'Thank you, Mrs Neuberger. We'll be back sometime to speak to your husband, as you suggest. We wish you the best with your baby.'

Jack had asked her what the men had looked like. The description tallied with that of the two men who'd been to see him at his chambers.

As soon as they'd left, Renee had called him at his chambers.

'But why didn't your wife tell you all this over the phone?' Vera asked.

'She was afraid. She thought that perhaps their visit wasn't just to ask questions. Maybe they'd come to plant a device or something.'

'So that's why we're walking in the park.'

'I didn't want to take any risks. It's probably silly – they're just trying to intimidate us. But nevertheless... I want to make sure that you understand what we're dealing with. We're going to have to be careful about what's said in the office from now on. Just as a precaution.

'What are you going to do, Jack?' It was the first time she had ever used his first name. He was aware of the whole range of reasons why that might be and he appreciated them all. She had been part of this case with him and it had brought them closer than he'd ever imagined possible at the start of her working for him.

'About the men? Nothing. Just wait and see what happens, whether they pay me another visit or not.'

'What about the case?'

He was silent.

'I know this isn't my business and I have no right to interfere, but I want to say something.' They had reached the small boating lake and begun to walk round the edge, skirting past little children riding tricycles, women throwing stale bread to the ducks, gardeners pulling up weeds in the flowerbeds next to the path. The gravel was crunchy underfoot. Jack noticed that Vera was struggling a bit in her high heels, her gait awkward and wobbly, as her shoes got caught between the small pebbles. 'I don't think you should do anything risky. You've got a wife to think of and a baby on the way. Your duty's to them, not to anyone else.

I know how you feel, Mr Neuberger' – she was back to the more formal form of address – 'I know you have principles. You're a liberal and all that. But this country's a bloody mess, if you'll pardon my language, and you're not going to be able to sort it out single-handed.'

He was taken aback by the intensity in her voice, the directness with which she expressed her feelings.

'These aren't times for heroism, you know, Mr Neuberger. You've got to be smart, not stupid. Those men, those Special Branch people, you're on their list now. They're interested in you. And if you're not worried for yourself, then think about your wife and what's best for her and for the little kiddie on the way. What's that word you sometimes use, "shtum"? Keep shtum. What my mother calls keeping your trap shut. Best all round.'

'You seem very sure about this, Vera.'

'I am.'

He didn't reply and they walked on in silence.

'Just think about what I'm saying, promise me that. There are a lot of people relying on you. You don't want to let them down.'

They turned off the gravel path, out of the wrought-iron gates and back onto the road. When they reached the chambers, he suggested that, since it was already late afternoon, she might go home early. No point in coming back in, just for half an hour, when everyone else in the building would be getting ready to leave. She thanked him, said she hoped she hadn't said too much, taken any liberties or caused offence, then walked off towards Wale Street and her bus home.

He watched her go, then climbed up the steps to the front door of the building. As he entered, Charlie greeted him.

'Those two men, Mr Neuberger, they were back here again. They said I had to let them go up to your office. So I said OK. Not for long though, just five or six minutes, then they came back down again. I thought I should let you know. Did I do the right thing?'

'Thank you, Charlie. It's not your fault. You had no choice – you did the right thing.'

Vera knew what she'd been saying. They did mean business. And now he was going to have to decide what that meant for him. For Charlie, it had been simple; he'd done the right thing. But what about him? For him, what might that be?

CHAPTER 23

'Your honour, my esteemed colleague Mr du Toit, members of the jury...'

The moment had finally come. He was ready to set out on this journey. He'd been born and raised on the Voortrekker Road. He'd already travelled a long way, from sitting swinging his legs on a sack of beans in the Handyhouse and wetting his pants in the schoolyard of Parow Elementary School, sitting next to Terence in the car on the way home from Hout Bay, to now standing up in court as advocate for the defence of an Afrikaner of high standing, in a case that had made it into the newspapers, with crowds of people jostling each other on the front steps of the courthouse, clamouring to get in.

The last few weeks he had slept badly. He woke in the early hours, going back over every detail of the case, rehearsing each move he thought he would make, getting up quietly so as not to wake Renee in order to jot down fresh questions to put to his client, to Laura or to the small band of church members who had, in the end, agreed to speak for the defence.

In the mornings, he went into his chambers with his head buzzing, still unsure of whether he was doing the right thing. Renee had refused to advise him on his decision – 'The way things are at the moment, with the baby on the way, I'm not sure you'd get a sensible view from me. All I can say is, whatever you end up doing, I'll do my best to support you. The decision has to be yours.'

When he told her what he was planning on doing, she'd listened carefully, nodding from time to time, then taken his face in her hands and kissed him. Later that afternoon, she'd come to find him in his study and told him that she'd rather not know any more of the details about it, now he'd decided.

'If I don't know anything, I can't say anything,' she'd said. 'I'd rather not know, in case anyone asks me. It's better that way. And anyway, thinking about it all just makes me worry too much, for him and for us. I've got to start concentrating on myself and the baby now.'

He understood. She'd been extraordinary, selfless and determined in her preparedness to trust him and his judgement. Now, it was only right that she should leave him to get on with it, to follow it through for himself.

'Do you want to go and stay with your parents while the trial's going on? Would that be easier for you, to be out of town for a while?'

'Would you manage without me?'

'Of course.'

'Then maybe. That way, I'll be away from all the talk, all the chatter. And you don't have to worry about me and the baby. My parents will look after me.'

But in the end she'd stayed. 'I want to be here with you,' she'd said. 'When you come home at night, we can pretend everything's just like normal. I'll get the maid to cook you something nice and we'll eat together. We'll talk about other things, about afterwards, the baby and that nice long holiday we'll go on, to Hermanus, or along the Garden Route, to Knysna and George.'

The last meetings with Van Heerden had been tense. The closer they got to the trial the more agitated he had become, and, finally, it had needed his wife to agree to come along, to keep him calm enough to talk to Jack and take in what he had to tell him and agree on the best course of action. The more frenzied he had become, the more composed she was, the more able to take control.

'You have to do what he tells you, Johannes,' she kept repeating. 'You have to accept the situation you're in and let him help you to make the best of it. It's no good wishing that things were different. They're not. You just have to find some inner strength, to help you through. This is about you and me and our small family and our wider community, our brethren, but it's also about more than that. Whatever happens to us is part of something bigger. You need to remember that. It's the reason we were put here on this earth in the first place.'

And when he became emotional and began to voice his utter despair, she encouraged him to have faith in God, who forgave all men their sins and looked after them in their hour of need. Then Jack would leave them for a moment or two, to allow them to kneel down in prayer. And on his return, Johannes would be calmer and more able to talk about the case.

The night before the trial started, Sarah had phoned.

'I'm worried for you, Jackie! I read in the *Argus* this morning that this is no ordinary case. There are a lot of people taking an interest in it. They're saying you've got communist sympathies. They're talking about dangerous links with Russia. That's not true, is it?'

'No, Ma. It's not.'

'You're not going to do anything stupid are you, Jackie? You know, your Ouma and Oupa didn't come all this way to see you give up the life they dreamed of. They didn't board those boats and leave their shtetls to have more tsoros and troubles here in South Africa. They wanted to make a good life for themselves, and for us, their children, and for you, their grandchildren.'

'I know, Ma. I'm not doing anything stupid.'

'And your Pa, you owe it to him, after all the fighting between you and him, all the arguments, to prove to him that becoming a attorney was a wise thing to do, not a stupid one.'

'He's dead, Ma.'

'Yes, but you still owe it to him. In the end, though he never came out and said it to anyone, he was proud of you, Jackie, just like I am. And he wouldn't want to think of you throwing it all away for a bit of nonsense.'

'Yes, Ma. I know.'

'So you'll do what's right?'

'Yes, Ma. I'll do what's right.'

'OK, then I can go to bed and sleep peacefully. Good luck for tomorrow.'

'Thanks Ma.'

The courtroom was full. Agnes Small was there, standing behind her advocate and his junior, just a few steps away from Johannes Van Heerden; if they'd reached over the other people sitting between them, they could have almost touched.

To one side of the courtroom, in the press seats, sat the court reporters, from the *Cape Argus*, the *Cape Times* and *die Burger*. In the public gallery, he saw Miss Joubert and her brother, along with a few of the other members of the church who were not appearing as witnesses for either the defence or the prosecution. Otherwise it was packed with unfamiliar faces, people eagerly awaiting what looked to be a particularly interesting case.

'Your honour,' he said again, 'my client, Reverend Johannes van Heerden, wishes it to be known that he has decided to plead guilty.'

There was a moment of silence. The newspapermen paused in their scribbling to look up, shocked by this sudden turn of events. In the public gallery there was a rising buzz of whispered voices.

'My learned friend, the counsel for Mrs Agnes Small, will no doubt wish to make a similar plea on her behalf. But before he does so, I wish to make a statement to the court.'

'This is not customary procedure, Mr Neuberger.'

'I am aware of that, your Honour, but in the light of my client's decision and the rapid conclusion of the trial that will be the consequence of it, I beg leave to be allowed to speak, before Mrs Small's advocate rises, and before you close the proceedings to consider your verdict.'

Mr Justice Steyn hesitated for a moment. 'Very well then, if you can be brief.'

'My client wishes it to be known that he is guilty, if guilty is what it really is. He has been brought to this courtroom on a charge of immorality; he is accused of immoral and indecent acts. In one sense, yes, he acknowledges the immorality of his actions, but in one sense only. And that sense is the immorality of having betrayed his wife. That, for my client, is something for which he is truly sorry; he repents his actions for the hurt he has caused her and the wrong he has done her. He made vows to her, in his own church, under the eyes of God, and these are vows that he has broken. He has allowed himself to stray. His wife is a remarkable woman. She is a woman whom anyone in this courtroom should admire, a woman of great strength and courage. Despite everything that she has suffered, despite all the illusions about her husband's faithfulness and honesty that have been shattered, she has remained loyal to him, his true helpmeet and companion. She has forgiven him his sins and promised to stand by him, regardless of what happens in this courtroom today.

'Has my client committed other immoral or indecent acts, beyond that of breaking his marriage vows? This new law says that he has. This law holds that any act of intimacy between a white and a non-European is an illegal one, an act of immorality and indecency. What kind of acts are we talking about here, your honour, ladies and gentlemen of the jury? Two hands meeting, pressure on an arm, a kiss on the cheek? Are these not acts that all of us have engaged in, with our African nannies, when we were children, with our coloured maids, whom we have accepted into our families and sometimes known for many decades and across generations? Are we talking about a close embrace? A passionate kiss? Or acts of greater intimacy? Where does the boundary lie between the close relationships we may *all* have had with the non-Europeans with whom we have had dealings in our normal, everyday lives, and something that goes a bit further than that and becomes more personal and more deeply felt? Who here could say that at no moment in their lives have they felt something warm, tender, or even loving for a person of another race?

'One only needs to look at our population to see that over the years black and white people *have* taken that relationship further, that sexual relationships have not been exceptional or unusual; our large coloured community provides the evidence for that. And why should we forbid this? All too often, it is true, there have been elements of coercion and control in the miscegenation that has occurred; all too often, white men have seen it as their right to exercise their power, to force non-European women into sexual relationships with them. But not in every case. And this is not what has occurred here. In this case, two consenting adults of different races have allowed a loving relationship to develop between them. It has threatened their happiness, as well as that of people close to them. But should that be an *illegal* act? Only the colour of the skin of the two parties is what makes it so. Men and women commit adultery every day of the week, and do so without fear of legal action, or penalties. Yet my client and the other party, Mrs Small, are in danger of becoming criminals, losing their liberty. Seven years. That's the maximum sentence. More than the sentence for many other crimes. Commit robbery, burglary, bigamy, fraud, even common assault or the rape of a woman by a man of the same race and the term is often lower. Seven years for showing love towards another human being.'

'Mr Neuberger, I must stop you there –'

'I'm almost finished, your honour. I appeal to you in determining the sentence that is passed on my client, and to the decent people of the jury, the decent people in this courtroom and those beyond, South Africans one and all, who will read about this trial in *die Burger* and the *Cape Argus* or the *Cape Times*. I appeal to you all to allow decency to prevail. My client is accused of indecency. And yet the most indecent act of all is this very law, with its divisive, barbaric insistence on the differences between races. Laws like this put us as a nation to shame.

'My client is guilty under the law, yes. But what happens when the law itself is besmirched and soiled? It is the duty of all of us to stand up and be counted. It's our duty to speak out against it. My client will be sentenced and perhaps, if your honour sees fit, he will even go to prison, but his punishment will not be in vain, for people here and in other countries across the world will come to hear what our "civilised" society is capable of and one day it will be acknowledged that it is not my client's behaviour but this law itself, and the enactment of it, that is the true crime. My client will go down in history not as a criminal but as one who suffered from the wrongs and misdemeanours of a state, from the immorality of a whole nation, that for a period of time lost its sense of what was right and what was wrong and went down a path of gross indecency.'

He sat down. There was silence. His client Johannes Van Heerden sat looking straight ahead, stony-faced, bloodless and pale; it seemed that at any moment he might fall to the floor. His wife, Laura, looked towards Jack and very softly, almost imperceptibly, brought her hands together and began to clap. On her own, without accompaniment, and for what seemed like forever, in the stillness of the courtroom, Laura van Heerden applauded.

All of a sudden, and perhaps because of the power of her act of defiance as much as the momentousness of his own, Jack was overcome. He started shaking. He realised that under his gown, his shirt was drenched in sweat. He was gripped with fear, with doubt at what he had said, what he had done. Renee would be at home waiting to hear what had happened; Ma would no doubt read about it in the paper the next day; perhaps already two men were driving towards his office to speak to him. In a few days' time the court would be re-convened to hear the verdict; Johannes van Heerden would be sentenced, as would Agnes Small. Already the judge had risen and left the courtroom; he'd be hanging up his wig and his gown; already the ushers were clearing the court, making it ready for the next case. There were no winners, only losers. No one would come out of this laughing. But he'd done what he'd judged to be right, however hopeless it might be, however foolish or dangerous. He'd spoken. He'd spoken for Johannes and Laura; he hoped that Justice Steyn would reflect on his words and show leniency towards his client, that the judiciary might make a small stand of its own. But also for Terence, Jack said to himself, for Terence, Walter and May. And for himself and for every other decent man or woman who lived in Parow, Goodwood, Maitland, Bellville, up and down the whole length of the Voortrekker Road and way, way beyond.

*****

DIE BURGER

MAY 8TH 1958

GUILTY PLEA AND SENTENCING SHOCK IN VAN HEERDEN TRIAL

The trial of the Reverend Johannes van Heerden and Agnes Small for indecency came to a sudden close yesterday, with the unexpected plea of guilty by the two accused. This first case under the newly passed indecency laws has been seen as a test of the strength of the tightened legislation, and its power to curb the growing threat of racial integration and the moral turpitude that is endangering our society.

Van Heerden's defence counsel, Jack Neuberger, a relatively inexperienced young advocate trained under Jewish QC Louis Abrams, surprised the court with the sudden announcement that his client had reversed his decision on his plea. The jury was summarily dismissed but not before Neuberger had made a long statement to the court, going well beyond the bounds of accepted practice. Justice Steyn's decision to tolerate this impassioned outburst, eloquent though it may have been, demonstrated in no uncertain terms his underlying sympathies regarding the case and gave advance warning of his likely approach to sentencing.

Just an hour after announcing an adjournment to consider the facts, Steyn re-called the court to let his decision be known. He made full use of the discretion given to him in determining the sentence, by imposing a minimal fine on both van Heerden and Small. With the option of a substantial prison sentence available to him, Steyn's derisory penalty is yet another troubling indication of the trend in recent years for the judiciary to erode the impact of the legislation passed by our government.

It raises the spectre of undemocratic interference by our judges in the running of the country and poses more strongly than ever the question of whether the justice system itself is in need of serious reform.

Outside the courtroom, van Heerden and his family refused to answer questions put to them by the large crowd of waiting reporters. A highly respected member of van Heerden's church, Miss Clara Joubert, said that it had been a troubling time for the individuals concerned and for their small community but that she hoped that they would all now be left to re-build their lives, out of the public gaze. When asked whether the Reverend van Heerden would continue to serve as pastor for the church, she declined to comment.

Counsel for the prosecution, Willem du Toit, spoke to reporters on the steps of the courtroom.

'I would have liked the case to have been properly heard,' he said, 'I believe that the nation has a right to hear the full details in trials such as this, however distasteful and troubling they may be. Advocates like Neuberger play the system. They're not operating within the spirit of the law. Advocate Neuberger took a risk for his client and it paid off. But is it in the interests of our country, our society, for a man like van Heerden to get off so lightly? Is that the direction we want our legal system to be going in? This kind of outcome paves the way for people to flout our laws with impunity.'

Neuberger himself was not available to talk to *die Burger*. Court officials told reporters that the advocate had slipped out of the building by the back exit. His secretary was not answering phone calls at his chambers.

For a more thorough analysis of the implications of this trial, turn to our editorial pages, where Martin Oosthuizen asks the question, 'Racial intermixing and lax moral standards – is this the future for our nation?'

About the Author

Barbara Bleiman is Co-director of the English and Media Centre, has an MA in Creative Writing from Birkbeck and has had short stories published. She lives in London.

Off The Voortrekker Road is her first novel.

Reviews

If you have enjoyed my writing, I'd be very grateful if you would consider writing a review of *Off The Voortrekker Road* on Goodreads and/or Amazon.

Amazon Reviews of *Off The Voortrekker Road*

A South African version of *To Kill a Mockingbird*
★★★★★

A South African version of *To Kill a Mockingbird*. Beautifully written with a compelling central idea and engaging characters.

Laura Ballantyne, 28 July 2014

Wonderful, enjoyed it so much and could not recommend more highly
★★★★★

This is a simply stunning book, one of the cleverest I have read. It will appeal to anyone interested in the Jewish diaspora; apartheid in South Africa; justice and the law; in fact anyone who likes a good story.

H. M. Sykes, 26 Nov. 2014

Richly textured. Agonisingly observed
★★★★★

The sense of growing up in a Jewish family in South Africa after WW2 came across particularly strongly - acutely observed, agonised over ... When I think of the book now it is that rich texture that remains most with me, almost like a flavour on the tongue.

The glimpses of ritual, language, customs and culture are like stumbling over interesting shells on the beach. You want to pick them up and turn them over and examine them more closely.

Kindle Customer, 15 July 2014

Printed in Poland
by Amazon Fulfillment
Poland Sp. z o.o., Wrocław